# ED & Livvy

## IN THE NAME OF JUSTICE

### BRYAN TANN

ED & *Livvy*                    BRYAN TANN

Print ISBN: 978-1-947584-84-6

This edition published by Tann Media, and imprint of
ELK Publications in 2023, in the United States.

# "THEY LOVE NOT FOR THEIR VIRTUES, BUT IN SPITE OF THEIR FAULTS."

# —WILLIAM FAULKNER

ED & Livvy                    BRYAN TANN

# B RYAN  T ANN

ED & _Livvy_        BRYAN TANN

# CHAPTER 1

## ED

**E**d White walked among the inmates in the housing unit, a silent sigh escaping his mouth as he kept his eyes scanning through the area. Whatever chatter rang from the inmates, he just filtered out until it was just low-grade buzzing in his ears. He knew the boredom he felt was evident in his body language, yet he didn't seem to care as he made his rounds.

He stood just under six feet tall, his broad, muscular shoulders and chest coupled with his powerfully built arms barely fit in his near black uniform that drew as much attention to his dark brown skin as when he walked among the heavy crowds of white inmates. In a living area of sixty people, himself and two other inmates were the only people of color, and he always noticed. Each and every time he came to work. With each step taken, his thick, heavy boots made a loud *clunk,* alerting every inmate he walked by of his presence. Each of the men looking at him gave a nod of respect, in which he returned in kind.

1

His saucepan sized right hand ran over his smooth bald head as overheard conversations of armed robbery, police informants-rats-robberies, drug deals, and drug use attacked his senses repeatedly reminding him of everything from his childhood—and the demons he fought so hard to escape. Ed rolled his shoulders as he walked, the aches and pains within giving him no solace from the street fights and even sports he was involved in from his teen years living in the inner city.

*How the fuck did I get here?*

As he began to go through the internal browbeating he always put himself through when he asked that question, he heard a commotion from the one of the cells on the far side of the dayroom and rolled his eyes in frustration.

"Goddammit!" he growled to himself. He looked to the officer's desk at the back of the unit and saw his partner—a rookie male officer sitting at the desk—oblivious to everything going on but his chewing gum and the computer monitor in front of him. "Of course. Goddammit. Golden boy can't pay attention to dick around here!" he muttered to himself as he took off toward what he knew to be a fight.

"Code Three! Fight in Charlie! Repeat, Code Three! Fight in Charlie, cell 113!" Ed roared into his portable radio, as he made it to the scene not even bothering to wait for the rookie. "Lock down! Lock down now, goddammit!" The inmates began to clear the area in a massive migration. He couldn't help but feel a slight feeling of pride knowing he could get an entire unit to lock itself down with little more than his voice.

As Ed charged past them with a style and grace that was deceptive to his near three-hundred-pound frame. "I said lock the fuck down, goddammit!" he roared as he shoved past a tiny group of stragglers who were already on their way to leaving but couldn't resist peeking in on the fight.

Once the inmates were out of the way, Ed peeked into the cell and saw the confined melee. He reached for the keys on his belt, not bothering to look for his partner, or even make an effort to wait for him. When he got the door open, he felt the rage he had built up inside that had become routine in his life since dropping everything to move here—over five hundred miles away from his home. He looked over his shoulder before pulling open the cell door and saw the Golden Boy checking the cell doors.

"Martinez! Jackson! Cut this fucking shit out now!" he roared. As the battle ensued, Ed charged into the cell and grabbed the nearest inmate, whom he realized upon his grip was Martinez, by the back of the shirt and hurled the young, massive Hispanic man with enough strength to make the felon fly like a rag doll and crumple into a heap when he hit the ground.

Ed stood between Jackson, a tall and muscular young Black inmate, and the door. Jackson glared at Ed as though they were enemies in some urban jungle turf war. The younger Black man glaring at the man that was easily fifteen years his senior as though he were ready to attack.

"You don't want to ride this train, Jackson," Ed warned, looking over his shoulder seeing his partner putting handcuffs on Martinez. He turned his attention back to Jackson, the two squaring off like two alpha males ready to battle for dominance.

"Turn around and face the wall, Jackson. Heels and toes together with his hands behind your back. Don't make this harder on yourself than it needs to be, bro," Ed said, softening his voice hoping to diffuse the situation.

"Man. Fuck you, White! I ain't going to the goddamn hole, Nigga! No muthafucking way!" Jackson roared angrily with his body tightly poised for combat.

"Look Jackson, there's no way out of it. You stay chill, I will walk you down there myself. We'll go through what we need to go through. Let me see what I can do for you, alright? I've never lied to you since you've been here man, and I swear on my son that I'm not about to start now. But I need to level with you, brother, there's no way you're not going man. You can either go for a short amount of time, or a long amount of time. Listen, just trust me, alright? Let me try to help you out, little brother," Ed continued reasoning taking a slight step forward with his hands out to show he wasn't threatening.

"I ain't goin' to no fuckin' hole, White!" Jackson yelled again. Looking over Ed's shoulder, he could see more officers coming into the unit and he stepped back, going to his pillow and pulling out a makeshift knife made from a sharpened toothbrush. "Get them the fuck away from me, White! I swear to Christ I'll fuckin' kill you, mother fucker! I'll gut your fat black ass!"

Ed, seeing the knife, felt his insides go cold and harden. Nothing on him moved, he just glared at the younger man.

"Jackson, this ain't the way, cuz. It don't gotta go down like this," the older man replied in a tone several degrees colder than his previous. His speech slipping to a dialect that he used so much growing up on the streets. A demeanor that he'd put aside when he'd moved, he easily slipped back to his old self, standing his ground. *'You never lose who you are,'* he always told himself.

"You don't get what I'm sayin' do you, White? Huh, Nigga? You think this little shit hole means a goddamn to me? Nigga, I'm facin' life, mother fucker! You think I give a fuck about shankin' yo ass? Fuckin' Uncle Tom nigga! I got no problem killin' yo ass! Fuck you and yo' talks, nigga!"

"Look, Craig," Ed began, making a real effort to take the cold edge out of his voice. He didn't need eyes in the back of his head to know what was going on. He could hear the officers radioing for back up, reporting a weapon had been pulled. The cell extraction team would be coming in soon. "Look, I know it's fucked up, alright? You don't need to make things harder for yourself. Listen just—"

"Fuck that! Fuck that! Fuck you!" Jackson cried out, lunging toward Ed's throat with the knife.

All thought was gone. The instinct of his years of martial arts training, and street fighting took over. Ed's left arm shot out in a perfectly thrown block that connected with the young man's wrist like a strike, and then wrapped around his arm to neutralize the knife. His right hand shot out on its own and in one fluid motion of a strike followed by the crunch of the young inmate's trachea as blood spurted from between his lips. The death rattles warmed

Ed's insides and he was himself again. The blood free-flowing from Jackson's mouth as he struggled to breath was followed by his slumping body to the floor.

The officers behind him were stunned to silence. Ed looked at the body that used to be Craig Jackson, one of the few Black inmates in the jail. Ed had been called to Booking when the young twenty-year-old had been brought in with the U.S. Marshals. It was believed that seeing another Black man would keep him calm. The two had spoken at great length over the last few months, with Ed trying hard to keep the young man's spirits up despite possibly facing his maximum charge of life in prison. Now, he was no more, and it was Ed that had taken his life.

Ed turned to look to his coworkers, they were staring at him in disbelief. He reached to the mic on his radio, clearing his throat.

"Code Three. Medical in Charlie. Inmate down. Call an ambulance," Ed said solemnly.

He looked to the other officers and said nothing at first. He cleared his throat again, walking toward the officer's desk. Bob Potter, the shift supervisor, a tall and portly man with a military haircut and thick wire frame glasses, stepped forward from among the officers that had come into the unit, looking to him apprehensively, blocking him from clearing the scene.

"Jesus, Ed ...are you—?"

"I'm fine, Bob," he said shortly, inspecting himself to ensure there was no blood or other injuries on him. When he was satisfied, he looked down at Craig Jackson's lifeless body again. He expected to feel the cold dread that he'd heard people say they'd felt after taking a human life. He expected to feel sick, to want to paint the cell with the remains of his lunch. It almost scared him that he felt absolutely nothing at all, no fear, no sadness, not even a little bit of remorse. "I'm going to, umm, go get a shower. You need a report now, or should I just go home?"

"Are you hurt, Ed, or...?" Bob began.

"I'm fine, Bob," Ed replied, his tone sharpening, holding his hands out for his supervisor to see and taking a full turn around to show where the knife hadn't even cut the material of his shirt. Or so he hoped. When he wasn't alerted to any harm that he could, or couldn't feel, he softened his tone. "Do you want my report now or not?"

"Yeah, I mean while it's fresh in your head, alright? There's going to be an investigation of course, but—"

"Investigation?" Ed looked to Bob indignantly, his voice in a raised whisper, not wanting to get the inmates riled up more than he knew they would. "The mother fucker came at me with a fucking shiv! He was going to fucking put it in my fucking throat, Bob!" Ed said, his eyes began to blaze as the adrenaline threatened to control him. His voice slowly rose from his usual calm, controlled tone. "He was going to kill me—do you understand that? I wasn't going to be able to go home to my family! I was going to be fucking dead, right here with a fucking sharpened toothbrush in my fucking throat!" Ed roared, forgetting his desire to keep his voice low.

Bob looked to him with understanding on his face. He held up his hands, as though he were attempting to calm him. The yelling had begun to rouse the inmates in their cells.

"Yo! What the fuck's going on!" demanded a voice from the top tier.

"White fucking killed Jackson!" came the reply from the cell directly next to the late Craig Jackson's.

"Oh shit!"

The caged inmates began pounding and roaring loudly in rage fueled hatred, kicking, and pounding on their doors, roaring threats from behind the objects of their imprisonment. The sound of a lock disengaging could be heard as the nurse and other officers entered the unit. Bob, and Ed exited the cell as they made room for the nurse to examine Jackson.

When Ed exited the cell, the pandemonium intensified. Various other officers made their ways to cells, attempting to quiet the insurrection to no avail. Bob gestured to Ed, and he made his way to the airlock door to exit the unit. Bob used his own key card to exit into the main hallway.

"Come on. Let's head down to my office, okay?" Bob asked calmly.

Ed looked further down the hallway and noticed the EMTs pushing a gurney down the hallway, heading to C-Block. He nodded to Bob, walking toward the office—which was at the midway point of the hallway—passing the EMTs as he did. He entered the office and sat down in the seat in front of the desk. Instead of relaxing in the chair, he stayed rigid. His anger from the exchange just a few minutes prior was not forgotten. His eyes blazed in frustration, looking at Bob. He knew, rationally, that it was protocol and procedure. He just couldn't give his thinking over to being rational.

"Look Bob, bottom line is I fucking killed him. Period. Why the fuck do I need investigating? I've never..." He took a deep breath, attempting to choose his words carefully. "I've never done anything to deserve an investigation. You saw him come at me, right?"

"Yes, I did. But I didn't hear anything that was said—"

"Oh, what a bunch of bullshit, Bob!" Ed roared, standing up so fast his chair fell back. "You know me! I've worked here for five goddamn years! Five! I've always been up front! I've always worked the extra shifts I've done everything that was ever fucking asked of me! I do not deserve this!"

He wiped the spittle from his mouth as he roared. "I was trying to talk the kid down, Bob! Young Black man in a jail in the middle of nowhere, the only other black face he sees is mine! He's talked to me about everything going on with this life! Everything! I tried talking him down! He and Martinez were brawlin', and I was just trying to get him to settle down so I could take him to SHU! He lost it, pulled the shiv, and came after me! Fuck!"

Ed turned his back, not trusting himself to look at Bob anymore, at least for the moment. The adrenaline was building, and it was threatening to unleash at a moment's notice. A side of him that he always tried his best to contain was threatening to boil over the surface.

"Look, Ed... You know this is standard operating procedure. You know that. It's not going to be anything overly invasive okay? It's to cover—" Bob began.

"It's to cover your ass. I get it, Bob." He shook his head turning back to face him, looking at him disappointed, disgusted. "After all of these years, just

9

because I don't want to end up on a fucking coroner's slab, I'm going to be subjected to this?"

"Look, Ed—" Bob began, attempting to retake the situation in an authoritarian manner.

"No, *you* look, Bob," Ed growled. "I understand about standard operating procedure, and I understand about covering ass. But don't you fucking dare think that you're going to make me out to look like I did something wrong! He came at me with a shiv, and instinct took over. We are trained that when something like this happens, all bets are off, and they were." Ed glared at Bob. "He. Was. Going. To. Kill. Me." Ed said slowly. "Imagine if it was you! Imagine if that kid was going to put a shiv into your throat! You wouldn't go home to Sarah and Emily again!"

Bob's demeanor seemed to soften slightly, and he nodded. "I get it, Ed, I get it. We're going to do this right by you, alright? Why don't you just relax and take the rest of the day off, okay? Hell, take a couple of days man... alright?"

Ed looked to Bob and nodded. Without another word he swiped his keycard and exited the office. The radio chatter, other officers walking down the hallway, none of it registered. He made his way to the male officer locker room, stripped out of his uniform, and got in the shower.

The heated caress brought a sigh from his lips as he closed his eyes and allowed himself to be swept in the ecstasy. It was then interrupted by his mind replaying the scene of Craig Jackson dying right in front of him. As the scene replayed over and over, no remorse threatened to enter him. His thoughts were soon disturbed when he heard the locker room door open.

"Yo! White!"

Ed ran his hand over his head and let out a quiet groan of frustration. He wasn't in the mood to be spoken to, or bothered, or anything involving anything resembling human interaction. He cleared his throat, attempting to keep the annoyance out of his tone. Chris Grace supervised the second shift and had a reputation for making power plays, which included knifing people in the back, to get his position. The difference between his rise to supervisor and now that he was one was simple. Now he had the rank to further protect himself and his buddies. It took Ed a few minutes to remember that Grace was covering the shift for one of his and Bob's favorites. The clique mentality around the jail was enough to remind Ed of high school, and the thought of it brought a whole new level of irritation to light.

"Yo?"

"Hey, Bob says when you finish that report you head on home. We talked to the superintendent and he's okayed you to take a few days. Alright? We'll call you when we need you for the investigation, alright?" The mock sincerity that he perceived threatened to turn his irritation into flat out anger. Instead, he sat on it and coughed lightly.

"Yeah, sure," Ed said quietly. He began to lather his body, shaking his head in frustration. When he was sure Grace had left, he rolled his eyes. "Don't do me any fucking favors. Asshole."

After finishing his shower, he took an additional hour to finish his report. He put it where it needed to go and he punched out. Anxiously, Ed jumped into his white Chevy

Impala, looked through the rearview to his son's car seat and the toys that were all over the place, and then sighed lightly looking back at the jail.

"The fuck did I do to get myself in this shit hole?" he asked himself as he started the car and drove off. He didn't take his usual route home. He wasn't in the mood to go there, he just wanted to be left alone. He just drove, his eyes narrowed as he navigated the streets of the small town.

He still had another three hours before his shift was scheduled to be over, and under the circumstances, he couldn't help but feel glad for the time to himself. The idea of going home was heavy on him, and just thinking about it brought tears to his eyes, as it always did after he punched the clock.

He was six years removed from graduating with his Criminal Justice degree and moving from his hometown to his wife's, as he dubbed it, hick redneck hometown. When he first moved there, he'd hoped that he could find a nice, quiet place to set up his roots.

*"Going to be just like moving to Mayberry,"* he'd told his friends back home. *"Nice, quiet New England town where I can get a job and make a nice living and live happily ever after."*

"Yeah, that's a bullshit way of thinking," he said out loud as the memory replayed in his mind. It was nothing like he'd intended it to be.

Issue number one being among the only Black people in the area he was always subject to looks of scrutiny, and even distrust, from everyone that he encountered. He noticed it at jobs he worked, from the police, before he got his job at the jail, and even after.

Issue number two he was a Black man married to a white woman. "So much for living in a progressive society. Racism is alive and well in 'merica, y'all. Just in case you were wondering."

He'd worked a few security jobs until the jail job came through. After his first two weeks he realized he wanted to move back to the city right away and forget that he'd ever had the idea of moving to the small town. When he'd brought it up to his wife Laura, she'd begun to cry.

"You said you'd give it a fair try, Ed! You've only been here for a few months! Why don't we give it until... next year? I mean if you aren't enjoying it by then, then we can talk about moving, okay?"

He'd let the matter drop at that point, not being in the mood to get into the argument. Not to mention her mother—who in the beginning was supposed to only be living with them until they got settled, and Laura got a job—had walked into the room as they were talking to which he just left without another word.

Worse yet, Laura still had not found a job as she'd sworn too. She'd moved to the city with him while he was going to school and left a job that paid her fairly well. However, when they moved to Helltown, she hadn't put much effort into finding employment. When she found one, she'd quit after a few days.

"It isn't for me, baby," she said in tears. "The fumes are so gross in that place! I swear they're doing more than just providing medical supplies!" she vented. "They just make me feel so sick. I will find another one, just please don't make me go back there!" she cried.

"Okay," he sighed putting his arms around her. He remembered working night shift doing security, taking time away from his duties to comfort her. "You don't have to do it. Just, I can't be the only one working, babe," he reminded her.

"I know, Ed. And I promise you, I will find another job." She kissed him gently.

Her promise never came to fruition. The following month during Thanksgiving she'd hunched over, almost dropping the turkey and clutching her back. After a trip to the doctor, it was determined that she'd pulled a muscle near her sciatic nerve. When the muscle pull didn't improve, they'd gone back to the doctor and it was determined that she'd actually pinched her sciatic nerve and needed physical therapy.

"Baby," he groaned in frustration a few months later. "Your back isn't going to get any better if you don't do the exercises."

"Ed! It hurts!" she yelled.

"I get it, baby, I really do. Believe me. But you need to take it slow. The physical therapist said it's going to be hard, but—"

"Look, Ed! You are not my father! My back hurts, it's bad and I know exactly how much my back can take better than you! So just get off of my ass!" she roared.

It was then he decided he couldn't handle it anymore. After wrestling with the decision, he decided he was going to ask for a divorce. A few months later, when he decided that it was time to tell her, Laura surprised him with the news that she was pregnant. He'd forgotten his misery he stopped begging her to get a job, he even let his misery of

14

living in the tiny 'Helltown' go to rest and felt himself get into the idea of being a father.

The memory of it brought a smile to his face as he drove. He'd gotten out of the main town area, navigating the back roads that brought its own form of contentment. Seeing the endless trees, and the smaller amount of cars relaxed him.

"I fucking hate living here, but goddamn if it's not peaceful to just drive around," Ed said to nobody as he made a turn onto another backroad surrounded by nothing but trees.

The months leading up to Eddie, Edwin Jr., being born, he barely had time to realize he was being used. He never missed a doctor's appointment, working the nightshift didn't feel as horrible as it had been. Life felt lighter, more worth living. He even ignored his growing hatred for his mother-in-law, and the resentment he felt for his wife. He'd finally begun to feel like what he thought a normal man was supposed to feel like.

When Eddie was born, he went about doing his fatherly duties. He doted on his son and did all that he could for Laura. He even learned to tolerate Lorraine— Laura's mother—as well as the rest of her family, despite his lack of respect for their lifestyles of contentment and not striving to succeed.

Despite living with her family, working at the jail, and doubling at the fire department, life wasn't entirely bad, for a time. He'd moved to the first shift on a permanent basis after he came back from an unpaid vacation he just called 'paternal leave.' Being on duty when the inmates were awake allowed him to be able to speak to them more, and build a rapport with them that made his job a lot easier.

When Eddie turned one though, the feelings of anger and frustration returned. It was also then that he'd begun to break down in tears on his drives home from work or taking longer routes just to have time alone. He'd been told that a CO lasts for three to five years before he learns if he's not going to go career. He knew the heaviness of his heart meant that being a CO wasn't for him.

As he drove, he remembered coming home on a particular day almost year ago. He remembered that Eddie was sleeping, Lorraine was still at work, so it was just he and Laura.

"Hey honey, how was..." she began. Yet, she saw his face and the redness in his eyes and the tear streaks on his cheeks. "Oh my God, Ed, what's wrong?"

She came to him and wrapped her arms around him as he bawled into her chest. His body shook with every sob as he clung to her as though she were his only lifeline. "I can't...I can't do this anymore, babe. I just can't," he whimpered. "I want to go home I can't make it up here anymore! I can't work that goddamn job. I can't live where I'm the only Black man for miles around! I cannot live like this anymore!" he exclaimed bawling against her.

"Honey, I know this is hard. And you have been so brave. But you know I'm waiting for the disability money to come. Everything is going to be okay. It will mean that we can't just leave right away, but at least I'll be bringing in some more money. Just like you wanted. It'll be okay. I promise. It's going to be okay though, we can just find a new job until then, that's all. It will all work out, I promise."

A year later, no additional money, still at the same dead-end job. Now, he'd killed a man. He wiped the tears from his eyes.

"Why me? What the fuck did I do to deserve this shit? Married to a woman that won't even try to get a job, or anything else for that matter. What the fuck did I do?" he cried out. "Come on, God! Is this going to be my life? Is there ever going to be any kind of change?" he roared. "Because if this is it, you may as well just take me now! Either give me a fucking break or kill me now!" he screamed.

The memories and self-pity suddenly vanished as he saw a car cross lanes and head directly for him. His eyes widened in terror as he turned the wheel harshly to get out of the way. Yet the crossing car smashed into his rear side of his Impala causing Ed to fish tail at first and then flip three times with the stored momentum before it finally rested to a stop once hitting a nearby telephone pole.

Ed groaned as pain claimed every piece of his being. A large, thick gash leaked blood into his face as he was still in the seated position, upside down with the driver's side door resting on the telephone pole. He tried moving his right arm and felt a stabbing pain run through him as even his fingers refused to move to his will.

"Well, great end to an already fucked up day," he grumbled lightly, reaching in vain for the seatbelt cutter on his key chain. He could feel a warmth begin to spread slowly within his body. He tried to resist the urge, but the cough built within his chest and the intense jerking of his body followed as the fit ran its course. His eyes shut tight as pain seared through him like a burning hot blade had sunk deep within his flesh. He could taste the blood before his eyes opened, and the blood splatter on the steering wheel and dashboard alerted him to the danger.

"Oh fuck," he groaned as he felt a blackened haze claimed him.

# CHAPTER 2
## *Livvy*

Olivia Malone, or Livvy as she'd been called since she was a little girl, let out a soft yawn as she sat behind the triage desk in the St. Martin's Hospital emergency room. She'd come to work at the hospital six months earlier. She glanced at her naked ring finger on her left hand where the engagement and wedding rings resided for the last fifteen years of her life.

She was on her twentieth hour of her swing shift and didn't mind being the floating floor nurse, because she wanted all the extra hours she could get. She relished in the idea that work kept her mind off the hell that her ex-husband Martin had put her through.

Livvy normally worked in the Med Surge unit, where patients just out of surgery were taken. The other nurses—like most in hospitals everywhere—hated the Med Surge unit and Livvy was no different. Yet, like taking on the boat load of extra shifts her parents and siblings warned her against, it kept her from focusing on what she'd been through with Martin.

"You tired yet, honey?" came a voice from behind her.

Livvy looked over her shoulder, even being exhausted she felt a little jumpy and her hand instinctively reached for the nearest thing she could grab, in this case a pen, and held it defensively. Fran, the nurse everyone joked had been at the hospital since before time, smiled to her and handed her a Styrofoam cup of coffee. "Here you are, sweetie."

"Thanks, Franny," Livvy said, putting the pen down quickly so Fran wouldn't notice how close she'd come to having a pen jammed in her eye. "I really need this," she said as she sipped the liquid that legally couldn't be called coffee, but more like palatable river mud. Yet, she knew that the sludge would help her make it to the end of her shift and home so she wouldn't complain.

"No problem, honey. I've had that look a million times. What hour you on?" Fran asked taking a sip of her coffee. Fran looked to Livvy like one of the toughest women ever to exist. She stood five-foot-seven, four inches shorter than Livvy, and a short five-seven at that, as she appeared somewhat squat due to her muscular, yet rotund frame. Fran had been raised on a farm by a widower father with seven brothers, so she'd never learned how to be *just a girl*, according to her.

"Twenty and change." Livvy smiled looking at Fran's warm yet hard, lined face.

Fran had lines upon lines on her face. Laugh lines, frown lines, happy lines, sad lines. She'd seen lot in her sixty-three years she was married to the same man since she was eighteen. "And I wouldn't want those forty-five years back for anything!" she'd say jovially. They'd had twelve children two of whom she'd lost thanks to the Gulf War. Bobby and Charlie, her twin boys, had died in combat, in two separate branches and battles. Her oldest son, Willie Jr., had become a fire-fighter and died a few years later after in a four-alarm warehouse fire. Despite those tragedies, and losing the family farm at the economic crash of 2008, her marriage had never faltered.

She'd come to work at the hospital after the twins died, hoping to make sure that no other mother would have to lose their children as she did if she could help it. Fran was easily Livvy's favorite person at work.

"Why do you do this to yourself, honey?" Fran asked.

"What do you mean?" Livvy asked curiously, sipping more of the coffee sludge.

"Every time there's some overtime you're scooping it up. You're always working days at a time. You're going to put yourself in an early grave if you're not careful."

"I'll be alright," Livvy said with a smile, appreciating the concern even though from most everyone else she had no patience for it.

"Well, I'm not one to meddle in anyone's affairs..." Fran began, and Livvy rolled her eyes internally.

"I'm fine, Franny, I promise," Livvy interrupted. Franny had been trying to get her to open up to her since she trained her on her first day.

"Now I know not everyone is a chatterbox like me. And hell, I know how to keep things quiet and all, but you keep your thoughts, and everything locked down like this too much and it's not going to be helpful for you," Fran said with a nod to accent her point.

"I know, Franny. But I promise, everything is okay," Livvy said in a matter-of-fact tone, hoping the older woman would take the hint and back off. *God, I'm thirty-seven not seven!* she thought to herself.

"Yeah, I know." Fran smiled to her rubbing her forehead. "I know when to butt out, honey." Franny smiled wearily.

The ambulance bay doors suddenly opened and Franny and Livvy were on their feet with a young doctor, Dr. Greenblatt, at their heels.

"What do we have?" Greenblatt asked the two EMTs as they fell into step together wheeling the gurney.

"Edwin Michael White, African-American male, mid-thirties, MVA. Potential compound fracture of the right arm. As far other injuries, we can't tell. Wide gash on his head, causing what we think is concussion like symptoms. He's been in and out since he was extracted. We got him stable. He almost busted Robbie in the jaw while in the back," the EMT said.

"Good God! How has he been since then? Is he still violent?" Dr. Greenblatt asked nervously.

"He's been alright, I think he was just freaking out. But I would be careful," the EMT said.

"Fair enough. Has next of kin been alerted?" the doctor asked as Livvy got to checking his vitals.

"Yeah, his wife is on the way," the EMT said.

"Alright good. Let's get him to two, and we'll monitor him. Since it's just the arm and the gash, we can stitch the gash and get him to x-ray to figure out the severity of the break," Dr. Greenblatt said.

Livvy looked down at Ed who was still unconscious as they wheeled him into room two. She began to set up the monitors quickly and efficiently. He groaned weakly, and her attention was instantly on his face as he opened his eyes slowly.

Ed's chocolate brown eyes opened slowly, and he took in his new surroundings. He noticed the woman, obviously a nurse and blinked. Her brown hair, which looked like it had a hint of red, was tight and curly almost like it was kinky mane. Her black framed glasses concealed her brown eyes, but they fit her perfectly. Her pink scrubs made him smile ever so slightly. *So she's real girly,* he thought to himself. Yet, the look in her eyes showed that she wasn't a dainty flower. She was tough, no doubt about that.

"Hey..." he managed to whisper in a hoarse breath.

"How're you feeling, Mr. White?" she asked him politely as she continued hook him up to the monitors.

"Name's Ed... not Mr. White," he said faintly as he closed his eyes again.

"I'm sorry. Ed, how're you feeling?"

"Like I was in a car that got hit and flipped," he said with a slight grin.

Livvy couldn't help but chuckle at his frankness. "So I imagine you're ready to go for a jog?" she asked as she lightened her tone, thankful he wasn't whining like most people that came into the ER did.

"Oh yeah. Definitely," he said with a smirk.

23

"So I heard you took a swing at one of the EMTs?" Livvy asked.

"Yeah... cocky little prick, don't fucking listen," he said. Even in a hoarse tone, his voice sounded menacing.

"What do you mean?" Livvy asked as she took a hold of his left arm. "You're going to feel a pinch, just going to run your IV,"

"Fucker..." he groaned weakly. "Told the cocky little fuck that I was having pain in my stomach and around my back. I fucking spit blood while I was in the car," he said irritably. "He kept saying 'Okay, partner', but wasn't listening. Patronizing little piece of shit!"

"You were spitting blood?" Livvy asked, concern etched in her face.

"Yeah." He nodded. "I'm fucking exhausted... I can hardly stay awake. And it's not the concussion, I've had my fair share. That isn't it, this feels different." He groaned.

"Okay, Ed, well *I'm* listening," Livvy said in a soothing tone. "You said your stomach and your back hurt, I am going to touch your abdomen. It's going to hurt, but I need you to tell me exactly where it hurts okay?"

He looked to her and saw the concern in her eyes. He gave her a nod, gratitude spread across his face. *Finally, someone that listens,* he thought.

"Ok, how about here?" she asked as she light touched his sternum. "Here?"

"Fine," he said.

"Good. Here?" She lightly touched where she knew his spleen to be, and he roared in agony. "Okay, okay, okay, it's okay, Ed," she said nervously.

His roar of pain quickly subsided into a cough and as blood came from his mouth, her eyes widened in shock and fear. She took two hurried, gliding steps, and pressed the 'call' button repeatedly. "Dr. Greenblatt! Franny! Get in here now!"

"Alright, Ed, we're going to take care of you okay? We're going to take good care of you," she said, trying to reassure him.

Dr. Greenblatt and Franny came into the room quickly along with the EMTs.

"What is it?" Dr. Greenblatt asked.

Livvy looked to the EMT whom had been giving the report with a scathing glare. "Are you aware that you brought us a patient with internal bleeding?" she asked in a harsh tone.

"What're you talking about?" he asked with indignation.

"He almost punched out your fucking friend because he was trying to tell you he'd spit blood while he was trapped in the car! If either of you had been listening to the patient instead of trying to *tell* him how he felt, or pass him off on us, dammit if you would have thought for two seconds and listened to him!" Livvy hissed as she began to get Ed prepared to be moved.

"Okay!" Dr. Greenblatt shouted before the EMT could retort. "Let's move like we have a purpose we have to get him to the OR! Fran, call down and let them know we have one that needs prepped for surgery!"

"Yes, Doctor," Fran said as she was already in motion to make the call.

Ed groaned. He looked as if he were ready to pass out again, but he forced his eyes open and caught Livvy's eyes. Something about that look, touched her.

"Thank you... you're my angel," he said, and she knew he'd fallen into the void.

"I can't believe that son-of-a-bitch!" Livvy hissed as she leaned forward, speaking to Fran fifteen minutes after Ed had been taken to the OR for surgery. Livvy and Fran sat at the triage desk with their dinner in front of them. Livvy had forgotten her meal, as usual, so Fran had brought an extra plate of homemade baked chicken, rice, broccoli, and apple crumb cake made from scratch.

"It's absolutely ridiculous!" Fran agreed shaking her head. "That poor man! It's a good thing you were there," Fran said. "You saved his life."

"No I didn't." Livvy blushed deeply. "You would have picked it up if you'd gone in there."

"Maybe, but I wasn't the one in there with him. You were. Good job, honey. It's almost like you were destined to save his life or something," Fran said with a smile.

"Maybe," Livvy said with a smile. She couldn't get the image of his eyes out of her mind. She looked at his chart and grinned.

"Look at this. 6' and about 275lbs according to his license. Big freaking guy." Livvy chuckled lightly.

"He definitely proved he's all big bad man with what he did to Denny." Franny laughed.

"Yeah, but he was so nice to me, you know? I just listened to him, you know? I showed him that I cared about what he was saying, and he was just a great big teddy bear." Livvy chuckled.

"You got all of that in just a few seconds of conversation?" Franny smirked.

"Yes!" Livvy grinned. "What's that look, Franny?" Livvy asked when she was given a look that reminded her of her mother.

"You sound like you're having a crush or something," Franny said with concern.

"I don't have a crush!" Livvy retorted defensively.

"Are you sure?" Franny grinned. "You don't think he's a cutie?"

"Franny!" Livvy squealed. "I couldn't really tell considering he was practically covered with blood!"

"Yeah, you're right. I'm just teasing that's all. But you know, most big guys like that are sweethearts. Men are like dogs, honey," Franny said.

"They hump everything in sight?" Livvy asked.

"Well, besides that. But the usual rule of them about dogs is that the big ones are always the gentlest creatures, even though they look scary. But you will never find a more loyal, and faithful companion than a big dog. I remember, when I was a little girl, we had this big old Mastiff named Hercules. He was huge!" Franny laughed. "And, if he didn't know you, he would bark and bark and bark and if you didn't know him it sounded very scary. Once he got to know you, though. He was so sweet and tender. He was perfect with little babies and was so patient and loving with little kids! When he got mad though. Watch out!"

27

"I hope you have a story to support the whole 'watch out' part of it?" Livvy asked picking at the chicken.

"Oh yeah. My older sister was dating this boy, Oswald Fletcher, and Herc never liked him at all. Always barked at him, just all the time he was barking at him. One night we heard all of this commotion in the barn. Daddy ran out there and came back in with blood on his clothes. Turns out that Oswald got real grabby and my sister said no. He hurt her, and Herc damn near tore him apart." She laughed lightly. "Afterward, he acted like it had never happened before. Damn loyal dog."

"So what happened?" Livvy asked.

"Nothing. When Oswald's daddy tried to run his mouth, my father told him he was lucky it was only the dog that got at him because if it weren't for the dog, his son would have gotten shot."

Franny and Livvy shared a quiet round of laughter when Franny composed herself. "Herc lived until I went off to college. Ever since then, I've always owned a Mastiff. Loyal and smart dogs that are gentle giants."

"That's great," Livvy said. "So you're comparing Ed White to a Mastiff?"

"I think that man is a big rough and tumble guy that will put a person through a wall with no problem but is as gentle as a lamb every other time," Franny said. "A real protector."

Livvy was ready to reply when Pearl, one of the receptionists approached them. "Hey guys, Mr. White's wife is in the lobby."

"Oh, I will let Dr. Greenblatt know," Livvy said as she rose from her seat, cleaning her hands off on a napkin. She found Dr. Greenblatt in the lounge eating a TV dinner.

"Dr. Greenblatt, Mr. White's wife is here."

"Alright, how about you direct her to the waiting room for the OR and they'll have update her as soon as they can," he said calmly.

"Alright," she said, walking from the lounge and out to the lobby. "Mrs. White, I'm Olivia Malone. I'm one of the ER nurses."

Laura White stood up quickly from her seat and approached, her quickly. The first thing Livvy noticed was the striking gray eyes that looked back at her with the look of a person that was perpetually dealing with misery, no matter where she was or what she was doing. She stood a few inches shorter than Livvy, with long, unkempt blonde hair wearing old and battered sneakers, blue jeans whose belt line her stomach was hanging over, and an overly large T-shirt that did not fail to conceal the underside of her abdomen. Livvy immediately knew it had to be Ed's. She was also wearing another oversized sweatshirt that was unzipped. *She must have just thrown clothes on, she was worried,* Livvy told herself. Yet, there was something about her that rubbed Livvy the wrong way.

"Is he okay?" Laura asked quickly.

"He's in surgery right now," Livvy answered in a professional tone.

"Oh my God!" Laura cried out, tears in her eyes. "What's wrong with him? What happened?"

"He's got some internal bleeding, a broken arm, and a possible concussion," she said gravely. "He was awake and alert when he came in, however, which is a good sign."

"Thank God... when do you think he'll be okay to work again?" Laura asked immediately.

"Excuse me?" Livvy asked, taken aback by the question.

"Well, he needs to work. I mean... that's what he does. He works and he takes care of me," Laura answered.

"Mrs. White, your husband's injuries are quite serious," Livvy answered sternly. "A broken arm alone can take easily six to eight weeks to heal depending on the severity of the break."

"My Ed is a fast healer," Laura said with a fierce glare. "He'll be fine sooner than that. I can get to the OR through here, right?" Without waiting for an answer, Laura White walked off.

Livvy watched her walk away, and headed back to the triage desk, bewildered. She sat down and began to rummage her fork among the rice on her plate.

"What is it, honey?" Fran asked as she cut a piece of chicken and chewing it carefully. "I swear, Willie certainly outdid himself this time with the chicken."

"His wife has got to just be... just scared... there's no way she's that selfish of a cunt," Livvy said.

"What?" Fran asked almost choking on her chicken as she started to laugh. "What are you talking about?" the older woman asked, shocked at the vulgarity from Livvy.

"Well, Ed White's wife at first was asking if he was okay, and then started asking about when he could go back to work."

"Maybe he's a work-a-holic and being laid up makes him a pain in the ass?" Fran offered with a grin.

"Maybe," Livvy said. "But it was something else. She looked like she doesn't take care of herself and she didn't even really seem to care about him. You know? It was like she just expects him to get on the mend right away and support her. You know? It was almost like he was inconveniencing her by getting hurt! I mean, yeah he had just been in a car wreck, but you should have seen her! There's no reason those two should be together if she is really like that. There must be something wrong with him."

"Maybe. Or she could just have her own way to show her worry and grief, you know? Besides, it's not our job to worry about those things. We bring them in, and send them on their way. Okay?"

When Livvy didn't seem very well convinced, Franny put an affectionate hand on her shoulder.

"Honey, don't worry yourself too much about this, alright? You have plenty more with your own life to worry about. Besides, if you let yourself get too close to the patients that come in here, it's going to drive you crazy. Look at it this way its good thing we aren't therapists. Patients would probably drive us crazier than they already do," Fran said with a grin.

"I have a sister that's a therapist. She hates her clients she says all they do is take, take, and take. She has one that she says is an 'emotional vampire'." Livvy chuckled lightly.

"Yeah well, does it surprise you? From what you've told me about your sister, she doesn't like anybody," Fran said.

"No, Jeannette is definitely not a people person," Livvy said. "She probably tells her suicidal clients to do it and gets away with it."

The two women shared a laugh before returning to their meals. By the time Livvy finished, she saw Carla, her relief, head in.

"Alright girl, you're out of here," Carla said with a smile.

"Thank God," Livvy said, standing up quickly. "Franny, I'll see you Friday?"

"Absolutely," Fran said with a smile. "Be a good girl."

Livvy shook her head and headed to the locker room to get her purse and coat. She walked to the parking lot cautiously. It'd been six months since she'd left Martin, and even though she didn't think he was crazy enough to come and make trouble with her again after all this time, she wasn't so sure. She made sure to keep her Glock G19 in her purse as a precaution in case he was.

She drove home listening to the radio, barely taking in what the next bit government conspiracy was. While the idea of working helped keep her mind off of the mess that was her personal life, she was craving her tub, a mug of green tea, something mindless to watch on TV, perhaps a quick pleasure cruise with her battery-operated buddy, and her bed.

She was having a difficult time getting Laura White out of her head as she pulled into her parking spot.

"How in the hell did a thing like her get a man like him?" she asked herself out loud as she slammed her car door and made her way into her apartment building. She unlocked her door, turned on the main room light, tossing her purse and keys onto the kitchen counter.

"How the hell does that even happen?" she mused aloud as her cats, Sylvia and Platter, came padding out of her bedroom to greet her. "Tell me that, girls!" Livvy said as she pulled off her shoes and made her way to the bathroom and ran her bath water.

"I know I sound crazy, girls, but this guy that came into the ER today, right? I mean yeah, he was in a car accident, but he was practically God-like gorgeous. Well, his wife comes in and she looks like shit run over with a riding mower! And all she could ask about was when he could go back to work to take care of her! What makes a man so stupid to marry a beast like that? Honestly."

When the cats looked at her judgmentally, she rolled her eyes and turned on the water for her bath. She went to the kitchen to pour the cats their dinners and then went back to the bathroom, stripped out of her scrubs, and got into the hot water with a loud moan of delight.

"God I needed this. I can't believe that guy, why would he marry such a beast? Doesn't he realize he could do so much better?" she huffed. She used her foot to turn off the water, wet her washcloth and put it over her eyes as she lay neck deep in the tub, allowing the water to sooth her aching muscles.

When she finished her bath, she toweled off and was soon on her couch wearing hot pink shorts, a white tank top, her hot pink bunny slippers, and her pink bunny Snuggie with a left-over plate of chicken alfredo and broccoli. She flicked through the channels and stopped on the news channel when she saw a familiar face on the screen.

"Corrections officer in accident?" she asked herself curiously. She pressed the volume button, curious as to what the problem was.

*Corrections Officer Edwin White is the subject in an investigation of the death of federal inmate Craig Jackson who was housed in the Tri-County Correctional Facility earlier this afternoon was involved in a motor vehicle accident earlier this evening. There's been no update on White's condition other than he was taken immediately for surgery due to his injuries. In further news...*

Livvy's eyes widened in shock over the news report. She pressed the 'rewind button on her remote and looked at the picture of Ed in his uniform. His eyes were so much harder, colder than they had been when he'd looked to her earlier.

"A car accident after killing a man... oh my God," she said to herself. She pressed the home button for her Fire TV remote and scrolled to her favorite soap opera *General Liaisons*, then pressed the big circular select button to play the next episode while she finished her dinner. Setting the plate on the coffee table and curled up tighter under her Snuggie as the characters came to life on her screen, Sylvia and Platter curled up together on her stomach as the three got into their usual comfortable positions.

"This doesn't make sense, none of this makes sense. He's a stranger that's killed another human being. That isn't... God, why can't I figure this out?" she asked herself as her eyes started to slowly close. "Why do I even care about him?"

# CHAPTER 3
## UNHAPPILY EVER AFTER

Ed awoke with a groan, feeling his stomach lurch as saliva pooled in his mouth as it always did before he was going to vomit. He closed his eyes again willing himself to settle his stomach.

"What the fuck?" he groaned weakly.

He knew he had been in a car accident. Thanks to the nurse that actually listened to him, they'd gotten him into the operating room and saved his life. He closed his eyes and allowed himself to embrace the numbness the morphine provided. In that moment nothing mattered. Not his horrible marriage, not his horrible job, the death of the inmate, or the accident. None of it mattered.

He could feel the embrace of sleep coming to him when the peace and numbness was abruptly swept away, and a lurch of pain hit him in the stomach when he heard the voice outside of his room.

"How is my husband?" came Laura White's inappropriately loud voice.

"Mrs. White, please keep your voice down. Your husband and other people on this floor are resting," a woman's calm, low, voice requested in response.

"Well I'm sorry!" came Laura's obnoxious reply. "But my husband was just in a serious car accident and I need to know if he's okay! My Ed hates not working! He loves to work to take care of Little Ed and I!"

"I understand, Mrs. White, but your husband has just had surgery. He could have died, and he is going to need time to heal and rehabilitate," the nurse explained patiently.

"Well, how long is that going to take?" Laura asked impatiently.

"I'm not sure," the nurse replied in confusion of the questioning. "You'll need to talk to the doctor."

"Well, that's what I'll do!" Laura replied with a huff and stormed off.

Ed sighed lightly in relief. If she went to go and complain to the doctor, then he would have at least another ten minutes of peace before she returned.

"Ed!" came a shrill voice.

Ed groaned weakly, realizing he must have dosed off. He looked over and saw Laura sitting at his bedside with a smile. "Hi, baby!" she exclaimed loudly.

Ed closed his eyes, the loudness of her voice felt like a knife in his brain.

"Hey, honey. Can you, please lower your voice a little? I have a splitting headache," he said with a small smile.

"Oh, Ed!" Laura replied, her voice barely dropping an octave. "I was so worried about you! That stupid nurse and that idiot doctor said that you could be hurt for six to eight weeks before you can go back to work! What are we supposed to do?" she asked indignantly.

"Well, honey—" he began.

"And another thing! As far as that inmate that you killed? What happened with that? What if you lose your job?" she asked crossing her arms. "Edwin White, you have a family to support and…"

Ed had gotten good at tuning Laura out when she got into her indignant lecturing. He closed his eyes slowly, praying that either a nurse would hear her yelling at him, or he would pass out.

"You know, sometimes I just don't know about you. Do you even care about anyone but yourself? Or our family?"

"Huh?" Ed asked groggily. He opened his eyes, looking to her unable to grasp what she'd just said.

"That's what I'm talking about, Ed! You said that you would take care of me! You promised!" Laura hissed.

"I know. And you know what? The market sucks, I'm doing all that I can, alright? Maybe if you got a job it would help? You promised me that you would get a job to help remember? Do you realize what would happen if you got a job and helped me with the finances? We could move out on our own away from your mom and—"

"Ed, you know I can't work! My back hurts all the time and…"

Ed groaned as he heard the same old excuses again, his eyes closing slowly.

"Are you even listening to me, Ed!" Laura asked indignantly.

"Yes, I'm listening!" He sat up far too quickly yet ignoring the pain in his abdomen, his eyes blazing in anger. "I'm fucking hurting right now, Laura, and I'm not in the mood to have you talk at me like this, alright? Goddammit! I just fucking—"

He grabbed at his stomach with his uninjured arm groaning in agony and laid back down. "Shit! Look Laura, if all you're going to do is bitch at me, why don't you just go. I'm not in the fucking mood for it!"

"Ed, how dare you—" Laura began.

"Laura, either get me a fucking nurse and let them know I popped my stitches or go away and let me die in peace!" Ed grunted.

"Oh I bet you'd like that, wouldn't you?" Laura stood up in frustration. "You'd love to just up and die on me and Eddie, so you don't have to be a real husband and father. Wouldn't you, Ed?" She exited the room, as the door began to close he heard her call out. "The fucking idiot popped his stitches yelling at me!"

When the nurse came in to check on him, he could feel the black haze beginning in the back of his head dim his vision as his eyes folded closed.

Livvy came onto the Med Surge floor four days later wearing a bright smile on her face as she always did. The few days off had done her a world of good finally able to finish the novel she'd been spending so much time putting off because of work, able to sleep in until whenever she felt like waking up, and laps around the track with B.O.B had definitely loosened her tensions.

"Hey, Livvy!" a younger nurse with short, blonde hair, a squat figure, and friendly eyes called after her with a big smile.

"Hey, Melissa. How are you?" Livvy asked in a slightly dismissive but friendly tone, as she checked the floor chart for rounds.

"I'm doing alright. We had a little bit of drama around here the other day though," Melissa answered with a giggle that screeched like nails on a chalk board to Livvy's ears.

"Oh is that right?" Livvy asked, going over her work sheet and noticed the name 'E. White' written in.

"Oh yeah. Have you seen the news? You know about that jail guard guy that killed a prisoner who'd gotten in the car accident?"

"Yes. Mr. White. I treated him when he came into the ER. Why? What about him?" Livvy asked, her interest in the conversation piqued.

"Well, he had to go back into surgery about two days ago!" Melissa exclaimed in a hushed voice.

"Why? Is he alright?" Livvy asked nervously.

"Oh, he's fine. He popped his stitches. Apparently his wife, who looks like a train wreck on two legs, came in here and started yelling at him and they got into a huge argument." The younger nurse giggled.

"Why was she yelling at him?" Livvy asked, trying hard to keep her tone even, despite the surprising anger that continued to build.

"She started yelling at him about being hurt and how he needed to get back to work, and then yelled at him about the prisoner he killed and all of that. Then, he yelled back at her for not working to help and, it just got ugly.

Then, she just stormed out and just yelled at Jackie that he'd popped his stitches and said he was stupid or something. It was really ugly."

"Wow, so it wasn't just the moment." Livvy shook her head in irritation.

"What're you talking about?"

"Nothing," Livvy said dismissively. "Nothing at all. That's terrible though, is he okay?"

"Oh yeah he's fine. It wasn't anything major, he got stapled back up and then got told that he needed to not get himself so excited and to relax himself. So now, he just sleeps all the time anymore," Melissa said. "Too bad. How does a cute guy like that end up with someone like her?" Melissa mused.

"I have no clue," Livvy said as she set the paperwork aside. "These things just happen I guess. I'll go and check on him first and work my way around. See you later, Mel."

"Good morning, Mr. White. How are you today?"

Ed yawned weakly opening his eyes toward the window. The landscape wasn't bright and sunny as it was when Laura ruined it with her visit. He blinked weakly before closing his eyes again, the brightness of the room way too much to handle.

"Could you turn off the light please? It's way too bright," he asked weakly.

"Of course, Mr. White," replied the voice. "There you are. How are you feeling?"

When Ed opened his eyes again, he couldn't stop himself from smiling brightly at the woman before him.

"It's you."

"Yes, it's me," Livvy replied with a warm smile. "How are you feeling? I heard you went ahead and decided to pop your stitches the other day? Why would you go and do that? Not enough excitement in your life already so you decided to stay with us a few extra days?"

"Oh... that." Ed chuckled weakly. "For the purpose of remaining diplomatic, I tried to sit up to talk to my wife. I forgot about the stitches. How long have I been out?" he asked.

"About two days. You had to go back in for surgery and the doctor decided that staples would be best for you," Livvy replied, pouring him a glass of water. "I believe, before you took your extended nap, he told you about making sudden movements that could hurt you?"

"Yeah, he did," Ed replied sheepishly. "Well, if it weren't for you I wouldn't even be laying here to have been able to pop those stitches. You saved my life, Miss...?"

"Malone. Olivia Malone. It's nice to meet you, Mr. White." Livvy smiled.

"Ed. Just Ed. Mr. White is my father." When Livvy laughed softly, Ed couldn't help but smile looking to her. He was transfixed by her smile it was so bright and warm. She was the opposite of Laura in every way possible.

"Alright, Ed. Now, how about you tell me what really happened? Let's forget about diplomacy, okay?" Livvy asked him seriously. She began to check his vitals, taking a few seconds to give him a serious look to let him know that she expected the honest answer.

"Well, Laura came in yelling at me about getting hurt and everything that happened with my job that day." He sighed sadly, shaking his head. "I'm pretty sure you saw the news, right?" When Livvy nodded to him, he returned the nod and continued on. "She has it in her head that all I'm supposed to do is work myself into an early grave so that she doesn't have to do a damn thing at all, apparently," he said bitterly reaching for the covers to pull them up closer.

"Why doesn't she work?" Livvy asked, aiding him in pulling the blanket up, then grabbing the extra-large blood pressure cuff and wrapping it around his left arm.

"A few years ago she pinched a nerve in her back. All the fool did was make Thanksgiving dinner. I was watching her the whole time she turned maybe five inches to the left and all of a sudden she started crying." He shook his head. "God, I don't know how I got myself into this... I really don't." he cleared his throat lightly, closing his eyes again to hide his sadness from her and himself.

"Ed don't be hard on yourself. I don't know you, but you seem like a very nice man. I'm sure you wouldn't have married her unless you loved her. Right?"

Ed nodded lightly, but kept his eyes closed.

"Alright then. Maybe she really did hurt herself and..."

"No. I mean, well maybe she did, but she can still work. I mean, she has picked up our son with no problem on all kinds of occasions. She just doesn't want to work, that's all there is to it. I work three jobs with her mother living with us and I can still barely make it financially. If she would work... even part-time, we would be able to save a lot more money. But she doesn't seem to want to, makes me sick to know that all I am is her fucking slave."

Livvy finished taking Ed's blood pressure and placed her hand gently onto his shoulder and offered a sympathetic smile.

"I'm sorry, Ed. It sounds like you are having a very difficult time and I'm sure you didn't need that accident, or your wife coming in here and yelling at you." She gave Ed's shoulder a gentle squeeze. Despite the warm smile on her face, she felt her insides ready to boil to the point that they threatened to make her explode. *How dare she make him have that sad look on his face!* she raged internally.

"Thanks, Olivia..." he began.

"Livvy. I hate being called Olivia," Livvy interrupted with a smile. "The only people allowed to call me Olivia are my parents, and... well that's about it." She chuckled.

"I'm sorry. Thanks, Livvy." He smiled to her. "Definitely could've used not having a kid's blood on my hands also."

"I didn't want to ask you about that, I'm sure you don't want to think—"

"It's alright. The kid attacked me, and I defended myself. If I didn't kill him, he would have killed me. I feel bad that he's dead. But I don't feel bad for defending myself." He shrugged slightly. "I had the feeling he would do something, but I thought he would just try and pick a fight, and would go to segregation. Instead, he decided to try and kill me. It was going to be him or me, and it damn sure wasn't going to be me."

"Fair enough." Livvy smiled removing the cuff from his arm. "I'm sure it can't be easy though."

"No, it's not," Ed admitted, moving his free hand out to grab his cup to sip the cool water. "They tell you so much during training that you are going to be assaulted, but you're never fully prepared for it. No matter how many scenarios they run you through, you know what I mean?

And then, knowing that you've used what you know and it killed someone. Well, let's just say that this morphine helps me out a lot with sleep. But enough about me, what're you doing here? I thought you worked in the Emergency Room?"

"Oh, I'm a floating nurse, a swing shifter. I was covering for someone the night you came in. I'm primarily here on the Med Surge floor," Livvy admitted while writing on his chart, handing him a glass of water he was trying to reach for himself.

"Do you like it?" Ed asked, thankful for the cool water rehydrating his parched throat.

"A lot of people hate it. I don't mind it as much as some of the others." She considered the flat out lie she'd just told and shrugged it off. He was a patient after all, he didn't need to know the truth about her feelings about the job. "It's a job that I need after all, and it is much better than sitting at home being miserable waiting for a job offer." Livvy chuckled.

"Yeah, you're right about that. The idea of being broke and unemployed in this economy scares the shit out of me. I really hope I don't lose my job."

"I'm sure you won't. It was self-defense, they can't fire you for not letting someone murder you," Livvy offered with a gentle smile.

"If only it were that easy." Ed snickered.

"Well, Ed, I have to go and conduct my rounds. I will be back in to check on you soon, alright? I'm glad that you're feeling better. If you need anything, just ring your buzzer." Livvy smiled heading toward the door.

"Alright. Oh, and Livvy?" Ed called out as she had opened the door. "Thanks, for saving my life. If it weren't for you, I'd be dead."

"You're welcome, Ed. I'm just glad you're going to be okay," she replied warmly.

"No," Ed said seriously, shaking his head. "You saved my life. Nobody was listening to me. I could have died, but you... you listened. I mean, after Laura came in here, I wish you would have let me die." He chuckled sadly. When Livvy didn't return the laugh, he cleared his throat. "But I'm grateful. Thank you again... for saving me."

"You're welcome, Ed. Get some rest. I'll be back in a little while." Livvy smiled, slipping out of the room quickly.

Ed yawned loudly as he pulled his blankets up to his chin and closed his eyes.

As she exited his room, Livvy felt a feeling that she had only felt one other time in her life, and her hands ran over her empty womb sadly as tears began to fill her eyes.

"That fucking cunt," she muttered angrily under her breath. "How could she make her man wish he were dead?"

"Did you say something, Liv?" asked a passing orderly who looked at her curiously as she brushed her tears away.

"What? Oh, no. Sorry, Freddy. Was just thinking out loud, some damn eye lashes getting stuck in my eyes." Livvy laughed lightly as Freddy gestured toward the door to Ed's room.

"Poor bastard. You should have heard how much of a stir his wife caused when she came in. Doc Harper banned her from the floor for a few days." Freddy shrugged as he walked past Livvy. "I think he was faking being passed out

45

because when she came back about something to do with work the next day he didn't wake up. Soon as she was gone though, he was awake and watching TV."

"I don't blame him," Livvy said quietly as she watched Freddy walk down the hallway. She went the opposite way, pushing Ed White and his marital problems out of her head as she went about her routine.

# CHAPTER 4
## *WHEN IT RAINS, IT POURS*

Ed hissed in irritation. He was barely able to focus on the television. He'd found resisting the urge to scratch and tug at the thick cast on his arm getting more difficult. When a knock came, Ed grunted in annoyance still trying to get to the one itchy spot within the cast seemingly out of reach.

"Yeah, come in!" Ed called. He'd almost completely missed hearing the subtle knock, having become used to the nurses doing the quick rap on the door before just walking in.

"Mr. White?"

Ed finally turned away from his cast to see a man he'd never seen before. From what he could tell, the man was shorter than him by a few inches and rather skinny—almost sickly looking—with thinning gray and brown hair, thick glasses, and a freshly shaven face. Even with his obviously tailor-made suit, he was so small that the suit seemed to envelop his thin body as though it were a curtain. Ed knew whatever he was selling, he didn't want it.

"Yes, I'm Ed White. Do I know you?" Ed asked curiously.

"No sir, I'm afraid you don't. My name is Robert Coleman. I'm an attorney representing the county," the man replied.

"Oh, alright. Well, I'm recuperating right now, can't this wait until I'm out of the hospital?" Ed asked in slight irritation.

"Unfortunately, sir, I'm afraid it can't. I need to discuss with you the events of your altercation the other day. It seems as though the family of the inmate who lost his life is looking to sue the county, and well . . . you, personally."

"Well, I kind of figured that would be coming," Ed said with groan as he attempted to sit up. He held his stomach in pain, the staples still tender. He laid back flat but turned so he could look at the attorney more carefully.

"Yes, sir. Unfortunately, the altercation took place in a cell so there is no surveillance footage to protect you," the lawyer stated as he sat down in a nearby chair.

"Alright. But you have my report and the report of the other officers that were in the cell, right? I mean, that was clean. He came at me with a shiv, I deflected, and instinct took over. It was either him or me and it wasn't going to be me!" Ed said, his voice starting to slightly raise a little.

"Yes, we do have the reports. I, however, need to speak with you in depth about this. You have to understand, Sergeant White, that this is a very serious situation. That young man was a federal inmate, and being a young African American man, a lot of media attention is—"

"Woah, now wait one damn minute here!" Ed exploded, interrupting Coleman. "They're trying to make

48

this about *race?* Look Coleman, you may not be able to tell by looking at me but I'm Black. Alright? Take it all in here, buddy, I'm Black the same as he is! He came at me with a fucking shiv! He could have murdered me! Do you all get that?" Ed's eyes blazed in fury as his breathing became erratic.

"Sergeant White, I can completely understand your feelings on this, I truly can. However, this is going into the court system and we need to cover all of our bases. I am sure that you can understand that, can't you?"

"God, this is beyond unreal!" he roared angrily before wrapping his casted hand over his stomach, feeling the pain of the staples resisting being tugged. "Alright, alright." Ed groaned, as he took a deep breath to compose himself. "Fine, I'll take this in stride. I can do that. Now, what is it that you want to know exactly?"

"Was there any animosity between you and Mr. Jackson?" Coleman asked, pulling a micro digital recorder from his briefcase, and set it on the nearby table.

"No. Actually when he first came onto the facility I spoke to him and offered him words of comfort. I spoke to him daily to help him get adjusted to being in the jail. I was connecting with him as best as I possibly could," Ed replied, slipping in his CO tone almost effortlessly.

"How so?" Coleman asked.

"Well, I would try to help him adjust to being in the jail and how to deal with the residents of this area as they come into the jail. At one point, he was ready to fight just about everyone in the unit due to feeling like he was being discriminated against for being black. I would also talk to him about my time as a young man and things that I did when I was his age. Essentially, I just tried to stay polite, and relate to him so that he wouldn't feel alone. It was a complete shock to have him come at me the way he did, and..." Ed sighed lightly, clearing his throat.

"Go on," Coleman replied.

"I mean hell, I should've seen that other car coming! But I was distracted and I got hit. Why? I couldn't get the whole thing out of my mind. Poor bastard driving the other car? Just another poor bastard like me driving home, from what the cops said, and he just lost control of his car! I mean, I've never killed anyone before. I never wanted to kill anyone, but he could've killed me. I was afraid. I was justified in what I did. Doesn't mean I don't feel horrible about it all!"

"Listen, Ed, I'm no therapist, but this doesn't sound unreasonable. You were in a life-or-death situation, and I can't pretend to know what that's like. None of us can." He gave a small nod. "I think that I have enough for right now. I wouldn't worry though between your report and the report of your fellow officers, I don't think you should have any problems. I will, however, remind you that it is the policy of the county that you speak to a therapist about this once you are able." Coleman stood up making his way to the door when Ed remained silent.

"Oh, and Ed?"

Ed looked up to the lawyer, the itchiness in his cast forgotten as he was deep in thought.

"Looking into your file, you're a good man and a great officer. Don't let this get you down. Everything is going to work out just fine." Coleman offered a small smile before exiting the room.

Ed watched as the lawyer left and gave a slight nod adjusting himself to get comfortable. He thought about the life he'd taken, and despite himself, guilt clutched at his chest bringing a tear to his eye. Ed reached for the remote to change the channel on the tv hanging on the wall across the room. The itch in his arm cast returned but Ed was too occupied with his thoughts to really care at the moment.

# CHAPTER 5
## *PAINFUL MEMORIES*

Livvy did what she could to avoid Ed White's room through most of the day. It scared her how she felt so protective of him, how much the buzz on the floor about how Laura White had made a fool of herself by yelling at her husband, or how badly she wanted that woman to pay for treating him in such a way.

She kept her usual cheerful smile and demeanor up as best as she could. She refused to be like the other med surge nurses that forced professional demeanor but carried a serious hatred for not just the job but the occupants of the floor.

*Poker face. Poker face,* she told herself inwardly over and over.

Ed White's situation reminded her so much of her own painful marriage. The White's marriage—if continued—would probably be the death of him. The thoughts of such a disastrous union brought back memories upon memories that she'd worked so hard to get over the last four years.

As the old recollections fought their way to the surface, she made her way to the empty break room, shut the door, and let her tears flow as she sobbed silently at first until the sobs turned to bawling. She let the emotion run over her, praying as much as she could during the displays of emotion that no one would walk in on her.

Olivia Malone met Martin Rhodes in college. She'd looked forward to finally being able to get away from her overbearing parents and her four younger brothers in an effort to finally have some real fun. For three years that was exactly what she did parties, parties, more parties, and enough sexual exploration to put *Letters to Penthouse* to shame. She had no shame in any of it, it was her life to lead.

*Life's too short not to live it!* she told herself again and again. One night, during her senior year, while home on Christmas break, her friend Susan had come home from school excited to tell her about her new boyfriend Tommy who had brought back a friend of his named Marty.

"Livvy, you have to meet Marty! He's gorgeous!" Susan exclaimed wearing sweats and a t-shirt laying sprawled out on Livvy's bed.

"Sue, I already told you a thousand times I don't want anything serious while I'm in school. I want to just have fun! I have plenty of time for all of that serious stuff when I graduate!" Livvy said as she took another bite of her slice of pizza.

"Oh Livvy, come on! What's one date going to do? Kill you? Besides, you won't be alone! The four of us can go to the movies and maybe go to the skating rink after!

Marty is supposed to be a really good skater! Besides, you used to love roller skating!"

"Yes, I know I love skating, Sue, thank you," Livvy said with an acid etch to her tone. "That doesn't mean that I want to go on a double date with your idea of 'Mr. Wonderful' for me, okay?"

When Susan looked at her, her head hanging upside from the bed with her pouty lip, Livvy's eyes narrowed.

"Don't."

Susan continued her pout and sniffled lightly.

"Damn you, Susan Marie, don't you do that to me! You are not going to guilt me into this, now I mean it!" Livvy said angrily as she tossed her half-eaten slice of pizza into the box a little harder than she'd intended.

Susan kept eye contact, as she rolled over onto her stomach to look at Livvy. A few tears starting to flow down her cheeks.

"Damn you! Fine! Okay? One stupid date and that's it! Don't you dare expect anything, don't you dare think that you're going to get me to do anything else! Do you understand me?"

"Oh thank you, thank you, thank you! You're not going to regret this! He's so cute! He looks like he was cut out of a dream!" Susan exclaimed happily as she charged off the bed to pull Livvy into a bear hug.

"Okay, okay! Get off me! I'm not happy about this! I mean it!" Livvy said angrily. They both knew it was nothing but a ruse, Livvy could never stay mad at Susan.

The next night, Livvy was dressed in a long, flowing red dress that complimented her long full legs and breasts perfectly. She and Susan had spent the day at the salon,

Susan's treat, to get ready for their big date. She'd made sure to pack a pair of jeans and a shirt for after the dinner and the movie so that they could go skating later.

"Oh my God, Liv! You look gorgeous!" Susan exclaimed. She was a few inches shorter than Livvy and a little bit skinnier, but the two were known to be among the most gorgeous girls in town.

"I know I do, Sue. Thank you. I'm still not happy about this, and you know it," Livvy said, still a bit irritated by the emotional blackmail.

"Trust me! You are going to have a great time. I promise!" When Livvy's eyes remained narrowed, Susan whined loudly. "Oh come on, Livvy! If you don't have a good time, then just think about it you got a full day of spa treatment on me!"

"Yeah, you're right," Livvy said with a wide smile. "I forgive you." As the two girls hugged close, the doorbell rang.

"Livvy! You have company!" roared her younger brother Jackson.

"Better than having a doorman." Susan grinned as she opened Livvy's bedroom door and led her down the stairs.

As they made their way down to the living room, Susan squealed loudly and ran into Tommy's arms kissing him passionately. Livvy looked to Tommy's friend and even though she remained cool outwardly, inwardly she felt her stomach flutter. He stood at least six-foot-two and appeared to be a slender, yet muscular type. He had dark blonde hair with stormy blue eyes and a slight tan to his skin reminded her of the cowboys on her grandfather's farm that she always had crushes on.

"Hi," the tall cowboy said to her with a slight southern drawl. "I'm Martin Rhodes. It's a pleasure to meet you," he said extending his hand.

"I'm Olivia. Olivia Malone," she replied sweetly, taking his hand.

"Pleasure to meet her, huh, Marty?" Tommy chuckled. "You've been bitching the whole way over about not wanting to do blind date bullshit."

"Oh don't worry about it, Marty," Susan said with a chuckle. "Livvy has been doing the exact same thing all day. Looks like you two have a lot in common already!" The two lovers laughed in unison as Livvy and Martin looked to each other with an understanding of loathing toward their friends.

"Well, sideline commentary notwithstanding," Martin grinned, "let's get going. We have reservations for six and the movie starts at eight-forty-five."

Martin offered his arm for Livvy with a smile, and she accepted it warmly. She looked over his outfit and couldn't help but be impressed by the aroma of cologne that was just perfect, and the shoes with the high shine, light gray pressed slacks, and matching gray suit coat and white shirt.

Her memories of that first date made the pain of the recollections even worse. She'd fallen in love with Martin Rhodes that night and when they kissed, she never wanted it to end. She remembered how gentle his touch was, and how he had talked so much about his hopes and dreams. He'd gone to fight in Iraq during Desert Storm, and when he came back, he'd started his own ranch as he had grown up around horses all of his life.

It made her smile, about the dreams that he'd told her about. How he'd wanted to have a gaggle of children on a large patch of land where he would run his ranch. All he needed was to find the right woman and they could live happily ever after. He'd told her that he thought she was the one, and her heart fluttered.

He'd proposed after she graduated, and she happily accepted. After that first date, all of her sexploits and partying had ceased. She promised herself that she would always be loyal to him and love him because he was her prince.

She'd moved into his ranch house with him. He wanted at least two hundred plus acres, and he knew he would get it after a few years of working. He'd begun to build the house there and had already purchased a few horses.

She'd insisted on helping with building his dream, since it was now *their* dream. She got a job at the nearby hospital as a nurse and when she wasn't working there she wrote articles for the local newspaper.

Over the next few years, they had slowly begun to build up the acreage he'd been hoping for. As they began to slowly turn a profit, they expanded the ranch considerably. Sadly—despite their attempts—the children had not come yet. He'd assured her that it would happen soon enough, it just wasn't the right time. She let the thoughts and worries go, thinking that it was for the best.

"You're still not pregnant, Livvy?" Susan asked in astonishment as their fifth anniversary party had been in full swing. "It feels like whenever Tommy comes anywhere near me with his pants off, I get pregnant!" Susan said with a laugh as she rubbed her growing baby bump.

"I know!" Livvy said, trying to hide the bitterness in her tone. "This is number four now, huh?"

"Four and five," Susan said with excitement.

"Twins?" Livvy exclaimed.

When Susan nodded, the two friends hugged each other close and squealed as though they were back in middle school listening to the newest *New Kids on the Block* cassette.

Throughout the party, Livvy did all she could to keep a happy demeanor. Yet, she couldn't escape the jealousy she felt for her friend. She'd been with Martin for five years, and nothing. As a nurse, she knew the issue may not be just within herself but could be his. She just didn't know quite how to approach him about that.

"Honey?" Livvy said to Martin as they crawled into bed that night. She began to massage his stomach lightly before moving in to kiss his earlobe. A small purr exited from her lips as she began to slide her hand further down his waist as she began to suck lightly on his neck.

"Livv, not tonight, baby," Martin said curtly.

"What?" Livvy asked, not really understanding him as she took his manhood into her hand and began to massage him gently.

"I said," he grumbled gruffly as he reached his hand under the covers to grab her hand, "not now." His eyes glaring at her, his lips curling into a slight snarl.

"I...did I do something wrong?" she asked, tears in her eyes as she moved away from him slowly.

"I just don't want to be bothered, alright? Quit pressuring me to have kids and let me go to sleep? I'm not a goddamn machine!" He rolled over so that his back was to her, turned off his lamp.

Livvy looked to his back his outburst surprising her to tears. She'd been so happy as it was now their fifth anniversary, and she was hoping for him to be happy too. Instead, she rolled over keeping her back to him and silently cried herself to sleep.

The next morning, when she woke up, Martin was gone. It wasn't anything completely new, as he always got up early to tend to the animals. She couldn't help but feel lonelier than ever before. As she showered, more tears followed.

She made her way to the kitchen to make breakfast, as part of their routine before she went to work, and she noticed some mail had been left on the counter and sighed lightly seeing the bills for the feed.

"What are you doing?" came Martin's irritated tone.

She dropped the bill quickly and looked toward him. "What do you mean?" she asked, slightly defensive.

"What do you mean, what do I mean?" he said angrily. "Why are you looking at the bills?"

"Martin, you do remember I am your wife, right? And I do have a right to know—" she began.

"You mind your own goddamn business! This land? This house? The ranch? That is my dream! It was my dream before I ever met you!" he roared, snatching the bill from the counter with speed and intensity that made her jump back with terror. "And I am sick and tired of you pushing at me about having a fucking kid all the damned time! Do you think I care thing one if that bitch Susan is knocked up again? I am trying to build this fucking business! I do not need a fucking kid right now!"

Livvy looked to him as though he had slapped her, fresh tears falling she stood up quickly. "What the fuck is wrong with you, Martin? Why the hell are you treating me like this? I'm your wife! You told me that your dream was *our* dream! You told me that you wanted kids and—"

"Well . . . I changed my fucking mind! I don't want any kids right now, not sure if I want them at all!" He shook his head running a hand through his hair as he tried to calm himself. After what felt like an eternity, he spoke in lower, forced tones to keep his anger under control. "Look, I'm sorry, okay? The ranch isn't doing as good as it had been. Could be nothing, could be something, okay? And, I'm worried and I'm stressed out and if we bring a baby into this situation, it's not going to be good. Okay? Look, I'm sorry that I'm..."

"Why didn't you just tell me, Martin? Why are you snapping my head off? Why are you making me feel like you don't love me?" she cried. "I'd do anything for you! You know that! Why would you think you need to hide this from me? We are supposed to be a team. This is not just the Martin Rhodes show, you know?"

"You're right," Martin said, as her words cut him. He put his arms around her and just held her close. "I'm so sorry, honey. I really am. I'm sorry that I ruined our anniversary." He kissed her softly on the lips.

In spite of herself, she returned his kisses. She clung tight, just wanting to be close and to feel loved. The small kisses soon turned into deep, passionate kissing. Before she knew it, he was carrying her to the bedroom. As her clothes were slowly, and gently removed with great care, and she felt his tongue touch the warmth between her legs, she felt pleasure exploding within her. It wasn't something he did regularly, and when he did she always felt that it was the most special thing.

And when he entered her, and she threw her head back and moaned loudly in pleasure, her tears were forgotten. She felt her climax erupt within her repeatedly, one after the other. His gentleness, his thoroughness, and attention to her every want and desire made her forgive him easily.

"Lying bastard," she hissed as her jaw clenched tight. She quickly wiped her eyes of tears when the sound of visitors approaching snapped her out of her haze.

"Oh, Livvy. How are you today?" the plump, older woman asked. She was much shorter than Livvy, but the head nurse Margo reminded her a lot of Franny, so she instantly liked her. She didn't pry as much as Franny, and she saw her more, so Livvy's soft spot for Margo was a bit gooier than it was for Franny. Her graying black hair and thick glasses reminded her of an old librarian that she'd known when she was a little girl growing up.

"Oh hi, Margo. I'm doing wonderful thank you." Livvy smiled warmly to the lead nurse.

"Great! Listen, Livvy, I need you to focus on a patient for me for a few days, if you wouldn't mind?" Margo asked.

"Sure, who is it?"

"Ed White. He just chewed out Becky something fierce a little while ago." Margo sighed lightly.

"Well that's not surprising," Livvy responded with a slight edge to her tone. "Mr. White doesn't take very well to authoritarians common sense can tell you that just by his profession. But why ask me to focus on him?"

"Well because he said to me when I came in to diffuse the situation, and I quote, 'Get this annoying bitch out of my face and get the only person in this hospital that has a brain in here! If I see another nurse in here that's not Livvy I am going to snap!' end quote." Margo chuckled. "Seems the life that you save is the life that is loyal."

"I didn't save his—" Livvy began, remembering Franny's comparison to big teddy bear type men.

"Olivia, please give yourself some credit? The man came in here speaking of a symptom that the paramedics didn't seem to care too much to pay attention to. It's a mistake that cost them their jobs, and you paying attention to it saved his life. No one would have caught that in time, he literally had minutes to live. You gave him a new lease girl. Accept it."

"Judging by the way he avoids his wife when she shows up, maybe I didn't do him any favors." Livvy chuckled.

"Liv, stop tap dancing. You saved a life. That life wants you closer. I'm just saying that, for a few days, pay some closer attention to him. As he starts to calm down a little bit more, start to slowly phase your way out. He's only going to be here for another week or so anyway, so it shouldn't be too hard. Okay?"

"Alright, Margo. I'll do it," Livvy said with a slight groan. "But I don't think it's going to do him any good. I mean—"

"Why do you keep doing that?" Margo asked.

"What?"

"Why do you keep denying what you've done? Why won't you allow yourself just this one thing? You saved a life, Olivia!" Margo stopped, realizing that her voice had started to raise, took a deep breath, and returned to her normal, calm tone. "You saved a life, Olivia. You did something that very few people, even in our profession, truly get to do. And you did it. Allow yourself to take some joy that you were able to make a difference."

Livvy said nothing, wiping the fresh tears from her eyes as they began to fall. Margo stepped forward and wrapped her arms around her and just held her gently, brushing her back gently.

"I know you're hurting. I wish you would open up to me, someone, anyone, but that is your choice. Maybe if you help this man, it can help you too. So, get yourself straightened up and head on into that room and do some good. Alright?"

"Alright, Margo," Livvy said, putting up a stiff upper lip that seemed to satisfy her boss. As Margo turned to leave, Livvy moved to the water cooler, filled a paper cup, and sat in the first available chair at the small round table in the center of the room. She first sipped then gulped the water down, letting the bitterly cold liquid rush down her throat before standing up slowly, taking another deep and cleansing breath, and made her way to her new best friend's room.

# CHAPTER 6
## *LIFE... OR SOMETHING LIKE IT.*

"**Oh** fuck," Ed groaned to himself when he heard the knock at the door. "If it isn't Laura, it's idiot nurses and doctors." He rolled over as best he could with the cast on his arm to keep his back to the door and closed his eyes.

When the knock came again, he wasn't surprised when the door opened and closed. He kept his breathing light and calm to continue to feign sleep.

"I know you're not asleep, so you may as well roll over and talk to me, Ed," Livvy said with a chuckle.

Ed rolled over and was greeted with her bright smile. He returned it effortlessly with a wide grin and began laughing loudly.

"Didn't expect to see you again for a while. Let me guess *Nurse Ratchett* went and whined about me so now you have to deal with the big, bad, Black man?"

"Strangely enough, you're right," Livvy said with a laugh as she sat down in the nearby chair. "Why did you ream Becky out like you did?"

65

"Because she's a little bitch," Ed said simply. "She came in here trying to tell me what to do and just being rude as hell and well, I wasn't in the mood for it anymore."

"I can understand that," Livvy said with a nod.

"Yeah?" Ed chuckled bitterly. "Liv, before I moved here I wasn't the same guy. I was a nicer person, I really was. But I didn't take shit from people either, you know what I mean? Suddenly, I move here, and I'm turned into a fucking doormat."

"What do you mean?" Livvy asked.

"I graduated top of my class in school. I was ready to move out west and get some private security work. By now, I would be making close to six figures! Instead, I'm not even bringing home two grand a month. I have a wife that would rather fake disabilities, and badly I might add, than do anything to help us build a life together. We've been living with her mother for the last seven years. I'm always working two jobs, if not more, because she would rather lay on her ass and watch TV and baby the kid!" he lashed out angrily.

When Livvy said nothing, Ed laughed bitterly.

"Do you realize my son is just turning three and he still isn't close to potty trained?" he asked sitting up in his bed, his eyes starting to blaze.

"You're kidding!" Livvy exclaimed. "How the hell does that happen?"

"Because I'm working my ass off while she sits on hers!" Ed roared. "You want to know the extent of our 'marriage'?" Ed used air-quotes to emphasize the last word as best he could with all the hoses and hospital equipment still hooked up to him everywhere.

Livvy nodded, almost afraid to get the answer. Her anger toward Laura White beginning to build again, mixing with the hatred she had for her ex-husband and her own memories.

"I wake up in the morning, she is downstairs sitting in her little easy chair with the kid on her chest like he's a damn baby baboon."

Livvy couldn't help but snicker at the visual, "Oh, sorry."

"No, it's cool," Ed said, a smile spreading across his face. "I meant to give you the visual. I barely see her as a human being! But I shouldn't insult baboons, they at least do something. She just lays on her ass and eats chocolates and watches TV all day. But anyway, she tells me she will see me later. I go to the goddamn jail, and I get to look at grown ass men and women and play fucking babysitter. I hate that job! Do you realize that a good chunk of those people are in there on non-violent drug charges?" He took a sip of his water and smirked.

"Seriously! Now I don't know about you, but I've smoked weed in my life and it's not a big deal to me. Hell, you want to do drugs, that's your damn business so long as you're not hurting anybody. Hell, most of the people in there are doing drugs because they have nothing else better to do!"

"Nothing else better to do?" Livvy asked quizzically.

"Yeah. They've been fired, or laid off, or they have no education whatsoever, so they just get high. And I've seen people go to prison over that shit, meanwhile a goddamn pedophile bounces in and out of the jail like it's nobody's business! I've even seen criminal domestic violence, you

know, wife-beaters do the same thing! As if they're there on
a damn fucking vacation. It's unreal!"

"Oh my God!" Livvy exclaimed putting her hand to
her mouth in shock. "How do they justify that?"

"Fuck me with a chainsaw if I knew," Ed said with a
chuckle. "But that's the way it is. I grew up hating cops and
now I'm laughing with them all buddy-buddy while they
pull their bullshit on people. I hate this goddamn job I hate
this fucking system! But I do it to take care of my kid, and
that fucking lazy tub of goo," he said with disdain.

"So why don't you leave her, Ed?" Livvy asked. "If
you hate her this much, why don't you just leave?"

"Because then I lose my son," he said quickly. "It's the
system, Liv. The man, especially a Black man living in
damn lily white-ville. I wouldn't stand a chance! She'll get
the kid I'll never get to see him and then I am paying child
support from so deep in my ass that they're pulling it from
my damn brain stem!" he shook his head. "No. I'm better
off just... just being miserable for a time. Besides. Maybe in
the next ten years or so she'll die. She doesn't take care of
herself you know."

Livvy looked to him, almost shocked at how flippant
he was with the idea of his spouse's death. And then, a grin
spread across her face. Realizing at that moment, she liked
Ed White.

"You seriously think that?" she asked.

"Well, I'm hoping for it anyway."

"Knowing your luck, she'll outlive you," she said
lightly. "After all if she's as lazy as you say then she is
completely well rested. You'll be dead by forty-five working
your ass off to support her."

"Wow listen to you!" he chuckled. "We're speaking on the same level!" they both laughed at the statement as they realized just how true it was. "But I'm a little miserable now too," he said with a smirk.

"Oh, really? Why now?" she asked with a quizzical glance.

"Because that'll mean I'm supporting her before, during, and from beyond the grave." Ed rolled his eyes. "She'll get all of my pension money and live like a bloated rat. Wait, shouldn't insult them either because they serve a purpose." He snickered. "I keep verbally abusing animals, the ASPCA will try to put me in animal jail." He laughed but abruptly stopped when Livvy didn't share in the joke.

"Can I ask you something frank, Ed?" Livvy asked cautiously.

"Livvy, you saved my life. You can ask me anything you want whenever you want and twice on Sunday."

"Why did you marry her?" Livvy said simply. "I mean you had to have had some indication of who she was when you were just dating. So why would you have married someone that you hate so much? What was your reasoning? What was your point?"

"Honestly?" Ed took almost a full minute to answer as he appeared to be racking his brain for an answer. "Desperation I guess."

"What do you mean *desperation*?" Livvy asked, unable to fathom such a gorgeous man being desperate for anything.

"Well, I wasn't all that great in high school."

"What does that even mean, Ed?" Livvy said boldly. "Don't bullshit me. We're not just patient and nurse. I'm supposed to be babysitting you to make sure you don't snap out on anymore nurses. They think that because you're nice to me that I can control you. I have no clue what the hell I'm supposed to be doing, so I'm just talking to you like..." Livvy had the word in mind, but didn't want to stencil it in.

"A friend?" Ed asked.

"Yes. Like we are just two people talking. Hell, you can even think of me as a therapist. I took a few psych classes in college anyway. So I'm just a friendly therapist person."

"Alright, but don't go thinking that you can control me now. I hate that shit," Ed said.

"Of course not, Ed," Livvy said quickly. "I was just saying what they seem to think, that is all. We're equals here. Anything you say to me stays between us, that's a promise." Livvy smiled, putting her hand on his, letting it linger longer than she intended to, then pulled away when she realized the contact. Ed looked at her hand on his and then back to her, smiling to her warmly.

"Well in high school I wasn't like the big man on campus. I was fat and afraid of my own shadow. I was bullied all the time for being the fat kid in grade school and it continued on into high school. I tried out for the football team and got cut because I sucked because I didn't know how to play, and I was afraid to try. I sucked at wrestling for the same reasons. I was always just too scared to do anything, you know what I mean?

"Girls didn't like me, and my only friends were the Hindu and white trash kids that no one liked because they were outcasts just like me. When I switched schools I went into a kind of loner stage, and then I made just a couple of more friends who were outcasts like me. I started working out harder to compensate for feeling like a loser and started snapping at people to keep them at arm's length. I finally snapped on some football players that were trying to give me grief, and started denting lockers with my forehead and fists just to scare people off.

"So because of doing stupid shit like that, I never had a real serious girlfriend because everyone thought I was some crazed psychopath. Didn't help that when I had to leave school for a few weeks for my grandfather's funeral, my best friend told people that I had killed someone and was in jail."

"Are you serious?" Livvy exclaimed.

"As a heart attack," Ed replied. "He said that he only did it to keep people from asking questions about my business. Which was nice, but it became a constant cock block. Fuck, I only lost my virginity at eighteen because of a mercy hump from a slut that I'd known since grade school."

Ed laughed bitterly at the memory.

"Worst sex of my life. You know how a guy, during his first time will cum like after two little pumps?" he asked. When she nodded in affirmation, he smirked. "Well I lasted for forty-five minutes and didn't cum. It was one of the worse experiences sexually in my entire life until I met the cold fish a.k.a. Laura," he grumbled.

"Hell, the internet was the best thing to happen to me. I could flirt with girls online and do phone sex and, hell, a couple of times I would travel to go see them. We'd have sex and that was my life, or something like it."

"That doesn't answer my question, Ed," Livvy said, keeping a firm expression that she remembered seeing her psychoanalyst sister make whenever she played therapist with their mother.

"I'm getting there, doc," Ed said sarcastically. "I bounced from fake relationship to fake relationship. I ended up meeting this girl Nina. She was alright. She had two kids, Antonio and Alena and I loved those kids to death. They called me daddy, the whole nine yards."

"What happened to them?" Livvy asked, ignoring for his manhood's sake, the tears that were forming in his eyes.

"I came home from work and found Nina fucking her friend Byron. Fuckers made it like I was the asshole for catching them. So I left and never saw those kids again."

"Damn, that sounds rough. I suppose you two haven't kept in contact either?"

"Not for a few years. I found her online a while ago. We flirted online a bit, and I got her to send me naked pictures because Laura and I weren't having sex. Funny thing is, after I broke up with Nina that's when I met Laura. I go back to my ex to get some sort of sexual release because my wife wouldn't touch me. Pathetic isn't it?" When Livvy didn't respond, he continued.

"I moved up here and married her within a few months. She told me all of the things that I needed to hear you know? 'You're so special! So handsome! How dare she treat you like that!' then came 'I'll never hurt you, Ed. I would never treat you like that, Ed!' Well, she's right. She's a hell of a lot worse," Ed said, staring off into space with a hard glare set on his face.

"What do you mean, Ed? What do you mean by worse?" Livvy asked.

"Well, I knew something with wrong with Nina when we weren't having sex anymore. I mean she was a selfish lover, but... at least I was getting laid. And she worked. Hell, we went to the same school and she would work. She actually asked me to quit my job and I could get paid to be the babysitter of her kids by welfare. Laura? Please! Not only is that bitch lazy and selfish in bed, but we haven't had sex in months! Literally! Do you know how frustrating it is to have to beat off on the computer with your wife laying a few feet away because she won't fuck you?" Ed caught himself, realizing that he'd begun to shout and laid back.

Livvy did her best not to laugh at the fact that she'd never seen a Black man blush before. She knew she needed to choose her words carefully at this point. He was in a vulnerable place he was hurting, and angry.

"So... must suck having your right arm in a cast then, huh?" Livvy shrugged.

Ed looked to her as though he had never seen her before in his life. He then looked to his cast and then began to laugh loudly. Livvy responded in kind, feeling her own weighted shoulders start to unburden ever so slightly.

"Well, I'm a lefty when it comes to that so, I'm not really skipping a beat." He smirked.

The revelation brought a thick blush of crimson to her cheeks.

"Ed!" Livvy coughed, reigniting the laughing fit between the two.

"Sorry." Ed grinned.

"No, it's okay. I just wasn't expecting you to say that that's all," Livvy said.

"I can tone down..."

"No, really Ed, it's alright. I want you to feel like you can talk to me. I want you to feel at ease and relaxed. You... you seem so sad and alone. You can be yourself with me. I'm not going to judge you."

"Damn," Ed said, looking to Livvy with a smile.

"What?"

"Why couldn't I have met you sooner?" he asked dreamily.

"What do you mean?" Livvy asked curiously.

"Nothing," he replied, dismissively.

"No, seriously, Ed. What's that supposed to mean?" she asked seriously.

"I wish I would have met you sooner. Would've been nice to just, have someone to talk to. I've been so lonely for so long..." he said sadly.

"Well, I'm here to listen, Ed. I promise." She smiled.

"I'm glad." Their eyes locked, and Ed could feel something within him beginning to stir.

"So what're you going to do about this situation?" Livvy asked seriously.

"I don't know," Ed replied with a defeated tone that sent pain running through Livvy's body. "I really don't. But I've got to do something. I can hardly feel anymore," he said seriously. "I just feel like I don't feel any more, Liv, and if I don't feel, then I don't care. And if I don't care, I die."

That night after work, Livvy soaked in the tub as she normally did and finally released the tears that had been building up the entire day. Her memories, mixed with the pain that Ed White shared was too much for her to handle.

When she finally pulled herself out of the tub, she looked at her red eyes in the mirror and a sudden flash of Ed White's face etched itself into her memory. When he laughed, his face lit up. That was the look she wanted to see from him all the time. That big, strong, funny man that it turned out was so creative. It had taken some coaxing, but he'd revealed to her that he wrote poetry and short stories as a way to keep himself sane. She'd even been able to get him to promise to share some of his poetry with her sometime.

Her sadness began to subside, and she saw Ed White in another light. She realized just how much she enjoyed that vision of her patient. The smile, the strength, the stories of his training. He definitely was the big and gentle type that had the potential to be dangerous if what he loved was threatened.

"And that cunt... she hordes him and abuses him. She doesn't deserve him," she said to herself, looking at her frowning face in the mirror. "If he were mine," she said to herself. And the thought sent a wave through her, and she felt her nipples harden slightly.

Before she knew what she was doing, she was in her room with B.O.B. in hand. She imagined those powerful hands on her body. His soft and full lips claiming her own, and the tender flesh upon her neck, and her breasts. Her hands clinging to his broad, muscular shoulders while she felt him filling her brought her to an intense climax.

"Oh my God! Oh Ed! Yes!" she screamed as her entire body went rigid with pleasure. When she finally went limp, she only had enough energy to turn off her friend and lay completely still. As she drifted to sleep, the visions of Ed White remained in her mind as she slept peacefully.

While in his room, Ed waited for the night nurse to check on him and leave before he moved his hand under the sheets and into his pajama pants where his excitement was most evident. As he manipulated himself, his thoughts stayed focused upon the one person that seemed to care about him.

He, unknowingly, shared his desire's visions. Their lips, their bodies, their souls becoming one as they each brought each other something that they only believed existed in erotic fairy tales. As his climax struck him and soiled his pants he shuddered with desire, wishing that he could have enjoyed his fantasy of her just a little while longer.

# CHAPTER 7
## THICK AS THIEVES

Over the next week, the two of them spent almost every hour Livvy was working together, just talking. Neither discussed their fantasies for one another. Livvy constantly reminding herself that Ed was still married made their time together bittersweet.

*He isn't yours,* she would tell herself out loud when she was alone. *He's still with that monster, and if he's too blind to see how you feel for him, then let him suffer with her!* her angry, vengeful side lashed out. *He fucking deserves it! If he can't see that a perfectly beautiful woman—with a much better body than that monster, and would be willing to use it would treat him like a king—wants him, then he deserves to be miserable!*

Her anger at him being unable to pick up on her subtle flirting and make a move did not stop her from anxiously speaking with him or using B.O.B. to be a stand in while she screamed his name, lusting for him, night after night.

*You're married, asshole,* he said to himself while she was in the room, and when she left. Even as he would bring himself to climax to the thoughts of her, he continued to repeat the mantra.

*What would a woman like that want with your ass anyway? You're stuck with that beast, and that's where you're going to be. Get over it!* he would echo. Yet, whenever she came in to sit with him, his excitement, and growing feelings for her took over all thought.

When he'd received word that he was going to be discharged, he couldn't help but feel saddened. Livvy had become the only constant in his life. The thought of her was the only thing that allowed him to stomach Laura's visits, which usually put him back in depressive moods.

"When do you think you'll be able to go back to work, Ed?" she would ask. "Do you think this whole you-killing-a-guy thing will get you fired?"

"I don't know, Laura. We'll have to wait and see, just like I told you the last times you've asked. I'm still on medical leave, and the lawyers and the commissioners haven't decided one way or the other. It's still a waiting game," he replied as patiently as he could.

"Don't they know you have a family to support?" she roared.

"I am still getting some money coming in. I'm on leave *with* pay after all," he retorted his irritation starting to build.

"Yes, I know. But once you're able to work—"

"Laura!" he boomed, unable to take the questioning anymore. "I've told you before, hell I literally *just* told you that they've put me on paid administrative leave until all of this is over! Can't you just leave it alone!"

78

"Fine! Excuse me for trying to be the practical one!" Laura retorted. "I swear I can't even talk to you when you're like this!" Laura cried as she stood up.

"At least the insurance company fixed the car so that's something," she said, resigning to leave him alone for now on his work situation. "What time do you want me to pick you up tomorrow?" she asked as moved closer to his bed.

"About noon I guess. The hospital will call you and let you know when I'm being discharged," he said.

"Alright, well I'll be ready." She kissed him on the lips. "I'll see you later. Love you, Ed," she said making her way to the door.

"Love you too, Laura," he said halfheartedly. When she left, he could barely contain his excitement as it meant Livvy would be stepping into the room soon.

True enough, within ten minutes Livvy walked in wearing purple scrubs which accentuated her figure a bit more than he thought she knew. Her hair was tied back by a purple scrunchie allowing her flawless jawline and neck to help further his fantasies about her.

"Hey, Ed." Livvy smiled as she sat down beside him.

"Hey yourself. God, I thought she would never leave." Ed sighed, pouring himself a glass of water.

"How was it? Did she bitch at you again?" Livvy asked.

"Of course she did. Bitching and moaning about work and blah, blah, blah. I cannot believe her. God I hate her!" Ed growled.

"Then leave her," Livvy said.

"I can't lose my son," he retorted, to which Livvy just stayed quiet, despite wanting to scream in his face that she would never allow him to lose Eddie. "You know what I was thinking?" he asked.

"That you want a steak for dinner instead of the roast beef?" Livvy asked with a smirk.

"Well, that too." Ed chuckled. "But honestly, I was thinking that if she isn't going to have sex with me, I should just find someone that will."

"Really?" Livvy asked ignoring the tingle she felt between her legs. "You're willing to have an affair?"

"I think so," Ed responded. "I mean, what am I supposed to do? Live like a monk?" he asked.

"No, you shouldn't," she replied. "I mean people have needs that are more than just biological. Umm... do you have anyone in mind?"

"I don't know," Ed admitted. "I mean, I don't know many people around here and who would want to." Ed muttered.

"Oh don't be stupid, Ed! You're a handsome man! I'm sure you could get anyone to sleep with you if you just took the chance," Livvy replied. *Come on, you idiot! I'm sitting right in front of you! I will show you things that bitch couldn't even imagine in her own dreams!* she shouted inwardly.

"Yeah, but who? I mean... it's not that easy," he replied.

*You clueless bastard,* she roared internally. "Look Ed, I won't judge you one way or the other," Livvy said to him. *Yes, I'm a lying, vindictive, fucking bitch. Sue me. Goddamn you, Ed White, if you never get laid again, I*

80

*won't feel the slightest bit of sympathy for you!* "If you feel that's something you need to do for your own sanity then I say you should," Livvy replied.

"Yeah, I guess," he said before trailing off.

When he didn't offer anything else on the subject, Livvy decided it was time to change it, her frustration for him continued to threaten to make its way to the surface. "So, how do you feel about being discharged tomorrow?" she asked after he'd gotten out of bed and slowly made his way to the bathroom

Ed stood in the bathroom looking at himself in the mirror, putting shaving cream on his face preparing to whittle down his stubble. He looked over to her and shook his head.

"Not really feeling it, you know? Not looking forward to going back to that house, and eventually back to that bullshit job." He went back to running the blade over his rawhide like skin.

"You can't be wishing you were staying here, can you?" Livvy asked him with a grin.

Ed said nothing as he continued to shave. As Livvy moved toward him and saw blood starting to dribble from his neck, she quickly grabbed a paper towel and put it to his wound. "Ed, what's wrong with you?"

Barely flinching, Ed just stared at the two of them in the mirror, his eyes empty.

"I don't want to go back to that life, Livvy. I don't," he said. "I just can't. I don't want to go back to the way things were. I hated it then, and I hate it now. I mean, God, almost dying made me feel so alive. And being here, and talking with you, for the first time I didn't feel like... like I was just around so someone could live the easy life. You treat me like I'm an equal."

"Ed, you're a good man. Why wouldn't I treat you like an equal? I'm not Laura." Livvy held the tissue to his neck, looking into his eyes furiously. "And I'll be here for you when you need someone to talk to. We're friends right?"

"Friends?" Ed chuckled bitterly. "I don't have any friends left. No friends, no family, no one. It's like that bitch just—I swear, you ever seen *Roots*?" he smirked. "I feel like a slave yanked out of his homeland and just completely cut off from all human contact."

Livvy burst out laughing shaking her head as she pulled the paper towel from the cut and checked it to make sure the bleeding had stopped and tossed the paper towel away shaking her head.

"You are the most overdramatic person I have ever met do you know that? I mean, my God listen to you! You're the only Black man I have ever known in my life that would compare his marriage to slavery in the Old South!"

"Please, woman!" Ed smirked. "I'm probably the *only* Black man you have ever known in your life!"

"You wish," Livvy said moving out of the bathroom, followed by Ed. She moved to help him get into the bed and he waved her off slightly.

"I've got it," he said, holding onto his stomach as he slipped into the bed.

"How's the pain?"

"About a six. Better than it was a few days ago," Ed replied as he grunted to sink into his covers.

"Well, you aren't supposed to be working for at least another month to make sure that everything inside is good."

"What about my arm?" Ed asked.

"About another month and a half or so. It's only been a week, Ed," Livvy said with a worried tone.

"Yeah, yeah. 'Don't rush yourself, Ed.' I remember," he said, his eyes rolling in annoyance.

"Well, you want to rush it and fuck your arm up even worse, that's your problem. Don't come whining to me when you're a gimp," Livvy shot back.

"No, I said I would do it the smart way and I'll just... shit... I've got to find a way to get away from that woman," Ed grumbled. "I mean Jesus, I just told you how she was when she came in. It's all about *her* and how I need to go to work and take care of *her*. Its fucking disgusting how she treats me!"

"It's been traumatic for both of you, Ed. Maybe she just wants some normalcy in the household?" Livvy suggested. *I agree with you, you stupid bastard,* she growled within. *But how about we disregard your feelings for a while since you keep disregarding mine! Make me fall in love with you and just ignore that I'm here in front of you, will you?*

"Nope. She's just a lazy bitch that would rather have me do all of the heavy lifting while she lives like some kind of a damn fucking princess," he replied angrily, looking at her from the reflection of the mirror.

"So then, why don't you leave her if you're that miserable?" Livvy retorted yet again. *I am going to make you keep running this same loop until you see it my way.*

"You know why!" Ed shot back, irritation rising in his voice.

"Then if you're not going to leave, Ed, then you're going to have to find a way to make it work," she said with a harsh tone. "You're going to drive yourself crazy. Well... crazier than you already are." She chuckled lightly hoping to calm him. She could see he was ready to erupt in frustration. "Sorry," she said with a sigh. "Have you given anymore thought to what I suggested yesterday?"

"A shrink?" Ed snorted back a laugh remembering the mention of a therapist during idle chat the day before. "No fucking way, Liv. I told you that! I've been that route! All shrinks do is twist your words around, and either lock you in a funny farm or shove pills down your throat or up your ass depending on their mood that day! No thanks. I'd rather slit my wrists with a knife dipped in shit."

"Jesus, Ed, do you have to be so graphic?" Livvy asked, feeling her stomach turning from the visual.

"Well, yes." He grinned. "Part of me being me." When she didn't share in his laugh, he looked at her nervously. "Yo, Livs, are you okay?" he asked sitting up.

Livvy yawned loudly and waved him off.

"Oh yeah, just a little tired that's all," Livvy said with a smile.

"Yeah, you're here like night and day all the time. I mean jeez, don't you date or have anything else to do than spend all of your time with my crabby ass?"

"I have my kitties and I take care of them. I don't stay all night, don't be a dork," Livvy said with a grin.

"You didn't answer my question. Don't you date or anything? I mean I know you're divorced, but..."

"No," Livvy said abruptly. "No, I don't date. Besides, you're almost charming enough to enjoy spending time with."

"Well thank you so much," Ed said. He looked to her. "You look really tired. Well, I'll be out of here, so you won't have to worry about being bothered with me anymore."

"Whatever shall I do?" Livvy said with a smile.

"Well, I still have to do physical therapy. We can, you know, have lunch or something right?" Ed asked with a smile.

"I don't know if that's a good idea, Ed," Livvy said. A soft frown spread across her face. "You're a married man, and it wouldn't look good."

"Yeah, I guess you're right," he replied. His voice was downtrodden. "Figured, we could still be friends when I'm gone from here. I mean you did say that you'd..."

"I know what I said," Livvy shot back. "But let's be honest with ourselves, just for a minute? You're married with a kid, I'm a divorced cat lady that works in the hospital."

"You saved my..." Ed began.

"Yes, I saved your life. But I'm not building up this Florence Nightingale thing with you. It's been nice getting to know you and I hope that I've helped in your recovery, but we need to get back into reality, okay?"

Ed looked at her his face marred with shock at her display. She kept her face firm and her stance ridged as she got to her feet as the saddened look on his face threatened to kill her resolve. A cold, impassive mask.

"Yeah, you're right," he replied expressionless. "Well, Nurse Malone... I appreciate you wasting your time and my time over the last week. Go ahead and let yourself out." He picked up the remote control and began to flip channels.

"Ed..." she began.

"Good night," he said with a more forceful tone. "You're right. You've already done the good nurse thing. But yeah, we need to get back to reality. So, go do whatever the hell else you would've done before you decided to hang out with me."

"Ed..." she pleaded as the tears that welled in her eyes began to roll down her cheeks and threatened not to stop.

"Good night!" he said between clenched teeth, finally setting the television on a horror movie.

When Livvy saw that he was now ignoring her completely, she left the room doing all she could to keep her tears in check.

When she left, Ed was just staring blankly at the television screen.

Livvy went to her locker to get her purse and keys with a loud yawn. She could hear the shower going full blast and hoped that whoever was in there would not come out until she'd left. Her hopes were dashed when she heard the shower shut down.

"Livvy?" Becky asked with a towel wrapped around herself. "You're still here?"

"Yeah, heading home now," Livvy replied closing her locker.

"So tonight is your last night spending time with Mr. Personality, huh?" Becky chuckled as she began to pull her clothes on.

"Yeah, so it would appear," Livvy said dismissively.

"You're a damn saint, Malone, I'll give you that." Becky chuckled.

"What do you mean?" Livvy asked.

"Well, I mean come on! He isn't the nicest guy in the world. I won't shed tears for a prisoner, but he still killed a guy and he seems to have a constant chip on his shoulder. I mean, he *is* an asshole."

"Yeah," Livvy said looking to Becky, resisting the urge to wrap her hands around her neck and squeeze until her eyeballs popped out of her head. *How dare you talk about my man like that you bitch!* she seethed. *He just hates you because you're an idiot! You fucking cow!* She just shrugged at Becky, forcing the thoughts out of her as she made her way to the door. "I suppose you're right. Good night."

Livvy exited the locker room without another word. When she got to her car, she hissed angrily, "Bitch. He may be an asshole, but... but he's *my* asshole."

When she left, Ed glared at the door before focusing his eyes back on the television screen feeling the loneliest that he'd remembered feeling in his entire life.

"'Florence Nightingale' well fuck you too then!" His eyes narrowed as he felt a surge of emotion. "Why the fuck didn't you just let me die! Goddamn you!" He laid back, closing his eyes tight as he felt stinging tears running down his cheeks when the phone rang.

"Hello?" he asked, composing himself.

"Hey, baby," Laura greeted.

"Hey," he replied coldly. *What the fuck do you want now?* he grumbled internally.

"So are you excited about coming home?" she asked warmly.

"Yeah, it'll be nice to not be in the damn hospital, that's for sure," he replied, despite the fact he'd already answered this question, he knew it was time to start getting used to this again. *She doesn't hear anything she doesn't want to here, remember that.*

"Look, Ed..." Laura began.

Ed rolled his eyes knowing exactly what was coming.

"I'm sorry about the way I acted, I was... I am just scared. I mean, first that inmate and then the car accident? It's a lot to happen in one day. I didn't want to leave things like that you know? That's why I'm calling."

"Hey, it's okay, Laura. Nothing for you to worry about. Let's just... let's just put it behind us, okay? I don't want to go on and on and on about it, I really don't. It happened, let's just put it behind us and work on it." He kept picturing Livvy's retreating back, and he knew he wouldn't see her again. *I just have to make it work,* he told himself. *What choice do I have?* "Look, Laura, I mean hell, we can even try therapy to figure this shit out. How's that?"

"Ed, I think that would be wonderful," Laura choked out. "I love you, Ed."

"Yeah, I love you too," Ed replied, putting his index finger to his temple, and pulling the imaginary trigger.

"So I will see you in the morning. What time again?" Laura asked.

"Shoot for about noon, but I will have the hospital call when they are discharging me. That way we can both get a good long rest because I'm not going to be taking meds once I get out of here, and you won't have to be waiting around."

"Alright, Ed, no problem. I will see you tomorrow, honey. Good night."

"Yeah. Good night." Ed hung up the phone, his eyes narrowed. "Counseling. What the fuck?" he muttered to himself. "Fuck it. Maybe I'll find someone to talk to. Not like I have friends around this mother fucker or anything."

# CHAPTER 8
## *ONE YEAR LATER*

Ed patrolled around the dayroom, keeping his eyes on the goings on of the inmates. It'd taken him almost ten months to return to normal working duties thanks to the extended medical leave as a result of complications from physical therapy for his arm, and the administrative leave due to the trial. Now, on the one-year anniversary of the incident that claimed the life of an inmate, and his own brush with mortality, he was back to work and life weighed on him more than ever.

He couldn't help but muse at how many inmates had come and gone in that year. Some were victims of the revolving door effect of the system, with others transferring in from other facilities. Despite where they came from, local or otherwise, all had read about him in the newspaper and even after a year, the whispers hadn't stopped. Inmates regarded him with a combination of awe, resentment, and fear.

Ed didn't know if he should attribute the new aura around him to the fact that he'd killed a man, or because he was leaner than he had been. After the accident, his

91

appetite wasn't anywhere near what it was. He'd lost over forty pounds since the fateful crash. His body mass hadn't decreased by much, it was leaner, harder, and his stomach was now hidden from view by his clothes, no longer poking out to give him the look of a powerfully built sumo wrestler.

First returning to work, he was kept in more administrative duties and worked in the facility control room. He hated having to answer phones but being left to his own devices to listen to music while punching people in and out of secured sectors of the facility suited him. The novelty got old very fast and soon he was complaining to Bob to get him back to his normal duties. It took almost three months for him to get back into a dayroom. Even then, he was not put into Charlie unit. It took another four months for that to happen. He simply accepted the situation at work as the new 'business as usual' and went with the flow.

"2:30... thank God. I'm ready to go home," he muttered out loud as he watched the different groups of inmates just passing the time. Some walked in circles around the unit. Others hung out at the tables and played cards or board games while others watched television or took their turns going in and out of the recreation area. The monotony of life in a county jail had always been boring. Now, it was downright aggravating.

He'd already been disenfranchised with his job the lack of pay, the lack of promotion, it was the most dead-end job he'd ever had. *May as well work in a damn burger joint for all of this shit!* he'd begun muttering internally.

"Got a hot date tonight with the missus there, White?" John McGuinness asked him as he held the unit headcount sheet, tallying the numbers to report.

"Yeah right, hot date nothing! It's counseling night again," Ed replied with a bored expression. "Hot date, I should slap you for saying something so stupid. My wife hasn't given me any ass in months. I regrew my man-hymen." Ed snorted.

"Jeez you guys are always in counseling!" McGuinness smirked. "Sucks about the sex though, man. Also, a bit more information about your body than I care to hear about."

Ed smirked at his new partner and gave him a nod. John McGuiness was in his early thirties but looked like he was still in high school. He stood just under six feet tall, and was a little smaller in stature than Ed. Unlike Ed, however, McGuiness had a youthful light in his eye that seemed eternally happy while Ed's eyes were just dark and cold, with an occasional bounce of happiness in them.

"Yeah well, we do couples counseling and then I have my own individual counselor."

"Yeah I hear you, man, but how is it going? Is it helping?" McGuinness questioned. His body language and tone let Ed know that he wished that the conversation had never even progressed to this point.

"Yeah, something like that," he replied as memories of the trial flashed through his mind, as they did each day. The looks of hatred from Jackson's family weren't anywhere near as bad as the Jackson family's minister's antics in the media.

"Edwin White? Yes of course! You can tell by the name, the stature, and the attitude! This man is a stereotypical Uncle Tom that seems to enjoy killing off his own people to satisfy his masters!" the minister Jerusalem Jones would proclaim to the media. "Not once has he appeared to show even the slightest bit of remorse! He just sits in that courtroom and just stares like a fool toward the witness stand and refuses to talk to the media or even myself, a man of the cloth. A man of God. And I tell you good people, he has been invited to and been asked to present a press conference with an official apology!"

He wanted so badly to defend himself against the allegations, but he was forced into silence instead of taking it up on his own, which just made it worse. He'd been told repeatedly that he would have his chance to speak his side, but it didn't make sitting through the hearings any easier.

Despite the department reports, and the internal investigation finding that he had acted within the scope of force, wasn't enough for the Jackson family. When the District Attorney had initially refused to prosecute, Jerusalem Jones and the court of public opinion pressured the DA's office to try the case anyway.

"Trial, home, karate, home, repeat," he'd told himself every day during the entire process. When he was finally found 'not guilty' the weight wasn't off his shoulders. Thankfully, when the family attempted to attack in a civil case, it was thrown out. Yet, the pressures still didn't die down.

"When are you going to get promoted, Ed?" Laura whined. "With all that you've done, especially during the trial, shouldn't you be making more money?"

He just bit his lip, keeping himself from exploding like he wanted to. The last thing he needed was to get in more trouble, especially after the trial. On the days when he felt particularly lonely, he thought of Livvy, and regretted their fight more and more. They'd only had a week together, but he missed her terribly, especially on nights when his physical needs rumbled within and Laura wasn't feeling particularly generous. He would go into the shower, and she would enter his mind. It was all that he could do to keep himself quiet.

He half hoped that when he started physical therapy that he would be able to see her and have just a few seconds of conversation. Unfortunately, trying to catch glimpses of her during his sessions was a waste of time since she wasn't anywhere near that wing. As soon as he was cleared from physical therapy, he stopped going anywhere near the hospital. It brought up entirely too many painful memories.

"So, Ed," McGuinness chuckled, cutting into Ed's thoughts. "Is she hot?"

"Is who hot?" Ed asked as he snatched the headcount sheet away to input it into the computer.

"Your therapist!"

"Oh c'mon, Mac, she's a therapist. What do I care?"

"Well, let's be real man, you don't get laid," McGuinness said.

"Neither do most married men. What's your point?" Ed asked defensively.

"Look man, I'm your buddy. You know that right?"

"Oh Christ, Mac, no conversation that has that tag line is ever a good one. Can you hold off until we aren't in the dayroom, please?" Ed asked.

"Fair enough, man. Fair enough," Mac replied.

When their relief showed, the two men walked down the hallway heading toward the locker room.

"Look, Ed," Mac started, "have you thought that maybe you and Laura aren't good together?" Mac asked.

"Look, I don't want to talk about this right now," Ed grumbled defiantly.

"Well do you talk about it with your shrink at least?" Mac asked. When the buzz from the control room indicated that the door was unlocked, the men walked through and headed toward the locker room.

"No," Ed said. "We've mostly talked about shit with the trial that's about it. I... I'm not really a big fan of talking about that personal shit," Ed replied as he opened his locker to get changed.

"Can I give you a nickel's worth of free advice?" Mac asked.

"You mean you weren't already?" he said a harsher tone than he'd intended. He released a sigh and looked at him. "Fuck I'm sorry. Sure, Mac. Whatever," Ed said, pulling his uniform off to change into his jeans and a T-shirt.

"Start talking to your shrink, man. That's what she's there for. She can't talk to anyone else about your shit, so just do it."

"No," Ed said in a matter-of-fact tone.

"Why the hell not?" Mac asked in slight irritation.

"Because my shrink is buddies with her shrink and I'm not getting into that sort of trouble."

"Yeah, but they're—"

"Come on, Mac, let's be real for a second, shall we? This is a small hick town in a small damn hick area of a practically hick state. People can do whatever they want, and they still get funded, keep their jobs, and otherwise be above the law and rules," Ed said bitterly. "Look, I get that you're trying to help, but we have both seen it happen. I start saying things to my therapist, she's going to say something to Laura's therapist and then it's just a big cluster fuck. I'd rather just avoid it."

"So what are you going to do, buddy?" Mac asked in a worried voice as he watched Ed getting out of his uniform before following suit.

"I don't know," Ed admitted, his irritation of being in a no-win situation building. "Maybe find someone else that I can talk to about these things. I mean hell, I bounce the shit off of you."

"Yeah, and then Meagan gets pissed when you do." Mac smirked.

"How do you mean?" Ed asked pulling a fresh t-shirt on.

"She says you're a major downer." Mac laughed pulling on his pair of jeans from inside his locker.

"Does this mean she won't let you come out to play anymore?" Ed asked pulling his jeans on and fastening his pants and buckling his belt.

"Only in small doses, although I do tend to get laid a lot more when I hang out with you, so plus there." Mac smirked.

"Yeah well, chalk this up to a small dose. I'll see you in a few days," Ed said heading out of the locker room laughing lightly.

"Days off, huh?" Mac asked.

"Yup. Took forever to get here too," Ed said. "Tell Meagan I said hey," he said as he headed out, not giving Mac a chance to say goodbye.

As he made his way to his car, he rolled his eyes in irritation. Mac was a good enough guy, and even though they talked like they were friends, their relationship was work only. Ed, however, didn't mind playing the game. It was nice to have someone to talk to, even if it was only just during the work hours and nothing more. He'd left all of his friends behind during the move, and very few of them kept in contact with him after he'd gone. He couldn't blame them he was never good at returning calls.

After a few months, the calls stopped coming. When he would make them, the conversations were more and more distant until finally, he gave up completely. It was then that he'd come to terms with the fact that he wouldn't have a real friend again. Laura wasn't much of a social type only ever wanting to go to see her families friends, the Bishops, who oddly and without his total input were also Eddie's godparents. It seemed to upset her that he had such a good relationship with them, and their children.

He pushed the melancholy thoughts out of his head, started up his car and drove off. Therapy was in a half hour and he was starving. Keeping his eye on the clock in his car, he decided to stop at the grocery store to grab a sandwich before heading in to see his therapist.

He walked through the grocery store on auto pilot, glaring at anyone that caught his gaze. He knew they recognized him from the news reports and the trial and wasn't in the mood for their oblong expressions. As he walked up the aisle, ready to snarl at the next person that looked his way, he stopped short seeing a familiar face. The entire world slowed to a crawl when he saw her. It had been a year and she looked more beautiful than she ever did. She wore a long, flowing violet dress, her hair was a little bit longer, but still slightly locked in style since it was so curly and in two braids. He looked to her large brown eyes that were covered by the same pink and white marble-colored glasses frame. Her perfect, curvaceous body and full breasts were entirely complimented by the sundress.

"Holy shit. Livvy?" Ed asked, as he walked up to the familiar, and his most favorite nurse.

Livvy, over the last year fell back into her same basic routine of work and nothing else. During his trial, she kept a close eye on the proceedings and cursed the mean, loud-mouthed reverend angrily for every attack that he'd launched against Ed. Even after the fight, and their estrangement, she couldn't allow herself to lose her protectiveness of him.

When he'd been exonerated, she celebrated with a bottle of wine and marathon session with B.O.B playing the role of Ed.

"Hi, Ed. How have you been?" Livvy asked with a small smile. *He's lost weight,* she said to herself, *but he's as built as ever.* She chuckled inwardly. His eyes looked older, colder, and she knew it was more than just the trial.

Her heated hatred toward Laura White never cooled, maybe mellowed to a simmer. Seeing her Ed standing before her again, and seeing the look on his face, it started to burn hotter than she remembered it ever being.

"I've been better, I've been worse. How about you?" he asked politely, a genuine smile finally cracking his stone face.

"Working. That's about all. Glad to see that things went your way in court." She smiled warmly and his heart began to flutter ever so slightly.

"Thanks. I... I really appreciate it. Going to jail or having to come up with a couple million dollars isn't my idea of a good time." He chuckled lightly.

"So, are you back at work or...?" Livvy asked.

"Yeah, back at work. But, I have court ordered therapy," Ed said with a groan.

"Oh that's not good. I remember how much you hate therapy," Livvy said sympathetically.

"Yeah, that's not the half of it. My therapist and Laura's therapist are buddies and..." Ed began defensively. He hated having to explain this to people away from his wife.

"...you're worried that the two therapists will discuss you and maybe even tip things off to your wife?" Livvy asked.

"Yeah, exactly. So, I sit there for an hour and go through the motions," Ed replied, shaking his head irritably.

"Smart move," Livvy said. "What do you really do when you need to get things off your chest?" she asked casually.

"The same as I always did I guess. Well not really. I'm working out a lot more. Figure that's better for me than eating my problems away."

"Yes it is," she agreed. "I see, you look good!"

"Thanks," he smiled at her.

"What was it like when you went home? Did things go back to normal after you got out of the hospital," she asked curiously.

"I mean, things were fine when I first got out of the hospital. But after a month, she went back to the same pattern after that. God, it's so fucking old," he replied, releasing the frustration effortlessly.

"Jesus, Ed, I'm really sorry," Livvy said, putting a hand onto his and giving him a light squeeze.

"It's not your fault. This is my bed that I made, got to lie in it. Whether it has smallpox or not. But I've been meaning to tell you that I'm really sorry about how I reacted to you that night," he said suddenly. "I really am. I mean you have done..."

"Ed, enough," Livvy said with a warm smile, pushing her hair from her face. "You had every right to be upset. I was never mad at you about it, and even if it I was, that was a year ago. I let that go a long time ago."

"Well, I appreciate that but can I... can I take you up on your old offer?" Ed asked.

"What do you mean?"

"Be my friend?" he asked hopefully. "The whole trial and all of that, and with how Laura is. It's just so..."

"Lonely?" Livvy offered.

"How the hell do you know me so well, Livvy?"

"Because I pay attention." Livvy winked. "And of course we can be friends. I haven't ever not wanted to be your friend. I'm here for you, Ed."

"Thanks, Livs. I appreciate it." He smiled to her politely. "So I have to go to this bullshit appointment. Do you think we can get together afterward?" Ed asked.

"Oh, slow down there pilgrim!" She laughed. "How do you know that I don't have a date, or something lined up? Do you really think that I am so pathetic that I have no life other than to anxiously await to want to hang out with you impromptu?" she asked.

"Yeah, you're right," Ed replied sheepishly. He did what he could to push down an enraged voice at the idea of her being out on a date. "I'm sorry I..."

"Oh my God, Ed!" Livvy laughed loudly shaking her head. "You are pathetic. Of course we can hang out for a bit. There's a little coffee shop near my apartment. It's on Smith. You know it I'm sure. Everybody knows it. Been here as long as the town has. But when is your appointment?" she asked curiously.

"In about twenty minutes, give or take," he replied, feeling a wave of relief wash over him when he realized that she was just kidding around with him. "And yeah, I know the one. Been there forever."

"Alright. Well then, how about you meet me at the coffee shop at about quarter after five?"

"Sounds great to me." Ed smiled. "Thanks, Livvy, I really appreciate it."

"What are friends for?" Livvy smiled. "Now, you go ahead and play nice with your shrink. I'm sure if you're a real good boy you may get a lollipop or whatever the hell it is shrinks give out." Livvy laughed softly.

"Yeah, very funny." Ed rolled his eyes but hiding his irritation behind a smile. "I'll see you soon. "Order me up a Mocha with no dairy for when I get there?"

"Sure. Now go on, get out of here."

At five thirty, Ed walked into the coffee shop, glad to see that there were very few people there. He saw Livvy sitting in the very back of the shop and walked toward her with a big smile on his face.

"Hey you."

"Hey yourself," she said with a grin. "So how was the doctor?" she asked intently.

"Oh you know. Blah blah blah and yack yack." He shook his head as he sat, raising the cup to his lips and took a long, slow sip. "Thankfully, I won't have to deal with it for too much longer. I only have another month and then I am done." He grinned as he took his seat in front of her. When he looked her in the eyes, he felt transfixed, the threat of getting lost in her gaze nudged him and he didn't care. It wasn't until she spoke that he was snapped back into reality.

"Well that's good," Livvy said. "Is it helping you at all?"

"What?" he asked, still slightly distracted. "No. Not even a little," he admitted. "I'm just giving this irritating bitch just enough for her to tell them that I am not a psycho. But I can't just open up to her, or anyone else for that matter, about things that I'm thinking about."

"Well, you're in luck because here I am." Livvy smiled as she put her arms in the air in a 'ta-dah' gesture. "And I'm not just anyone."

Before he knew what he was doing, Ed reached his hand out, took her hand, and held it firmly yet gently.

"Thanks, Livvy, really. You're... you're the most decent woman I have ever met," he said giving her hand another gentle squeeze.

The sudden contact shook her ever so slightly. To feel his large, calloused hands surrounding hers in such a gentle embrace, she felt a fire building within her that threatened to burn all of her inhibitions away. *He's heroin,* she told herself. *I can't do this much longer.* She blushed a deep crimson and Ed smiled to her. She licked her lips slowly, her breath caught in her throat.

"You're welcome. Like I said before, you're a good man, Edwin White. You need someone to be on your side," she responded in a soft, quivering voice.

"Well, you're the only one that is." Ed grinned. "Maybe its fate. Who knows?"

"You think so?" Livvy asked sipping her coffee. She then turned a sideways glance toward him, then offered a sly smile. "How do you mean? This should be the most stunning explanation I have ever heard."

"Do you want me to be honest?" Ed asked.

"No. Lie to me. I love it," Livvy replied sarcastically with a wink.

"Alright. Well, since the last time we spoke I haven't stopped thinking about you," he said quickly. "And I have felt terrible about how I treated you."

"Really?" she asked dismissively. *So you haven't been able to stop thinking of me? Interesting.*

"Yes, really Livs," Ed said, raising his mug to his lips.

"Well like I said before, you're forgiven. And I'm here for you now. So anyway, how's the sex life going?" she asked innocently. *I'll give you something to think about Edwin White.*

"Well..." Ed laughed nervously, suddenly feeling very self-conscious. "My sex life now is as uneventful as my sex life in high school."

"Jeez, really?" Livvy asked.

"Yup. The last time we'd had sex was almost six months ago. And even still it was so boring and like... God, I don't get why she is like that. She expects me to do everything for her, but she won't do anything for me," he replied angrily.

"Give me an example," Livvy asked, leaning forward with her chin in the palm of her hand.

"No that's okay, I—" Ed began.

"Edwin White, I am not a dainty flower. Anything you say isn't something I haven't heard before you know. Hell, I've probably done more things sexually than you have!" Livvy scolded.

The sudden dominate tone took him by surprise, and it showed. She folded her arms over her chest, and he couldn't help but notice the mysterious mounds of flesh that were pushed together. He felt his body react to the view, and his heart pounded.

"Okay, fine. For one thing, she just lays there like a damn dead fish, you know? She won't get on top of me or do anything other than lay flat on her back because she says it hurts! Then she makes these, these, I don't know weird noises. She sounds like a beached whale trying to force its way back into the ocean or something!"

Livvy couldn't resist, she snorted and laughed almost uncontrollably. Ed looked over his shoulder and saw a few patrons who heard his assessment of his wife laughing also. He looked away from them and back to Livvy, with a shrug.

"Well, it's true!"

"I don't doubt you!" she chuckled, trying hard to compose herself. She finally cleared her throat and shrugged. "Is that all? Is there more than her animal noises?" Livvy chuckled.

"Oh there's a lot more! She is so goddamn selfish!" he leaned forward to whisper to her, "She wants me to go down on her, all the time, you know? It sometimes feels like if I don't do it, I'm the worst husband alive. Yet she won't do it for me. And when she does, it's a tease," Ed said looking to her, slightly embarrassed.

"What do you mean a tease?" Livvy asked, deep interest in her face.

"Well, when I go down on her she expects me to keep doing it until she comes. Well, she won't even let me remotely get close. She'll go down on me for a few minutes, I start to get like really into it, you know? I mean I am getting really, really into it and then she just fucking stops! Then she just lays on her back and does nothing. She gives no indication that she's enjoying sex with me one

106

way, or the other, unless those weird noises are an indication of pleasure."

"Really?" Livvy asked. "Why do you think that is?"

"I don't know," Ed said. His eyes quickly turned sad. "Maybe it's me. She said, when we first met, that she was a sexual person. But she never wants to do anything with me. I've been thinking about just having an affair or something, but who would want me? Maybe I'm just some fugly person that's so horrible at sex that I can't even get off a beast person."

"You stop that right now, Edwin White!" Livvy said in a fierce tone that surprised even her. "You are far from fugly, do you understand! You are probably the sexiest man I have ever laid eyes on! You're smart, you're creative and talented, and you are just perfect in every way! And don't you even think of disagreeing with me! I'm serious, what about the book you said you wanted to write? Does she even remotely support you in that? Does she try to give you any ideas, or even read anything you've written? No, don't say a word because believe me, Ed, I know the answer it's no. And you want to know what else I think?" Before Ed could say anything, Livvy cut him off.

"'Well what is that, Livvy?' Well Ed, thank you so much for asking! You've looked at her to encourage you in some way with that book of yours, and you're not getting it. You were able to get a good bit ahead, but you're nowhere near where you should be because if she would show at least some interest in you as a person, who you want to be as a person, and where you want to be as a person, you could! Instead, she just sees you as a work horse who has only one mission in life and that's work yourself into an early grave so her lazy, fat ass can just sit in the same clothes all day every day, watch television, and pack on more pounds and bitch about life!" Livvy's eyes burned with intense hatred, so much she'd wanted to say about Laura White in the last year to someone, anyone, other than her cats or inwardly had come out with so much intensity it almost scared her.

"And furthermore, Ed, the fact that you stay with her tells me one of two things one, you're just a patron saint that enjoys being used, abused, and treated like shit. Or, you have so little self-esteem that you've sold yourself this crock of shit that this is what you deserve for whatever the hell you've done. I've been trying *so hard* to figure out why you'd lower yourself to be with a woman like that and I just don't get it! It makes me sick how she treats you, it makes me angry that you allow it to happen, and if you don't fix it, you are going to die a sad, bitter man and I hate that! I want better for you! I want you to be happy goddammit!"

The two just stared at each other for a few minutes, both shocked by her outburst.

"I'm... I'm sorry," Livvy said, finally getting a hold of herself. "That was out of line and..."

"No, it's okay," Ed replied, his face still molded in shock from Livvy's explosion of emotion.

"Yeah right. You only say that it's okay because I said all of that nice stuff about you and bad stuff about her!" Livvy chuckled nervously.

"Well, yeah, but it felt good to hear, nonetheless. That was kind of a kick in the ass that I needed to hear. But I have to ask do you really see me like that?"

"I told you I did, didn't I? I promised you that I would never lie to you, and that hasn't changed." Livvy smiled, but her eyes still blazed angrily as she took his hand into hers.

"Do you remember when we talked about me possibly having an affair?" When she nodded in affirmation, he took a deep breath. He could feel his heart starting to pound with anxiety. He sipped his coffee, trying to wet his suddenly dry throat. "Well if I were to have an affair, and you were interested, I would so have it with you," he said quietly, looking to the floor at first before daring to look her in the eye.

"I'm pretty sure I just told you that I would be interested. If that rant doesn't tell you that, then you're a bigger idiot than I thought," Livvy replied, a hint of mock irritation in her tone. A feeling of excitement building within her core, sending a tingling sensation to other areas.

"Yeah, so you did," he said with a grin.

The two stared into each other's eyes for a few minutes. Ed then reached to his back pocket and put a couple of bills on the table.

"Can we get out of here?" he asked.

"Absolutely," Livvy replied, standing up to put on her jacket. "Follow me to my apartment," she said abruptly.

"Sure."

As they made their way to the parking lot, Livvy's stomach twisted into tight knots. She could feel his eyes on her and could see his body in her mind's eye. She'd imagined it so many times, since the first day they'd begun to spend time together. She'd fantasized about him so many times, brought herself to so many orgasms with his

109

name on her lips, yet now she felt nervous. He was all that she'd wanted for over a year, and now she felt anxiety.

*What if he really is terrible? God I don't want another case of Martin on my hands!* she screamed inwardly. *Stop it! There is no way that he could be that bad. He is so pent up he is going to have to be good! I'll show him what he wants. He can't be terrible. Please God, don't let him be terrible.* She prayed as she got into the driver's side of her car and drove off. She looked into her rear-view mirror every two seconds ensuring that he was still with her.

He stayed close to her tail, his heart pounding within his chest in a way that he'd never felt before. He couldn't believe he was about to do this. He had made the vows of marriage, and he'd taken them very seriously. He'd never had any intentions of violating them, other than occasionally wanting to flirt, until he'd met her. And now, he was about to do more than violate them he was ready to obliterate them in a wave of passion that was more than just a need for sex. He looked to his left hand, noticing the wedding ring on his massive ring finger, and then looked away quickly.

He remembered how it felt to put it on for the first time. How for the first month of their marriage he looked at the ring as though it were all just a crazy dream until he finally got used to the idea that it was there. He wanted to just pull it off, throw it out of the window. However, he knew he couldn't do that. Not just yet.

The short drive to her apartment felt like an eternity until she finally pulled into her parking spot. Her body flushed hot in anticipation as she put the car into park and shut it down. She slipped out of the car and saw him pull in beside her. When he got out of the car, she felt her knees get slightly weak.

"You okay?" he asked calmly as she stood there, just staring at him.

"Great," she replied breathlessly. "Never better." *You are so fucking gorgeous,* she said to herself. *You're going to know what it feels like to be a man when I get done with you.*

"Are you sure this is what you want?" he asked her, noticing her hesitation.

"Are you?" she asked him. *What if he's changing his mind? Oh my God! I am such a selfish bitch! But God I want him so bad! Please be sure you want this, damn you! If you don't, you're an idiot! You had better not turn me down now, you bastard!*

"What do you mean? I'm here aren't I?" He stepped forward, taking her hand into his, squeezing it assuredly.

"Yeah, you are," she said. "But are you sure this is what you want? I'm not a whore, Ed." She didn't know where the proclamation came from, or why she'd even said it. *I'm better.* Her eyes set, her body rigid.

"I know you aren't, Livvy. I know."

He pulled her close to him and kissed her gently on the lips as he wrapped his muscular arms around her. As she melted into him and moaned into his kiss, she felt his body fold into her equally. She broke the kiss, massaging his cheek.

"Let's go upstairs. Okay? We can deal with the other stuff later. Okay?"

"Alright," he said, kissing her again. "Lead the way."

Leading the way to the building, then to her apartment, the walk felt longer than the drive. When she finally got the apartment door open, their arms claimed one another as their lips locked with the intensity of lovers that had long been separated. The last of her sanity told her to push the door shut as their hands searched and claimed their new territories.

He released her lips just long enough to move his lips to her neck, suckling on her passionately. She felt her body already threatening to explode in pleasure just by the feeling and anticipation of him. She shuddered and gripped him tight, as his hands moved between them to massage her breasts.

"Oh God you feel so good, Ed! I've wanted this for so long, baby!" she gasped as she felt his hands move down below her waist, under her skirt to grip her and lifted her up so that her legs could wrap around him. "I would marry you in a second, baby, oh fuck I love you, Ed!"

He moved his lips from her neck and looked her in the eye, and he stopped, still holding her effortlessly.

"Is... is there something wrong?" she asked him fearfully.

"Do you mean it?" he asked. "Did you mean what you just said, or is it just lustful 'I'm ready to fuck' talk?"

"I'd never lie to you, Ed. You should know by now that if I didn't mean it, I wouldn't say it. I'd never treat you like she does, Ed. Not ever." She massaged his cheek gently, kissing him gently on the lips. "You're precious. She doesn't know it, she's a stupid fucking bitch, and I hate her for how she treats you."

Ed carried her into the bedroom and laid her onto the bed where she sat up to look him in the eye. He smiled, massaging her cheek gently.

"Yeah, she is," he said with a nod.

"You remember what you told me? About how selfish she is?" Livvy asked while massaging his thigh.

"Yeah, I remember," he replied in a husky voice.

"I'm nothing like that. Ready to see?" She winked and didn't give him a chance to respond.

She moved forward unbuckling his belt and then unbuttoned his jeans. She reached within his pants to feel his excitement, a purr escaping her lips. She pulled him from his denim prison and gripped him lightly, massaging him gently. Keeping him in her hand, using his own body as a leash directed him to the edge of the bed, and pulled the jeans down past his hips then pushed him to a seated position on the bed, before stroking him again.

"How can she be so mean? How can she not appreciate this?" she asked as she leaned forward and wrapped her lips around him. He cried out loud at the sensation of her mouth claiming him as he was barely able to keep himself from falling limp.

She looked up at him and grinned removing him, she smiled when his eyes opened wide. "I'm not stopping, baby. I'm just getting comfortable. Why don't you just lay back and enjoy yourself? Go on now." She gave him a gentle nudge to the shoulder and sent him back, sprawled.

"Take a look at me, baby," she said in a deep, passionate voice. She stood up and kicked off her shoes, then lowered the straps of the dress down her shoulders and pulled her dress the whole way down her body, over her supple thighs, standing before him in a black strapless bra and matching black panties. Running her hands over herself with seduction in mind, she licked her lips, "I wore these just for you. God, I have been fantasizing about running into you. I hope you like them. But I have to ask you something very serious is my body better than hers?"

"She's not even in your league. She's not even in the same damn sport," he replied, barely above a whisper.

Livvy chuckled lightly sliding her panties down her thighs and to the floor. She seductively moved her hands up her thighs, emphasizing to him her freshly shaved bikini area before reaching behind herself to unclasp her bra and allow her full breasts freedom.

"I'm glad to hear it. I'd hate for you to think you were downgrading," she said with a smile, massaging her breasts, bringing a moan to her lips.

"I don't see how anyone could see you as a downgrade," he replied, looking over her in all of her glory. "Oh fuck... you're so perfect." He began to sit up and she shook her head.

"No," she said in a firm tone. "Don't you fucking move another inch do you hear me?" She moved over to him and began to unlace his boots and pulled them off along with his socks. "You have spent your entire time with her serving her wants. Hell, I bet you've spent your entire sexual life serving everyone else's wants. Now, for a change, someone is going to service yours. And I'm going to give you exactly what you want. And you are going to lay back and you're going to love it. Do you hear me?" She finished pulling his jeans off of his body, leaving him lying half-naked on the bed.

"Yeah... I hear you," he replied.

"Good." She lifted his shirt up over his head and off.

"Look at your body. How the fuck doesn't she appreciate you?" she asked running her hands over his chest. "Your body is so hard, so strong. Did she ever compliment your body?" she asked.

"Not in a long time," he admitted. "I can't remember the last time she complimented me."

"What a bitch. She doesn't deserve you." She massaged his stomach gently and moved down his body and accepted him again with a muffled moan. She chuckled inwardly as his hips arched toward her chin and his moaning intensified.

She continued to work him into a sexual frenzy for several minutes, groaning over him as she did. Hearing his approval of her made her happy to be putting her talents toward someone that would appreciate them.

"Oh fuck... I'm... I'm so... so close..." he cried out as he moved his hands to her head as though he were going to move her away.

She grunted at him, keeping herself in place and continued working him. She knew he was close before he said so. She accepted his explosion with great delight, never once letting him go as he spilled himself, not allowing herself to miss a single drop of him.

When she was sure he was finished, she allowed his remains to wash down her throat and finally released him with a purr and moved up his body kissing him passionately. He returned her kiss with equal intensity as he clung to her tightly.

"I bet she never did that for you, did she?" she smirked.

"Not even close," he replied, his eyes closed.

"There's plenty more where that came from if you want it," Livvy replied, nipping his bottom lip.

"I want it all. Every last bit of you," he said, trying to catch his breath.

"Do you really? But what about your wife? What about your son?" she asked massaging his stomach gently.

"I do not want her. I hate her. Fuck," he said.

"What?" she asked with a grin.

"That's the first time I've ever said that out loud. But I do, I fucking hate her," he said with conviction. "I don't want her. I'll file for divorce I don't care anymore."

"You're ready to file for divorce after one blow job?" she chuckled lightly.

"It's the best blow job I've ever had." He laughed. "Plus, you're the only one up here that has ever taken the time to just listen to me and not judge me or tell me how I'm being such a downer."

"Who told you that?" she asked. "Who says you're a downer?"

"Well, my buddy at work, Mac. Anytime I call to talk to my parents, or my brothers, or any of my friends from back home, all I get is how negative I am. You never make me feel like that. You make me feel like you actually give a shit."

"Because I do give a shit, you idiot." She giggled, slapping his stomach playfully. "Do you think I would have spent all that time with you if I didn't care? Do you think you would be here in my bed right now, if I didn't give a shit?"

"No, I wouldn't," he said. "I mean it though. I will leave her if that's what it takes. I want you, Livvy."

"I won't make you do anything that you don't want to do, Ed. But I do not sleep around, and I don't do the one-night stand thing. If this is really what you want then, I'll trust you. Don't play with my heart. So help me God if you're playing with me I *will* kill you." She looked into his eyes and he could tell that she wasn't joking.

"Believe me, I am not playing. I'll tell her tonight that I want a divorce. I promise you," he said running his fingers through her hair.

"I'll hold you to that." She looked up to him and grinned. "You look like you're ready to go for real now."

"For real?" he asked.

"Of course for real. You think that's all you were going to get?" she laughed. "I gave you something you wanted. Now, you're going to give me what I want."

"And what's that?" he asked curiously.

"You." She locked her lips to his, moving her hand down between his legs to massage him and snickered approvingly when she felt his body respond to her instantly. She climbed on top of him and adjusted herself and released a loud cry of pleasure feeling his thick hardness enter her, and her body working to fine-tune itself to his girth.

He cried out loudly at the sensation of her tightened walls adjusting themselves to him. As she rolled her hips over him, his hands moved to massage her breasts as their tongues flicked and swirled over each other. Their cries of pleasure mixed into a cacophony of passion and desire as their bodies came together in a perfect fit in all, as though they were made for one another.

As she continued rolling and grinding herself over him, he quickly rolled her over and took control, pushing his hips into her as he refused to release his lips from hers until he discovered her breasts again and suckled upon her nipples with great desire. She screamed his name as her orgasm struck her like a lightning bolt.

He continued his assault on her despite her orgasm. The gentle passion slowly turned aggressive and desperate as she bit down roughly on the flesh of his shoulder, causing him to push harder into her with a growl of feral craving. She could barely contain herself as another wave of orgasm struck her and sent her into a stratosphere of pleasure, screaming his name as loudly as her body would allow her too.

His movements inside of her picked up in intensity as he felt his own explosion drawing near. Hearing his grunts of pleasure, she dug her nails into his back and held him close.

"That's right, baby. Show me that I'm yours. Come on, baby, make it yours! Come on, baby. I've been dreaming of this forever! Don't make me wait, Ed! Give it to me now! Claim it! Claim it, Ed! Now!"

He pushed harder within; her encouragement driving him into a state of desire he never knew existed and when he felt himself at pleasure's door and the explosion brought a savage sound from him that he'd never heard before the world ceased existence.

The lovers clung to each other, their bodies slippery with sweat and desperate desire as their lips continued battering one another.

"I... I never thought it could feel like this," Ed gasped.

"What do you mean, baby?" Livvy asked. Her head rested on his chest, cuddling into his side.

"Whenever I'm with that bitch, I have to put my brain elsewhere to get off," he said with deep bitterness.

"What do you mean by that?"

"It means that to even get off, I have to either think about people I've had sex with, people I want to have sex, or think about porn."

"Is that right?" she asked.

"Yeah," he replied.

"So, what did you think about the last time you two had sex?" She chuckled.

"The six times or so that she and I have had sex in the last year? I've thought of you. Hell, when I'm in the shower I'm thinking of you."

"Oh please," she said, giving his stomach a slap. "You've already had me. You don't have to lie to me."

"I'm not lying. The first time she and I had sex, I had to think of you just to get off. You've been in my head like mad. Hell, I almost came to your floor when I would go to physical therapy."

"Why didn't you then?" she asked.

119

"Because I didn't think you would want to see me after that last conversation," he replied.

"Well, if you had, it wouldn't have taken this long for this. I couldn't turn you down, Ed. Not ever." She placed a gentle kiss to his chest.

"Good to know." He smiled. "So, how are we going to do this?"

"What do you mean 'how'?" she asked.

"Well, when I go home I'm going to tell her that I want a divorce. That's all there is to it."

"Okay, so what is your question?" she asked.

"I don't know. This is just... I don't know, it's a new situation for me that's all." He chuckled lightly.

"If you really want to know how you do this you tell her you want a divorce and then you get an apartment of your own. I hope you didn't think you'd be living here?" She smirked. "This is only a one bedroom and you still have little Eddie to think about."

"Yeah, I know. I will get an apartment around this area so I'm at least close by. I figure that at first she and I will do the joint thing until we get into court."

"Do you think you'll be able to handle this nicely?" she asked, looking up to him. "I don't want you to get cheated."

"I think so. I mean, we've talked about the 'what ifs' before. She promised me that she wouldn't keep him from me and that we could find ways to make it work. I've been good to her it shouldn't turn ugly at all." He nodded pulling her closer. "Don't worry about it. We can get this done and then focus on the future."

"Sounds like a good plan to me," she said with a gentle smile, placing a few kisses to his stomach. "Do you feel any regrets?" she asked.

"Actually, I do," he said.

"Oh," she said. Her body ran cold as she tried to control the tears that were threatening to swell.

"I regret that I didn't do this sooner," he said placing a small kiss on her forehead. "Ow!" he cried when she smacked his stomach sitting up.

"You asshole!" she hissed angrily. "That was so mean!"

"I'm sorry, baby." He chuckled as he pulled her closer to him. "I'm telling the truth though I only regret that we didn't do this sooner. All that time we spent sitting and talking was the only thing that kept me from giving up."

"What are you talking about?" she asked, her eyes still narrowed.

"You saved my life, but with her showing up to the hospital the way she was..."

"You wished I hadn't," Livvy finished for him. Her eyes dropped in that moment but she quickly recovered.

When he nodded to her, and embarrassment crossed over his face, she placed a soft kiss on his lips.

"I understand. I do. Believe me, I've asked myself at least a dozen times a day why you would marry someone like her. If I were with someone like her, I'd probably want to kill myself too."

"I've wanted to. I would sit in the bathroom when she'd be asleep with a knife to my wrist. Before the accident and ever since," he said looking to her. "She just... she makes me feel like such a loser. Anytime I'm happy, or excited, here she comes with some negative bullshit and makes me feel like complete shit. I seriously would rather die than even have to go home to her. I mean it."

"Jesus, Ed, I really don't know what to tell you," she said as she leaned up on her elbow to look at him. "Look, I'm off tomorrow. Do you want to just stay here tonight? Call her and say you'll be out late with some friends and you'll come home tomorrow?"

"I want to do that more than anything," he said looking to her. "But it may not be the best idea. We don't want her to start getting the idea that I'm cheating. I'll just say that after therapy I ran into some of the guys from work and we went for a beer and I had to sober up."

"Won't that make her think something is up?" Livvy asked.

"Nope. I texted her and said that I was going to have a few beers before I came in. I always back myself up." He chuckled. "Although I am anxious to break the news to her though. What if I went back to let her know that I'm leaving, then I can come back here. Is that alright? I may need to stay here until I get my own place if that's alright?"

"That's a quick change," Livvy said as she looked to him seriously as if searching him for any deception. After a few seconds she gave him a nod.

"That would be alright. If you're sure" she said. "So should I expect you sometime tomorrow then?"

"I will be back tonight." He laughed. "She'll probably just cry and try to manipulate me that way. When she sees it won't work, she may get pissed off. That's her angle usually. But I wouldn't want to stay under that roof with her anyway. I would rather be here." He smiled at her, running fingers through her hair. "You know I'm never going to let you go right?"

"Yeah right, Ed," she said with a grin shaking her head.

"I'm sorry, Livs. I'm never going to let you go. I've got you now, and I'm never letting you get away." He smiled, brushing his lips against hers.

"I'll hold you too that, Mr. White." She cupped his cheek in her hand.

"You do that."

# CHAPTER 9
## *TRUE COLORS*

"Here we go," he said to himself as he pulled into the driveway. It was an hour later, and as badly as he wanted to get this over with, leaving Livvy made him feel like he'd left a chunk of himself behind. "Must be what love is really supposed to feel like." He snickered as he turned the key to shut down the engine and closed the car door to head inside.

He checked his watch and knew that Eddie would be asleep by now or should be. If he wasn't, he made a mental note to bring that up to the litany of reasons why he was leaving her. He hated being made to feel like the bad guy just for establishing rules for his four-year-old son.

"I'm home," he announced when he stepped in the door. As he made his way into the kitchen, he felt his eyes narrow at the sight of his mother-in-law Lorraine. Everything about her drove him crazy from her tall, skinny stature, to her short gray hair, to her near toothless, blank expression, her thick voice due to years of chain smoking, completed by the fact that she existed at all.

"Hey. How was work?" Lorraine asked politely.

125

"Fine. Same old dog and pony show. Not insane yet," Ed replied as he went into the fridge for the carton of orange juice. On some days, he felt bad that he hated her so much. Then, he remembered exactly why he hated her so much she allowed her daughter to rule her life, yell at her, and essentially was completely subservient to her daughter's whims. And, on days when she got tired of her daughter yelling at her, she tried to take it out on him.

"Well, that's good. Eddie is in bed, Laura is upstairs," she said making her way to the front door to go outside to smoke.

"Alright thanks," he replied, claiming a glass for his juice, and opened the door to the microwave as he was about to heat up his supper that he knew was in there and made a face. "Fucking pork chops again? Goddammit!" He put the plate in the fridge and pulled out the bread and ham and began to make a sandwich.

He made his way upstairs after eating and groaned pulling off his boots as though he'd had a long day.

"Hey, babe," Laura called from the bedroom.

"Hey," he replied making his way into the bathroom.

"How was your day?" she asked as she set down her e-reader and made her way into the main room of their top floor apartment.

"The usual. Inmates bitching and moaning, administration full of horseshit, and still no promotion." He smirked as he started to get out of his clothes to get into the shower.

"I'm sorry to hear that. But at least you're back to work in full now, right?" she asked.

126

"Yeah, I guess so. I'm going to start looking for a new job though," he said as he turned on the hot water and stepped into the shower. When he did, Laura came into the tiny, compact, bathroom and sat on the toilet.

"Again?" she asked exacerbated.

"Yes, again," he said. "I told you before I hated it there."

"But it's a good job, Ed!" she said.

"Laura, it pays me like... ten bucks less minimum to other places! Plus we've talked about this I don't believe in this shit."

"Okay, I get that. But listen, it keeps food in your son's stomach and..."

"Laura, I can find other jobs to support Eddie. I don't have to be at the jail," he said as he let the water run down his back to ease his muscles.

"And where do you think you're going to get a job like that? I mean, anything else you get is going to pay less! You said so yourself," she retorted.

"Well, babe, why can't you get a job? You said you would help me out with this when I moved up here. That was like six years ago."

"Ed, please don't start this okay? I've had a long day and I don't want to fight about this again! My back isn't feeling any better!"

"You've had a long day? Did you go out today?" he asked, knowing the fight was coming.

"Edwin White! You know I didn't! You had the car and then decided to go out with your buddies! I was dealing with Eddie all day!"

"Laura, come on!"

"No Ed, *you* 'come on'! We've talked about this over and over again! Any job I get we would end up losing money because of childcare!"

"Laura, this isn't fair! You cannot expect me to do all of this myself! I don't want to live with your mother anymore, and it isn't her job to help pay the bills and such. You and I are supposed to be building a life together and that involves you having to put in the work too!"

"I am! I'm raising *your* son! I make sure *your* dinner is made!" Laura retorted.

Ed's eyes narrowed angrily within the shower.

"You know what? Women work and take care of their children! I cannot do this alone, Laura! I've told you this repeatedly, I need help!"

"What kind of fucking man are you, Ed? Begging me to help you? You're the man! You're supposed to work and take care of me and our kids! That's your job! My job is to take care of the home and raise the kids! You remember that? You remember you said that you wanted to be traditional?"

"Yeah, that was before the fucking economy went into the goddamned toilet! There are no married couples where only one is working and..."

"Ed, I am tired of this! I have had a..."

"A long day," Ed replied with her in unison. He turned off the water and grabbed his towel and dried himself off and exited the shower looking Laura in the eyes. "I can't do this shit anymore, Laura," he said walking out of the bathroom.

"What is that supposed to mean?" Laura asked following him out of the bathroom.

"I'm sick of having this same argument all the time. I can't do this."

"Well then stop bringing it up, Ed! My back hurts! I cannot—"

"No Laura, you won't," he said as he pulled a pair of boxer shorts from his dresser and pulled them on under his towel and pulled on a t-shirt.

"Ed—"

"No," he said abruptly. "I'm so sick of the excuses. I'm sick of working a job I'm miserable at while you sit here all-damned-day watching TV and acting like watching Eddie is the equivalent of hard labor. Most Mothers by now have their kids in pre-school or something and going to work. He isn't a baby anymore. But you would rather sit around and do nothing and keep with the same back excuse, while you probably hinder the poor kid's development by keeping him acting like a fucking baby! It's completely old. Your back isn't so bad that you can't carry him when he begs you to. It's only a problem when you need to do something."

"Ed—"

"No!" he hissed, trying to keep his voice down so not to wake Eddie. "I'm tired of it, Laura. I'm not your goddamn slave. I'm so sick and tired of you bugging me about promotions, and work, and all of this shit. I'm done being your slave. You want a slave? Jump in the magic car and go back in time and own a plantation. But you aren't living the high life on my back anymore that's for goddamn sure."

"What are you saying, Ed?" Laura said in a low voice, brushing tears from her cheeks.

"I'm leaving," he said simply. "I want a divorce. I'm done being your lawn jockey." He went into the closet and pulled out a shirt and some pants.

"Ed, no you can't," she started.

"Yes... I can and yes... I am. I'm going to file for divorce. I've been begging you for years to help me. And you just dismiss me with empty shit like 'It will be okay.' Or 'We'll find something.' I'm sick of it. It wasn't cute before, and it damn sure isn't cute now. I'm staying at a motel tonight. I'll be around tomorrow to pack some things. I'll do the filing."

"Ed, please we can..."

"No. I'm over it, Laura. I've been over it. You want to be a trophy wife, and my shelf just isn't big enough to deal with it anymore. I hope we can figure all of this stuff out without needing to involve lawyers because I want the best for Eddie. I hope we can at least agree on that?"

"Of course," she whispered as tears rolled down her cheeks.

"Good. I don't want this to turn ugly. I would like to at least be able to get along for Eddie's sake. Just because I can't stay married to you anymore doesn't mean that I want to fight with you and have hatred toward you." He went into his drawers, pulling out multiple pairs of underwear and socks and tossing them onto the bed, then pulling a gym bag from under the bed and stuffed the clothing into the bag, then shoving various pants and shirts from the closet in as well.

"I don't want you to hate me either, Ed," she replied.

"Good. I'll call you tomorrow before I head over to pack some things," he said as he went back for his boots.

"Don't do anything with my stuff, I will handle all of it, no problem."

"Alright. I... I'm sorry, Ed. I'm sorry that I'm a bad wife. I didn't mean to be," she said, as she sobbed quietly. Ed's eyes narrowed, the little respect he did have for her obliterated as he saw through her manipulation. *Not this time, bitch. Not this time.*

"Laura, I think we just rushed into this with different ideas on what it meant to be married. We should have, I don't know, figured out the rules of all of this before we did it. But better we do this now than do it later."

"Yeah. Like you said, we don't want to hate each other," Laura said as she brushed her hair from her face. "You said you're staying at a motel?" she asked.

"Yeah, either at a motel or I may just go stay at Mac's or something I haven't decided yet. I'll let you know what is what tomorrow when I've had time to sleep on it and think it through some more."

"Okay. Well, be careful and... let me know you've gotten to where you're going safely okay?" she asked with a sad smile.

"Sure. Good night, Laura," he said. He grabbed his phone and went to get his coat and got back in the car and took a deep breath. "Well, that was easy." He smirked as he put the car into gear and drove off back to Livvy's apartment.

He rang the door buzzer when he got back to the apartment and was buzzed up instantly. When he got to the door, she was wearing a robe that was tightly pulled closed, with wet hair and no glasses. He had his gym bag slung over his shoulder and smiled at her.

"Honey, I'm home." He chuckled.

She reached forward, clutching the collar of his jacket, and yanked him against her body and kissed him deeply. Once he crossed the threshold, he tossed the bag to the floor and pushed the door shut with a slam. He moaned deeply into her lips, moving his hand down below her waist to hold her.

"Mmm, I could get used to that type of greeting." He smiled looking at her.

"Is that right?" she asked, then looked to the bag and then back to him. "So how did it go?"

"Went as good as it could. She tried to guilt trip me but it didn't work."

"Did you eat?" she asked kissing him again.

"Yeah, had a ham sandwich. She made pork chops... again, and I hate how she makes them," he said with a glare.

"Do you want me to make you something?" she asked starting to move toward the kitchen. He kept his arms firmly around her waist and shook his head no.

"No. The only thing I want is you right now, that's all." He kissed her again.

"I think I've created a monster." She chuckled.

"Maybe you did," he agreed.

"Well big man, you know where the bedroom is. I will be right there."

"Where are you going?"

"Unless you want them mad at you, I need to feed the cats. Their dinner is already late, and they aren't happy." Livvy smiled and gestured toward his bag.

He turned and saw Sylvia and Platter clawing at his gym bag.

"Fair enough. Don't want them angry at me." He laughed pulling off his boots and leaving them by the door.

"No, you don't." Livvy chuckled. "Now go ahead, I'll be there in a minute."

Ed kissed her again before heading to the bedroom. When Livvy entered the room, he was lying in the bed with only his naked upper body visible. Livvy took off her robe, still naked, and climbed into bed with him and rested her head on his chest.

"Ed are you sure I didn't scare you with what I said earlier?" she asked cautiously.

"You mean about wanting to marry me?"

"Yes."

"No, you didn't," he admitted immediately. "I was thinking about it the entire drive to, and back actually."

"And what did you come up with?" she asked.

"Well, I know that I've been in love with you for the last year and being apart from you only made it stronger. I didn't realize it until today. And when I left, I just wanted to be back here with you."

"So what are you saying?" she asked.

"I'm saying that I'm going to have to get you a ring soon." He grinned placing a kiss on her forehead.

"Don't rush into it, Ed. Just because I was serious doesn't mean that I want you to feel obligated to do

anything. I understand if you want to take some time and—
"

"Stop it," he said with his finger slightly pressed against her lips. "I don't do anything that I don't want to do. This is something that I want to do." He placed a kiss on her lips.

"Well then buy a ring and ask me properly. This isn't a soup kitchen, White," she responded in a testy tone.

"Yes, ma'am," he replied.

He didn't give her a chance to say anything else. He locked his lips to hers and pressed his body against her. As they made love, he felt all of the worry and anxiety of his life fade away. There was only the two of them and their bodies claiming one another in the moonlight. Two lovers finally finding one another, after a lifetime of separation.

"So you finally did it?" Mac asked a few days later as the two were preparing for the start of another shift.

"Yeah, I did." Ed nodded. "And I tell you what, I feel like I was just paroled."

Mac started to howl in laughter getting the attention of the other officers in the locker room.

"The hell is so funny?" one of the officers asked.

"Oh you didn't hear, Delaney?" Mac answered after composing himself.

"Hear what?" the officer named Delaney asked.

"Laura and I are getting a divorce," Ed told him calmly.

"Seriously? Damn man, sorry to hear that."

"Don't be, D," Ed replied. "Like I just told Mac here, it's the best decision I could possibly make."

"What about your kid?" Delaney asked.

"Well I filed the paperwork yesterday and got a bit of my stuff together already. I'm probably going to try and get him since she doesn't work," he said. Delaney shook his head shutting his locker door. "What's the head shaking about, D?" Ed asked.

"This is going to get shitty for you, White. I'm just telling you that right now," Delaney replied.

"How you figure that?" Ed asked.

"Bro, you can't be that dense. She's the woman. She is going to fight tooth and nail to keep that kid. Shit, he's gonna be her meal ticket to easy street, just you wait."

"We said we were going to try to come up with something that's best for him," Ed retorted.

"Yeah, she says that now. But once it sinks in, she's going to be pissed that you're leaving her, and she's going to try and take you to the cleaners and back again. You'll be lucky if you can get the kid for weekends. Believe me, I know. When me and my ex split, we had this whole plan in place. After about a week, it turned. Now, I see my kid every other weekend and I'm paying over a third of my check for child support. Now, she's trying to move which means I'll never get to see him, but I'll still be paying out the ass for support. Don't be naïve, man," Delaney said as he exited the locker room.

Ed and Mac looked at one another. Mac put a hand on his shoulder and shrugged.

"Maybe you should get yourself a lawyer, bro. Just to protect yourself."

"You really think so?" Ed asked.

"Couldn't hurt. Come on, we got to go and punch in."

Livvy walked the Med Surge floor with a wider smile on her face than usual. Ed had been at her apartment for only a day before having to go back to work, and she realized she didn't want him to leave for anything. They'd barely made it out of bed the next day other than to eat, and of course, use the bathroom. Now that it was time to go back to regular life, she was able to happily reflect on their time.

After making another round on the floor, she walked past the nurse's station and was greeted by Becky and Margo.

"Hey Livvy, your sister called for you a little while ago," Margo said handing her the post it note.

"Okay thanks, Margo. Must be that time of the month sisterly lunch time." Livvy chuckled picking up the phone to dial her sister's extension.

*"Hey, Livvy,"* Jeanette answered on the fourth ring.

"Hey, Jeanie. You called?" Livvy asked.

*"Yeah. Are we still on for lunch today or are you going to reschedule again?"* Jeanette asked.

"I'm okay for lunch. Same place?" Livvy asked.

*"Yup, little Japanese place out of the way. I'll be there at about one-thirty. I have a client at noon and she always runs over."* Jeanette chuckled. *"She called and said that her husband was leaving her, so I'll have to allow for a lot of time."*

"Is that right?" Livvy asked with a dismissive tone.

*"Yeah, but she's the needy type so now that her husband is leaving, she will probably be even more needy,"* Jeanette said. *"I'll tell you a little bit about it later. Talk to you soon."*

"Alright Jeanie." Livvy hung up and laughed to herself.

"Okay, what's his name?" Margo asked.

Livvy looked at Margo curiously.

"Oh come on now, you are positively glowing!" Margo said. "And, not to be crude, but you're definitely walking a lot differently than usual. So that definitely means that you've been having a lot of... shall we say... fun." Margo winked.

"Exactly." Becky giggled. "So come on, what's his name and how good is he on a scale of one to ten? Although judging by the way you're moving, he's definitely higher than a seven."

"Off the charts." Livvy winked mischievously. She paused for a moment when Becky asked about his name. She looked at Becky as if to size her up and realized that she didn't trust her, or Margo for that matter. "Damon," she said instantly. "His name is Damon."

"Damon, huh?" Becky asked with a grin and leaned forward with a whisper. "Is he... you know?"

"Is he what?" Livvy asked with a sharpened tone.

"Oh, nothing," Becky said with a wicked grin.

Livvy watched her closely as if trying to decipher the other woman's intentions with her questioning, but finally just let it go.

"So you say he's off the charts, huh?" Margo asked with a grin. "That good, huh?"

"Best I ever had," Livvy replied, giving Becky another look over before looking to Margo with a smirk.

"Is that right?" Margo asked. "Do tell! I want loads of details! I'm sure if it's good enough, Floyd will be thanking you tomorrow."

Becky let out a loud giggle before containing her giddiness with her hand over her mouth. Livvy did her best not to laugh out loud herself, hiding the it with a cough.

"Well I'm not one to kiss and tell, but he is just... amazing," Livvy said with a slight blush.

"That's so sweet," Becky said, a light tone of sarcasm in her statement. "Now is it... that he's good at what he does or is it the equipment or both?"

"Both." Livvy grinned. "He appreciates what I do for him, and the things he does to me... I've never felt from anyone."

"Is that right?" Becky asked. "Well give me more! I need to live vicariously through you!"

"You'll just have to guess," Livvy said as she stood up. "I have to get back to my rounds."

"You're a cruel bitch, you know that?" Becky laughed standing up to go in the opposite direction.

"Speak for yourself," Margo said. "I have an overactive imagination."

Livvy pulled up to her favorite Japanese restaurant a few hours later, glad to be away from the hospital, and all of the questions. It hadn't taken long for the news to circulate amongst the staff that Livvy had found a new guy, and everyone wanted in on the information. She'd always been so guarded about her private life, for reasons that were obvious to her.

She knew that no one in the area knew Martin, but she was always terrified that someone would find out and tip him off to where she was exactly. She felt a slight shudder of terror run through her at the idea, but the cold chill was quickly replaced with the thought that she now had someone that would protect her, and the idea brought a wide smile to his face.

"You're definitely going to be rewarded for that later, Mr. White." She snickered to herself.

Walking into the restaurant, the wait staff all knew her and greeted her with smiles and gestures toward her normal table, where Jeanette was already seated with a cup of tea and a glass of water in front of her, and a matching set across from her for Livvy. She walked over to the table with a smile.

"How long did I keep you waiting, Jeanie?" she asked politely, removing her jacket.

"Not long. Five or ten minutes. I was finishing up some case notes," Jeanie replied.

"Anything interesting?" Livvy asked taking a sip of her tea.

"Always. And if I tell you it would violate HIPPA tremendously."

"All the more reason for you to tell me." Livvy giggled.

"Of course," Jeanie replied, looking around the restaurant ensuring that they were alone. "I got something major league good."

"Oh yeah? What's that?" Livvy asked.

Jeanie went quiet instantly when the waitress walked over to take their orders. After ordering her usual, Shrimp Tempura and hibachi chicken, Livvy looked at her sister with an excited glance.

"Come on already!"

"Alright, alright!" Jeanie replied. "Jesus you're like an annoying kid on Christmas!"

"Oh shut up," Livvy snapped back playfully. "You know you do the exact same thing whenever I have dirt on Mom, Dad, or the boys." She chuckled.

"Yeah, you've got me there," Jeanie replied. "So you remember that hypochondriac of a client I have?" Jeanie asked.

"Yeah," Livvy replied. "What about her?"

"Well you know how I told you that she always bitches at her husband about money and everything?"

"Yes."

"Well there is a lot more to it than that." Jeanie grinned, going quiet again as the waitress brought their soup and salad.

"Okay, like what?" Livvy asked, starting to grow impatient with the build-up.

"Well for one, she is married to that jail guard guy that killed the prisoner last year. Remember when that was on the news?" Jeanie asked.

"Yeah..." Livvy replied as casually as she possibly could despite her insides clenching instantaneously.

"Well apparently he told her that he wanted a divorce the other day. She came in bawling her eyes out, saying how he's such an unreasonable bastard expecting her to work when she is so badly injured," Jeanie replied rolling her eyes.

"Is she?" Livvy asked carefully.

"What? Injured?" Jeanie asked. When Livvy nodded, Jeanie chuckled. "Fuck no. She's a total fucking liar she just doesn't want to work. She told me like, a long time ago, that there was nothing wrong with her, but he's so stupid he'd just put up with her not working. When he'd start to get fed up with it, she'd act like her back was bothering her to play on his sympathies. Problem is, she's told the lie so much she believes it. She is a classic case of a pathological liar and a seriously sociopathic con artist." Jeanie chuckled.

"Wow, what a cunt," Livvy replied with her teeth clenched. She wanted so badly to wrap her hands around Laura White's throat knowing now that her lover's suspicions were completely justified.

"The sad thing is," Jeanie continued, "that her husband is the sweetest guy, you know? He used to come to her appointments, always had a polite word and a smile. He would like totally wait on her hand and foot. When their kid was born, she told me, he didn't sleep at all the entire time. He got in the birthing tub with her and went really above and beyond what a man does in the delivery room. I think she said that he didn't sleep for almost three days straight between the delivery and taking care of the baby."

"He sounds like a great guy," Livvy said shortly. Her jaw still set tight, trying hard to calm the rage inside of her.

"Oh yeah, he is. She used to tell me all the time how great he was. But the poor guy is so dumb. She gradually became more and more blatant with her manipulations of him and he didn't notice. And even if he did, he wouldn't do anything because he was afraid of getting a divorce because of the child support and not seeing his son. She figured she had him. Well, turns out he finally got sick of it."

"Why do you think that is?" Livvy asked.

"Well, I think a lot of it is that he went back to work and it's too hard to deal with after the trial. Plus he goes to see Alyssa and he knows that Alyssa and I know each other so he won't talk to her. I actually feel bad for him," Jeanie said. "But anyway, that's not the half of what happened."

"Oh?" Livvy asked plainly. "It gets worse?"

"Much worse." Jeanie sighed. "So apparently, she figured he was going to get tired of the whole thing. Apparently she'd been setting him up from the very beginning. So she comes in and says to me 'Jeanie, if I tell you that I'm afraid of my husband and that I think he's going to hurt me, you have to do something about it right?' and I told her 'Yes, of course.' So then she says 'Well, I'm afraid of him. He told me that he wanted a divorce and if I tried to take Eddie away from him that he would kill me.'"

"Are you fucking serious?" Livvy shouted expectantly, so loud that the staff in the restaurant stopped what they were doing to stare at her in surprise.

"Livvy, you're going to have to play it a lot more casual than that or I'm not going to tell you anything else," Jeanie hissed.

"Sorry, that's just so fucking rude and disgusting!" Livvy exclaimed in a whisper.

"I know!" Jeanie replied. "So I asked her if that truly happened or not, because she had never mentioned him ever being violent. I even reminded her how she'd told me about how he was so gentle and loving and that he would never hurt a fly and how she would share a laugh with him whenever doctors would ask her if she was in fear at home. She got pissed and told me, 'You can't ask me that. I'm in fear of my life do something about it.'."

142

"So what did you do?" Livvy asked.

"I did what I had to do. I had to get her in touch with domestic violence counselors and..."

"Jeanie, no!" Livvy exclaimed with shock.

"Livvy, I had to!" Jeanie growled. "If she doesn't come right out and tell me that she is lying, and just says that she has that fear, I have to take it to the proper channels. If I don't, I could lose my license."

"I know, I know," Livvy replied sheepishly. "I'm sorry, I don't blame you. What a fucking..."

"Yes she is, but that's not the worst part she told the domestic violence people that he'd been beating her up and raping her for years and that he had started to molest their son too," Jeanie said.

"I... I'm speechless," Livvy replied, the rage in her building to four alarm fire status. "But he never..."

"He's a molestation victim!" Jeanie exclaimed. "Since their cases are in the same office, they both signed agreements which said that Alyssa and I could reference notes to help with their treatment. He was molested as a child Livvy. I looked it up, it was a horrible story, absolutely terrible. From his psychological profile, I know she's full of shit Liv. There's no way he did that. But the DV people believe her. So now, he's not going to get to see his kid until they go to court because they've put her in a shelter and are trying to get a protective order to keep him away from his son. She wants to leave the state with the kid. And you want to know what's even worse?"

Livvy tried to answer, but her mouth wouldn't even move so she simply grunted.

"She's only doing it to have a free place to stay. Her mother can't afford the rent on the house on her own, so she is just trying to find someplace to live because where her mother is going to move to, she isn't wanted. So she wants to run her husband's name through the mud even more so, just for a free roof over her head."

"Oh my God that is... that evil fucking..." Livvy growled lightly. Her jaw was beginning to ache from keeping it clenched so hard.

"Are you alright, Livvy?"

"Yes. Just..." she started.

"Oh, I'm so sorry, honey. I really am," Jeanie replied. "I didn't even think! You saved his life after his car accident!"

"It's not your fault," Livvy said in a darkened tone.

"No, but I should have been more sensitive, I... I mean you took care of him round-the-clock and got him on his feet. You know him better than anyone I bet. I know you know it's all bullshit! I know how you feel about him..."

"It's fine, Jean," Livvy snapped as she stood up. "I'll be right back I have to use the bathroom."

"Okay, take your time," Jeanie replied as Livvy walked off.

She barely made it into the bathroom before she screamed. She had to slap her hand over her mouth to muffle the noise so that no one would hear. So many thoughts and feelings rushed through her mind as she ran over in her mind what her sister had told her. She began to weep for Ed, hating to have to see the look on his face when he found out the allegations and that he wouldn't be able to see his son. To know that things that he still hadn't told her, which were traumatic for him, would now be used against him.

"How can I protect you?" she asked herself out loud. "What can I do?" She looked at her phone and saw that it was still too early for Ed to be out of work. She clicked her contacts and sent him a text. *'Get in touch with me the minute you get this. I mean the instant. Everything is bad.'*

Ed went to his locker during his last break and grabbed his phone and raised a brow when he saw the message that Livvy had sent two hours prior.

"What the fuck is this about?" he asked himself as he dialed her number.

"Oh my God, what took you so long?" Livvy asked before the phone could even ring one time the whole way through.

"I just got on break, babe. What's going on?" he asked worriedly.

"Listen, are you working overtime today?" she asked quickly.

"No, I get out at my normal time why?"

"Listen, don't ask me any questions okay? Just do what I tell you and then come right home after you've done it. Do you understand?" Livvy asked hurriedly.

"Baby, I..."

"Listen, Ed, I'm not even supposed to have my phone on me right now. But I kept it on me because this is something that is very serious, and you just need to trust me. Don't ask me any questions because I do not have time to answer them the way you want. Just trust that I'm telling you what's best for you right now and you need to do it, otherwise you are going to be royally fucked. Now do you understand me?" she asked in an agitated tone.

"Yeah, I understand," Ed replied bewildered.

"Alright. As soon as you get out of work you are going to go directly to the court and file what's called an *Ex Parte motion*. Do you understand?"

"Yes. Why am I filing and Ex ma whatsup?" he asked.

"Because that goddamn, mother fucking, piece of shit ex-wife of yours is going to try and take Eddie away from you without you knowing. If you do not file this motion today, then you are never going to see your son again because she is going to take him out of state and fucking run."

"How the—" he began.

"Just shut up and listen okay? Stop asking questions and just listen and do what I say. I'll explain everything when you get home," she said hastily. "Go in and file the motion stating that she cannot take him out of state until your divorce is final. Do you hear me?"

"Yeah, I hear you," he said, his tone sounding slightly agitated.

"They're going to say that you have to inform her. So call her cell phone and tell her that is what you are doing and then just hang up. Don't give her any fucking reasons or anything like that. Just tell her. Do you understand me, Ed?"

"Yeah, I understand you," he said.

"Just trust me. Know that I'm watching your back, alright? I'm watching your back and I'm trying to protect you," Livvy said. "Now listen, I get off work at seven tonight. I will be home no later than seven thirty. After you file that motion you just go straight home, take a bath, and relax. I will explain everything when I get there. You just do what I told you to do."

"Alright, honey," he said shortly. "I'll do what you ask. I just... I don't understand."

"I know you don't. And believe me, I'll tell you everything I know so far as soon as I get home. Just make sure you don't fuck around and promise me you will file that motion."

"Alright. I promise."

"Good. I love you, Ed."

"I love you too, Livvy."

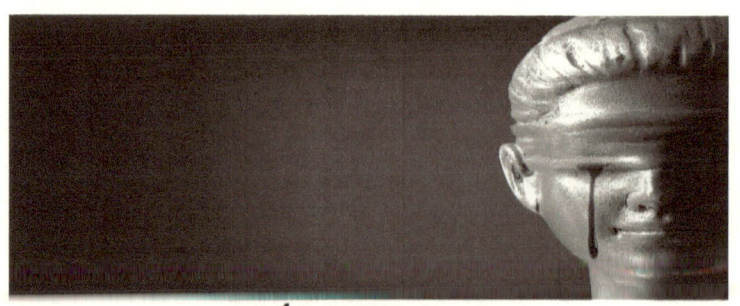

# CHAPTER 10
## PLAN OF ATTACK

**"S**he *what!*" Ed roared hours later when Livvy got home.

She knew he was going to snap when he found out what Laura was doing, and despite how frightening he looked, she was more afraid for Laura than she was for herself. She knew he wouldn't hurt her.

"I cannot believe that illiterate fucking inbred cow! That goddamn lying trailer park fucking degenerate! How fucking dare she do this! I was nothing but good to her all of those years and this is what I get out of it! Are you sure that—"

"Yes I'm sure, Ed," Livvy replied. "My sister wouldn't lie to me. Now you have to keep your voice down alright? And you need to stay calm because right now my sister is a spy and she doesn't even know it. But if you lose your head, this isn't going to work. Now just—" She motioned her hands like she was patting something invisible down gesturing to tone his voice down so the neighbors would be unaware of him.

"Where's my son?" Ed interrupted, tears in his eyes. "Where is he? I want my boy!"

"Ed!" Livvy shouted back. "Shut the fuck up and listen! Do you want to make sure you get your son, or do you want to fuck around and lose him?"

"I... I don't want to lose him," he replied.

"Good. Then get it together because now is not the time for you to be losing your shit. Now is the time for you to fight her back. Fire with fire. Do you understand me?" she asked calmly.

"Yes. I understand," he replied through gritted teeth.

"Listen, I know you're mad. You should be and you have every right to be. I'm pissed right here with you. You can take it out on me in a little while," she said. "Believe me you can pound me until you drop dead, then I'll revive you and you can start all over again. But right now I just need you to listen," she said. When he didn't say anything else, she pushed the thought of angry sex out of her mind.

"Now, she pulled this already, so she struck the first blow. But you going to the court counters a lot. So now she won't be able to steal him. However, if they can get the protection against abuse order pushed through, it'll be really hard for you to get visitation, so you have to see about getting into court. Now what date did they set for your hearing?"

"About three weeks from now," he replied.

"Three weeks? Why so long?" Livvy exclaimed.

"The court is backed up," Ed replied bitterly.

"Alright, well it looks like you won't get to see him for a while if that PFA does go through," Livvy replied in irritation.

"How good of a chance is it that it'll go through?" Ed asked.

149

"Pretty good."

"What! Why?" he roared. "There is no record of me having done anything to her!" he cried out.

"Because you were born with a dick," she said simply. "All a woman has to do is whimper abuse and the law will do everything it can to destroy that man as best as it possibly can. But, with you being a Corrections Officer, and having no record, it could save you," she said with a small smile. "So we've got that in our favor. The most important thing that you can do is just not let this bother you. You have to toughen yourself up and just deal with this. You're going to be alright. I *will* do everything that I can for it. Alright?" Livvy asked him hopefully.

"Alright," he said.

"I need you to trust me, Ed. Swear to me that you will trust me and do what I say."

"I swear," Ed replied with a straight forward tone. "I'll trust you and do everything you say."

"Alright good. I won't let her hurt you. I promise."

"But why?" he asked sadly. "Why would she do this to me?"

"She's had you played from day one. It was everything you thought it was and more. I'm so sorry, Ed. I really am." She wrapped her arms around him and held him close to her, protectively.

"There's something that... I never told you," Ed said with his face pushed against her chest.

"What is it, baby?" she asked softly.

"She's saying that I raped her and molested Eddie... you know that's a lie right?"

"It never even came to question in my mind that it's a lie. I know about your nightmares, but I figured that you would tell me in your own time," she said.

"Well... I was molested when I was a kid," he said quietly. "When I was four, my cousin... he..." his voice broke as he started to speak. "And when I was twelve, I..." his voice broke again, and he clung to her tight unable to say another word and bawled against her.

She hated the sound of his pain, hated to feel his burning hot tears soak through the fabric of her shirt. She hated the sound of his hurting, and she hated the source of the hurt even more. Not the molesters, but the one that was using his pain and trauma as a way to destroy him.

"That fucking bitch will pay," Livvy said as she massaged his smooth, freshly shaved head. "We will use the court to make her pay, I promise you, baby. I will not let her get away with doing this to you. I promise you," she repeated as she rocked him gently, whispering soothing noises to him as he bawled.

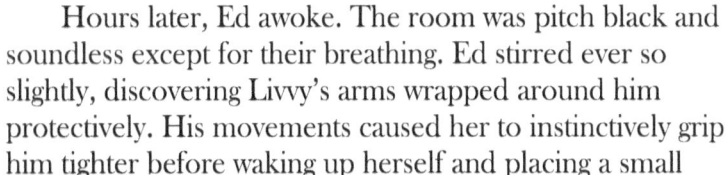

Hours later, Ed awoke. The room was pitch black and soundless except for their breathing. Ed stirred ever so slightly, discovering Livvy's arms wrapped around him protectively. His movements caused her to instinctively grip him tighter before waking up herself and placing a small kiss on his lips.

"What happened?" he asked weakly.

"You fell asleep," she replied massaging his cheek.

"I was just thinking," he said weakly, "we're going to have to keep 'us' secret for now."

"Why do you say that?" she asked arching a brow.

"Well if your sister is feeding you information, don't you think it will look odd to her and to everyone else that I am staying one step ahead of her? We both know this is a small area, and word travels fast."

"I thought the same thing. You're right," Livvy replied, her face sour.

Neither one of them spoke for several minutes as the severity of the situation, from each side, weighed on them.

"You're going to have to almost literally go through all of this completely alone," she said. "I'm going to have to sit in the background and watch all of this happen to you like I'm just some fucking stranger," she said bitterly.

"Yeah," he replied. "Wouldn't it get you in trouble anyway at the hospital? Us being together?"

"Not really. You're not a patient anymore, and this is a year later, so there's no rules being violated."

"Well that's good."

"It'll also mean you can't live here. If she were to get a good lawyer, they may try to figure out where you live. That'll make it hard for us to be able to get information."

"I cannot believe that bitch," Ed growled. "She had me conned from day one."

"Hey, it's going to be alright. There is no proof of anything she is trying to say. My sister says that if she's never been to the hospital for any of her injuries, or made any doctor's reports, then it'll be difficult for her claims will be substantiated."

"Can't your sister just tell people that she is a liar?" Ed asked.

"No. HIPPA, baby. And doctor-patient confidentiality. That pig is protected by the law. It's kind of like a lawyer and their client the lawyer will usually withdraw from a case if they know the client is guilty, but they can't tell people that the client is guilty. My sister can say that she doesn't want to be her therapist anymore because of Reason A, but she can't say 'My client is lying about her ex-husband so I can't have her as a client anymore.' Do you understand?"

"Yeah, I do. She can essentially lie, and just completely get away with it no matter what," he said bitterly.

"What makes me angriest," Livvy growled, "is that she lies about being abused and is living in a shelter right now. There are women out there that are seriously abused and can't get help because of people like her," Her eyes had a dangerous glint to them as she looked far off for a moment.

"Babe, can I ask you something?" he asked cautiously.

"Sure, what is it?" Livvy massaged his chest gently hoping to calm whatever anxiety was coming from him that she'd heard.

"It just seems like, you're taking this real personal," he started.

"And why wouldn't I? This evil, manipulative con artist is trying to destroy you!" Livvy retorted, anger starting to build up in her.

"Yeah, I know, honey. But I mean, it seems like there is more than that and—"

"Listen, Ed," Livvy pushed back from him rougher than she intended to, her temper ready to explode. "It's bad enough that, for the last year, I was in love with you and had to see you on TV with her at your side and you telling everyone how she was your chief supporter! I was the one that was fucking crying for you every night! I was the one that was ready to kill over you when that asshole preacher and that kid's family were running your name through the mud! That cunt would just sit on her fat ass and act like none of it bothered her! All she cared about was you going back to work so her ass didn't have to do anything but get fatter!

"And you, going on television and saying how much you love her and how she is the only one that cares so much for you? Asshole, I was in love with you before you even realized it! I was the one that got chewed out that night only because I was trying to think of you and not put you in a situation where you would have to compromise yourself!

"Now this bitch is looking to obliterate you! She's trying to steal your son and tell everyone that'll listen that you are an abuser! I've never heard of a situation where a woman is being fast forwarded through the DV center's system so quickly!" Livvy shouted. She turned on the nightstand light and the look of rage in her eyes made him sink back like a puppy being scolded.

"What do you mean?"

"Thanks for catching up with the fucking conversation!" Livvy growled. "They have her in a shelter, they're putting through paper work to get her a lawyer. A free lawyer!" Livvy growled. "And in case you have forgotten, this further makes you stand out because you are one of the few Black people around here! Do you know what that means?"

"Yes, unfortunately, I do," he said, his bottom lip stiffening, his body going rigid with anger.

"Yeah? What does it mean, Ed?" Livvy snarled.

"It means that a lot of people are going to believe it whether it's true or not," he said.

"That's right. You're the big, bad, black guy who was just on trial for a criminal, and civil case involving the murder of another human being. They're going to use that against you also. Get it? Just because you were acquitted before doesn't mean that there aren't people that are still going to think you were guilty! Doesn't that infuriate you?" she growled.

"You're goddamn right it does!" he roared.

"So why would you even ask me that question?"

"Because it seems like, there's more behind it and—"

"Listen, Ed, there are certain things that I am just not, not ready to talk about yet," she said, softening her tone. "I know what you mean, and I'm sorry I turned all psychotic just now, but let's just say that I don't want to talk about it right now, okay? I promise you I will tell you. Just, give me some time alright?" she pleaded.

"Alright, baby. Let's just get through this and we can cross that bridge when you're ready," he said softly, massaging her cheek.

"Thank you," she said with a gentle smile. "We need to get you through your situation first. Something tells me this is going to get a lot worse before it gets any better."

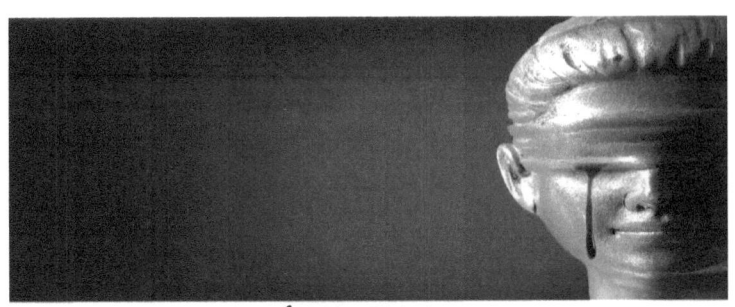

# CHAPTER 11
## *THREE YEARS LATER - ED*

Ed sat outside of the courtroom his eyes marred in disbelief. He looked at his phone, afraid to send the text to Livvy knowing how desperate she was to receive it. He knew he'd have to send something soon it was too long of a drive home for him to not send her anything. He just didn't want to.

"Mr. White?" came a nasally, weathered tone.

Ed looked up to see the shrunken, older man with the slight hunch of his back between his shoulder blades and liver spotted face looking down toward him with an almost irritated expression through a forced professional politeness.

"What?" Ed asked, his tone anything but friendly.

"Mr. White, there's no need to use that attitude with me. I did everything I could to—" the man continued.

"Oh bullshit, Paul!" Ed growled attempting, and failing, to keep his voice down. "Don't you dare give me that shit! You did not do all that you could for me, and you know it!"

"What outcome did you expect, Mr. White? This is how the law works!" the man replied.

"Oh really? What lawyer, besides you, doesn't fight to ensure their client has to pay as little as possible? You never tried to renegotiate with them, you never tried to even fight them on anything! You handled this whole case on auto pilot at best!"

"Mr. White!" the lawyer Paul replied as his voice raised, "You seem to have a very misguided view of the way the world, and the legal system works! You cannot be married to someone and not expect to have to come out of the marriage without paying something! Your, now ex-wife, doesn't work, as you well know and—"

"And how is that my fault, Paul? How? You told me when I first signed on with you 'Provost and Provost will do all it can for you, Mr. White.' Do you remember that, Paul?"

"Of course I do, Mr. White, but what you—"

"No, Paul! You did not do your best for me! Did you get any of the documentation from her files at the domestic violence center, or the various homeless shelters that she allegedly stayed in?"

"Mr. White, I told you that I did," Paul Provost grumbled. He wanted to end the conversation, but his years as an attorney, and his own personality, required him to get the final word.

"Then why the hell didn't you bring any of that up? How she'd been kicked out of homeless shelters, and domestic violence shelters for refusing to look for work?" Ed grumbled.

"Mr. White, none of that matters to the court. I've tried to explain this to you at length, however you seem either unwilling, or unable, to mentally grasp that it did not matter to the court."

"What did you just say to me?" Ed stood to his full height, towering over the smaller, older man.

"Mr. White, I suggest you sit down and not try to physically intimidate me." The older man glared. "Let me attempt to get through to you once again! The court has decided that you leaving, and thereby taking your income from her, that being why she is essentially destitute. And despite your acquittal of the murder case years ago, it still has a negative stigma on you. She may not have ever had any visible displays of abuse, but your past has worked against you. You even said yourself that she, and I quote from your deposition under oath, 'tended to stay away from people a lot of the time.' She was able to spin it that you physically intimidated her to remain separated from people so that her injuries would have time to heal! Her mother, herself, and various other people in her family testified to this... under oath."

"They're her family, Paul!" Ed bellowed. "What'd you think they'd say? You think they're gonna call her a liar in open court? You barely even tried to challenge them on any of their points whatsoever! I'm not even a lawyer and I could poke holes in their stories! If I'd caused her back injury with the severity that they're trying to say I did, she would have had to have gone to the emergency room!" Ed shook angrily as his adrenalin built within him. "Hell, I've even shown you video of her picking up Eddie and walking with him! Why didn't you introduce that into evidence?"

"Mr. White," Paul said in exacerbation. "It doesn't matter. You lost and you need to accept that your ex-wife has been granted full custody of your son, you have zero decision making, and you have supervised visitation the third Wednesday of the month for an hour. Be glad that you were not brought up on abuse and neglect charges."

"Abuse? Neglect? What the hell are you talking about?"

"Mr. White, the fact that your son had bruises on him—"

"I've never hit him! Never!" Ed cried out, his anger fading and despair claiming him.

"Be that as it may, it doesn't matter. Be glad that you do not have to pay alimony. The fact that the judge decided that the entirety of your pension was more than adequate compensation. You really got off very lucky. Be appreciative of that," Paul said.

"You don't even care do you?" Ed grumbled. "It's really no big deal to you that things went the way they did in there is it?"

"Mr. White, I did the best I could for you. It does not bother me one way or the other. Now, I suggest that you just be grateful for what did go your way and then try again in a few months at the court ordered mediation and counseling visit to determine if the court will amend its decision to allow you individual parenting time. However, with the display you've just made it will be difficult for you. Now, good day, Mr. White. My bill will be in the mail." With that, Paul walked off and shook hands with Laura's smug looking lawyer Marvin Lincoln with the rest of his ex-wife's family standing around looking back at him with equally smug looks.

Laura, her mother, her sister Lucy, her aunt Jenn, and her boyfriend Tim, who Ed referred to as a creepy old skeleton with a rat tail, regarded him with looks of disdain that one would direct toward a fallen enemy. Ed returned their looks with absolute hatred, yet it didn't matter. They'd defeated him, despite his best efforts.

He sat outside the court room for several minutes after they left in disbelief. It was impossible for him to figure out what exactly had gone so wrong in the last few years. Two years prior, Ed lost his job at the jail when the allegations of domestic violence had come at their strongest and finding a job in 'Hell-town' had become impossible, despite his best endeavors. He and Livvy had to live separately, as they'd planned. They attempted normalcy with Eddie, taking him places together and behaving like a family, until Eddie began to tell Laura everything about Livvy that he could think of. Slowly, but surely, Livvy and Ed had to keep their interactions few and far between as to not arouse suspicion as Jeanie was still unwittingly feeding Livvy information, and Ed received the information from Livvy.

Ed was granted residential responsibility of Eddie a few months after his first ex parte motion was filed, as the court was not happy with Laura keeping Eddie from him for almost three months. Ed thanked his original lawyer, Catherine, for this. However, a year or so into the divorce proceedings, Catherine suddenly withdrew from the case. Ed's mother had been helping pay his legal fees due to financial difficulties, and she began to miss payments.

"Well I'm sorry, Ed," his mother Rose grumbled. "But I'm not made of money. I'm on a fixed income, and I still have bills to pay."

"But Mom, you told me that you'd help with this!" Ed remembered crying out to her.

"And I have every intention to do so, but situations change."

Ed didn't speak to her for almost three months after that. He'd taken out loans from the bank to pay for a new lawyer. His three part-time jobs were barely enough to make the payments to the bank and take care of his bills. Thankfully, Livvy helped him out as often as she could, taking on extra shifts at the hospital. Unfortunately, this kept them apart even more to the point where they began to fight all the time.

*"Aren't you trying hard enough to get a full-time job, Ed?"* Livvy yelled at him over the phone during one such instance. *"I can't keep working all these shifts in a row! I'm only one person!"*

"I know!" Ed roared back. "I don't like this! I fucking hate it! And I appreciate everything you're doing for me, but no matter how many feelers I put out there, nobody is interested in me! I swear, it feels like I am blacklisted or something!"

*"Well you need to do something! I can't keep doing this, Ed!"* Livvy retorted.

"Then why the fuck are you even doing it?" he shouted back. "You fucking offered!"

*"Because I love you! You stupid asshole! And I'm loyal to you! But you need to understand that this is killing*

*me! I cannot keep supporting you! Help me! Please, Ed?"*
Livvy cried.

When they were able to spend time together, they kept their fighting to a minimum. When they could afford it, they would go out to dinner. And, for a few short hours at least, they were happy to be able to feel like a real couple. When they couldn't afford to go out to dinner, their time together were short, sexual rendezvous that they'd grown used to enjoying and appreciating. Their love and sex life keeping them together despite the difficulty his divorce was causing.

He hadn't spoken to his father, or his brothers in that three years. When Ed called him shortly after filing for divorce, his father laid into him about the spiritual consequences of divorce.

*"You made a commitment before God, son! You cannot break that! Your soul will be damned if you do this!"* His father's convictions regarding his church upbringing came strongly through the earpiece of the phone. Ed had to hold the phone away from his ear.

"Dad," Ed replied, "what about her side of the vows? She refuses to work! She's been lying to me from day one! Doesn't that make any vows null and void if you are tricked into it?"

*"Son, I will pray for your soul,"* Roland White replied. *"You are wrong. You need to figure out a way to make it work."* The discussion was further exacerbated when his stepmother Winifred informed him that she and his father were praying for his and Laura's reunion. Ed didn't bother to contact them again after that and his brothers, angered by his dismissal of them, dismissed him.

His friends that he'd left behind when he moved, after a few months, stopped responding to his calls when he would reach out for emotional support. Other than Livvy, he had nothing left. And, because of how difficult the situation had become and their constant fighting, he felt as though he were losing her too despite her swearing her loyalty and love to him over and over.

When Livvy was offered a Head Nurse position at a hospital in Manchester, a further distance wedge was placed between them. However, on days when he didn't have Eddie, he would drive there and spend time with her which made things a lot easier for them. She'd made sure to purchase a four-bedroom home so that they would have enough room for him to move in, with or without Eddie, when the divorce was final.

When he finally turned his phone back on, he saw dozens of text messages from Livvy imploring him to get in touch with her immediately. It was very apparent she was pleading to know how things turned out. They'd discussed what they would do if he lost the case. She'd reminded him that child support would destroy their finances and that he would also have to claim her income as well in the financial affidavit.

"You have to do what you can to fix this, baby. You have to protect us," he remembered her saying.

He looked at the phone as though it were a bomb with less than three seconds left before detonation. More text messages from Livvy caused his phone to vibrate as though it were ready to explode. He finally texted back. *'Bad news.'*

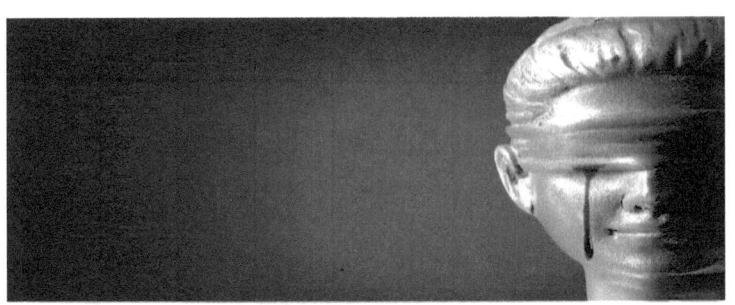

# CHAPTER 12
## THREE YEARS LATER – *Livvy*

Livvy had taken the day off and was pacing the living room floor frantically. She knew he was supposed to be in court by ten in the morning, and that court was supposed to last, at latest, until two in the afternoon. It was now three, and she still hadn't heard anything.

She'd sent him text messages throughout the morning sending him her well wishes and support. As three became three-thirty, she began to ask him to give her a quick update, and then finally began to beg him to get in touch with her.

She'd become so high strung since their relationship had begun. She'd initially wanted to keep her relationship with Ed a secret to protect her sister's license and so that she could get more information from Jeanie to help Ed to use the knowledge against Laura in court. However, as the news of the divorce and the allegations spread, it became essential to hide their relationship for her own career as well.

Ed's name was already tarnished because of the death of Craig Jackson. As soon as talk began to spread about the alleged domestic violence, Ed's name was like having leprosy. The small town soon began to develop rumors of Ed's mental instability. Anytime he lost his temper due to stress, it did nothing more but add to the fuel of the fire of his supposed mental deficiency.

Soon after he'd lost his job at the jail, she did what she could to help him until she'd been called into the hospital administrator's office to discuss her time spent with Ed. She realized quickly that she was being interrogated and her job was in jeopardy. When the Head Nurse position opened up in Manchester, she knew she had to take it. Her professional career wasn't safe there any longer. As things continued to play out, and she accepted the new position, she knew Ed would be forced into a worse position than he already was.

Worse yet, due to her anxiety over the situation, she continued to have nightmares about Martin. She wanted, so badly, to explain to Ed why she was getting so anxious, and angry. She knew though that with all that was going on with the divorce, he needed to stay focused. Her own past wasn't going to help him handle his situation any better instead, it would only make things worse.

She felt guilty, not to mention sheerly responsible, for the deterioration of their relationship. He was doing all he could to keep himself together, and so was she. The stress was more than either of them could handle, especially with how his family and friends were treating him. This, paired with the negative effect the situation had on her family dynamic made her feel as though she were slowly losing her mind along with Ed. It all came to a head during Thanksgiving the first year of the divorce as the family sat around to have dinner.

"So girls," her father had said during dinner, "how's work?" he asked.

"It's going alright," Livvy replied.

"Oh yeah?" her youngest brother Doug chuckled. "Do you still see the killer cop guy?"

"He isn't a killer cop, Douglas." Livvy glowered at her brother. "He was defending himself at work when he was attacked."

"Yeah, whatever. That's pretty cool. According to the news, he did some karate flick move where he ripped the guy's throat out, like fucking *Road House*! Is that true?" Doug chuckled.

"He didn't really talk about it much to be honest," Livvy replied.

"Well I hear," her brother Arnold, the lawyer, replied taking a sip of his wine. "From a friend of mine in the courts down there that a lot of people are paying close attention to that case even still. Locally, that is."

"Is that right?" her father asked.

"Well apparently he's getting a divorce and she's claiming domestic violence," Arnold said taking another sip of his wine.

"How the hell do you know that?" Livvy asked irritably.

"Because Marvin Lincoln from my firm is supposed to be taking the wife's case *pro bono,* and he only takes pro bono cases when he really feels strongly about it," he said, shooting Livvy a piercing gaze. "Apparently, his daughter was beaten up by a football player boyfriend, so he takes cases like these very seriously. That fucker is fried for sure," he said before shoveling a fork full of stuffing into his mouth.

"Well he took out some scum bag prisoner, no matter what his domestic life is," her father replied. "One less piece of shit sucking up the resources of the hard-working taxpayers."

"Well, his wife isn't much better," Livvy grunted.

"Olivia! What a thing to say!" her mother said in shock.

"Well Mom, she is faking disabilities according to him!" Livvy shot back.

"And I suppose he told you that while he was in the hospital recovering from his accident?" her mother asked.

"As a matter-of-fact he did, Mom," Livvy replied. "And I was there when he got brought in and all she could do was fuss over him going back to work to take care of her!"

"Well, that's what a man is supposed to do," her mother retorted.

"Mom, I don't have a man taking care of me and I do just fine. And even when I was married, I still worked," Livvy rebuked.

"Same here, Mom," Jeanie replied, having stayed silent about the whole subject until now.

"Yes, well you girls are doing very well for yourselves, but that's beyond the point," her mother retorted. "A man like that Ed White person is dangerous. He should just stay among his own kind where he belongs anyway."

"Mom, what the fuck is that even supposed to mean?" Livvy roared.

"Olivia," her father warned. "Watch your language toward your mother, especially at the table."

"All I meant," her mother responded, "is that from what the papers said he is from the inner city. Somewhere down south. Perhaps he should have just stayed there. It's a different world here."

"Why are we even talking about this?" Arnold asked, taking another sip of wine.

"The point is," Livvy said, unable to hold her tongue any longer, "he is a good man. I've actually spent time with him. He is a nice man who was just in a very terrible situation. Now, his situation is getting even worse. It's not fair that some work case of his is being brought into his divorce case."

"But if he was abusing his wife," her mother responded with a patronizing tone, "then perhaps he didn't have to do to that poor young man what he did? Maybe he truly is dangerous."

Livvy looked to Jeanie for some support, yet Jeanie just kept her mouth shut. On the surface, Livvy knew that it wasn't fair to expect Jeanie to stand up for Ed. She and Jeanie were always the closest of the family, and the two oldest kids. They discussed things with each other that they didn't dare say to anyone else. Jeanie's husband Frank shrugged.

"If he beat his wife, he is a low-down piece of trash that deserves whatever happens to him," he grumbled.

"How do you even know that he did anything, Frank?" Livvy replied.

"If he killed a guy in jail, what makes you think he hasn't started to lose his damn mind and start taking it out on his wife?" Frank retorted.

"Frank, you are so full of shit! One thing does not—" Livvy began.

"Don't you dare talk to my husband like that, Olivia," Jeanie replied, staring daggers through Livvy. She looked at Jeanie as though she had slapped her and was suddenly shocked to silence.

"Alright enough of this talk," her father said in a command voice. "This is a family meal I have no clue why we are even bothering with this. This is stupid. Now Doug why don't you tell us—"

Livvy didn't even bother to pay attention to her father after that. Her relations with her family cooled after that night considerably. Her lunch dates with her sister were now non-existent, and their phone calls to one another ceased as well. She was just as alone as Ed was. Worse yet, a few days later while shopping at the nearby mall, she saw her ex-husband Martin and felt her blood run ice cold.

She did all that she could to avoid him, ducking into various stores hoping not to have to see him. When she finally lost sight of him and continued her shopping, she heard a familiar voice behind her while looking at shoes.

"Hello, Livvy," Martin said calmly.

"What the fuck do you want, Martin?" she asked, her eyes narrowed to slits as the memories flooded back to her.

"I saw you, and just wanted to say hi," he said with a slight grin. "You look good, really good."

"Yeah? Well you look like the same piece of shit you've always looked like," she fired back, feeling her body go hot. She stormed off, yet she could hear Martin's footsteps following her.

"What the fuck do you want!" she roared at him.

"Calm down. You're making a scene," he replied calmly.

"Is there a problem here?" a mall security guard questioned.

"No. No trouble at all." Martin smiled. "I'll talk to you soon, Livvy," he warned, turning to leave.

Livvy immediately exited the mall and drove back to her apartment. She still didn't talk about Martin to Ed and didn't want to bring him up now. She knew that he had so much going on, he didn't need to be saddled down with her baggage as well. She made sure to keep it all from him, the conversation with her family, the confrontation with Martin, even her issues at work.

"Edwin, goddamn!" Livvy growled seeing that her texts were all going unanswered, even after it mentioned that he'd read them all. She continued to text him frantically, demanding his call. She knew that he could hear her tone of voice, despite her words being nothing but letters on a screen. He knew she was yelling at him she knew that he had to have known. Finally, she got the text back finally at 4:15.

*"Bad news."*

"Ed? Goddammit are you trying to stroke me out!" she roared into the receiver. "What time did you get out of court?"

*"At about two like I said."* His voice was flat, even, devoid of all emotion.

"Well then why are you just now getting back in touch with me? What was this shit about bad news?" she roared.

*"She won,"* he said flatly. *"The bitch fucking won. Lincoln tore me apart on the stand, Provost never even tried, baby. He never even tried. It feels..."* he said weakly. *"It feels like nothing."*

"Oh God," Livvy whimpered lightly. Her blood felt cold. The lack of feeling in his voice frightened her more than his yelling ever could. She remembered what he'd said to her four years earlier 'If I don't feel, I don't care. If I don't care, I die.'

"Ed, you need to listen to me, baby. Can you do that for me?" Livvy asked fearfully.

*"I can't fee—"* he began.

"Edwin! Do you hear me?"

*"Yes,"* he replied flatly.

"Come to me, Ed. Come here right now. Do not do anything but drive straight here. Do you understand? Can you do that for me, baby?" she pleaded, tears flowing from her eyes. It was almost a full thirty seconds before he spoke, but she could hear his breathing. She knew she couldn't push him too hard right now, or else she would lose him forever.

*"Yes,"* he finally replied. *"I'll come to you. And I'll do nothing until I get there. I promise you."*

Livvy felt the cold grow slightly warmer as she was able to pick up slight emotion in his voice. "Good. I promise you things are going to be alright. Just come home to me, baby."

Almost two hours later at the falling of twilight, Ed arrived at the house a quaint two-story home with a red door and massive yard that housed an even larger oak tree. The house was completely dark everywhere with the exception of the candlelight from the living room that he could tell from the curtain covered windows that flanked the front door which had a note taped to it that said, *'Come In'*.

The knob was unlocked, and Ed walked in slowly, closing the door behind him and locking it.

"Livs?" he called out curiously. He walked past the stairs into the living room where the candlelight was concentrated. The candles appeared to be leading him into the dining room where he saw Livvy standing wearing a soft violet colored spaghetti strap dress low cut that accented her cleavage.

"Hi, baby," she whispered softly.

"What is all of this?" he asked her curiously.

"We're celebrating," she said simply.

"What are we celebrating?" he asked. He realized that she was smiling warmly. "What is it Livs? Today went horrible. What could we possibly celebrating?"

"I went to the doctor today," she said with a smile.

"You did?" He walked closer to her and she took his hand into hers.

"You're going to be a daddy," she said with a bright smile.

"A... are you serious?" He felt the cloak of despair that he'd been clad lift from his shoulders instantly.

She nodded to him with a warm smile and wrapped her arms around him and kissed him deeply. He returned her kiss moaning gently against her lips.

"Livvy, will you marry me?" he asked softly.

"I thought you'd never ask."

# CHAPTER 13
## *SILVER LINING NOW DARK & GRAY*

"Ed, I'm telling you I'm alright." Livvy chuckled into her cell phone as she drove. "I'm going to the mall to get a few things for the baby and then I'll be right home." She loved how he fussed over her so much. It made her feel especially needed, protected, and valued. She looked down at the plain black and orange dress she wore, knowing it was his favorite. He liked it on her when she wanted to tease him and she had every intention of making him earn his loving later.

*"Yeah, but aren't you supposed to be keeping off your feet and taking less shifts?"* Ed asked on the other end of the phone.

"Will you stop worrying so much?" Livvy laughed. "Everything is going to be alright. My reduced hours start next week, and everything will be fine. Are you sure you'll be able to get the extra hours?"

*"It's already taken care of, baby,"* Ed replied. *"Matter of fact, my next class starts in about fifteen minutes."*

After her announcement, he'd moved in with her. Within a week, he'd gotten a job as a martial arts instructor at a nearby school, and even began to teach self-defense tactics at the nearby **YMCA**. It'd been so much easier for him to get jobs just two and a half hours away from Hell-town. There were people that knew who he was, but they knew nothing about the divorce. No one even really spoke of the trial as it had already faded from the big city's memory.

He'd been able to carry his weight easily, despite the child support order. They were both still estranged from their respective families, but neither cared. They had each other, and that was all that mattered.

Ed noticed, however, that Livvy was having trouble sleeping. Whenever he asked her about her nightmares, she always dismissed them as just dreams. He knew there was more to all of it than she was telling him though. He let the idea reside in the back of his mind, not wanting to stress her. He figured she would talk to him when she was ready.

She loved having him there, it was nice to wake up next to him every morning and not have to rush through sex, or even dinner. They finally felt like a normal couple in love, and that was all either of them ever wanted.

At her last doctor's appointment, she was told her uterus had some scaring on it and she needed to take it easy. That was over a week ago. She'd put in for a reduced schedule and was prepared to go on bed rest within the next few months under monitoring by her doctor. Ed adjusted his schedule as much as possible so he could make up the difference in income.

He was still restricted from Eddie due to the court order, but he was confident a new lawyer would be able to have it amended. Every attorney he consulted told him the same thing Paul Provost screwed him. He'd written a letter to the state Bar Association and was waiting to hear their ruling against Provost.

*"Ok baby, if you're sure everything is alright."* Ed snickered. *"Hey, what do you want for dinner tonight?"*

"I'm not sure, what are you in the mood for?" she asked, feeling her stomach rumbling just a little.

*"Honestly, I'm up for anything. How about I pick up some Chinese on the way home? You were talking about pork fried rice all morning I'm starving for it."* He laughed.

"No wonder you're perfect. You know what I like." She laughed.

*"Alright, honey. I'll talk to you later."*

When she ended the call, she got out of the car and made her way into the mall. The darkness of the last few years had finally lifted. She ran her hand gently over her stomach as if to give their unborn child a gentle message of gratitude.

"Let's go see what Mommy can find her little one. You're going to need a good and comfy crib, aren't you?" She smiled lightly walking through the mall window shopping for the most part before she heard a voice that she hadn't heard for years.

"Well hello, Olivia," came a female voice from behind her. When Livvy turned around, she was face to face with Laura White, and her heart began to pound angrily.

Laura White stood before Livvy wearing a pair of brown hiking shoes, blue jeans, and a dark blue T-shirt. Her unruly blonde hair had been obviously treated at a salon. Her stomach still hung out far, bending over her belt line. She saw young Eddie standing with his mother, his stomach hanging over his belt line the same as his mother's wearing black sneakers, a pair of sweatpants and a black hooded sweatshirt. His face looked as overweight as the rest of his body. Livvy looked at Laura and then at Eddie and then back at Laura, her eyes narrowed.

"Laura," Livvy replied, his voice hardened.

"How are you?" Laura smiled, looking as though she didn't have a care in the world.

"I'm fine. You?"

"Oh just great thank you. So you're still with my Ed are you?" Laura smiled coldly.

"He isn't *your* Ed, Laura. He hasn't been for quite some time," Livvy countered.

"Oh that's right, you were second choice weren't you?"

"Actually, he refers to me as an upgrade." Livvy grinned coldly.

"Is that so?" Laura asked, her smile faded.

"Yes, that's right. Now did you have a point when you walked up to me, Laura, or are you having fun being a pointless fucking waste?" Livvy snarled.

"You know, Olivia, I don't blame you for any of this. I don't even hate you. All I'm going to tell you is to just be careful. Ed is not a stable man. I'm surprised you haven't noticed that by now. What, with all of the pain and misery he caused me," Laura said rested the back of her hand against her forehead.

"Let's cut the bullshit, Laura," Livvy said, stepping forward keeping her tone low. "You're a lying cunt. You lied all throughout your marriage, and you lied all throughout the divorce. You turned this boy against his father, all because he was sick and tired of you taking advantage of him. Was all of it worth it? Was any of it worth it?"

"I don't know what you're talking about," Laura replied. "Ed promised to take care of me, and he broke that promise. He hurt me deeply. He couldn't keep his hands to himself and—"

"He never laid hands on you!" Livvy exploded. "He never hit you and you know he didn't! You lying bitch! What in the fuck is wrong with you!" she roared. "Does it just turn you on to be a lying bitch? Or do you actually believe the shit that you spew?"

"I'd appreciate it if you watched your language in front of my son," Laura replied, her look turning icy. "Just because you are in an abusive relationship and can't get out of it while I had the courage and strength to walk away, don't take it out on me," Laura said with a nod. "I thought that I could talk to you like a normal person. But you're so brainwashed, I'll pray for you," Laura replied with a look of pity before walking away.

Livvy watched her walk off, her blood boiling inside of her veins. She took a step toward Laura's retreating back and a sudden shooting pain in her stomach dropped her to her knees and she cried out in agony as the pain did not falter.

"Ma'am? Are you alright?" came a strange voice to her right. She kept her hand clutched to her stomach and began to cry loudly as she wrapped her arms around herself.

"This is Reynolds near Sector 7G," the mall security guard called nervously in his walkie talkie. "Yeah, I need EMTs at my location. Responded to the disturbance, we have a woman who appears to be having abdominal pains. We need someone here now." He holstered his walkie talkie quickly. "Ma'am, is there anyone you would like for me to call for you? Oh my God..." the security guard exclaimed noticing the blood that had begun to pool from between her legs.

"I... I want Ed... get Ed... please?" she screamed.

He gunned the motor of his car with no care of the vehicle's or the other motorists' protests. His eyes were locked on the road with single minded determination for one goal, get to Livvy at all costs. Tears streamed down his face as he revved the car engine driving faster still. When he heard the siren and the lights in his mirror, he didn't bother to stop. Instead, he pulled out his cell phone and dialed 911.

*"911, what is your emergency?"* came the cool female voice.

"Yes, my name is Ed White. I am currently on Wood Avenue headed toward St. Mary's Memorial Hospital with a cruiser on my tail. I received a call that my pregnant wife was taken via ambulance to St. Mary's. I have zero intention of stopping until I have gotten to the hospital, you may want to pass that information onto the officer following me," Ed said in a flat, emotionless tone.

*"Sir, do you know why—"*

"My wife is pregnant, and they said she collapsed with abdominal pain. I am not stopping until I get to the hospital and I will not submit to anything this officer attempts until I get to my wife and I know that she is safe," Ed replied in the same flat, even tone.

*"Please hold, sir,"* the operator replied calmly.

Ed paid no attention to the lights in his rearview anymore. It didn't matter to him what the operator said. Nothing was going to stop him from getting to his Livvy. Nothing.

*"Mr. White?"* the operator asked.

"Yes?" he replied still driving.

*"Where was your wife when you received this call?"* the operator questioned.

"She was at Eden Prairie Mall. That is all that I know," Ed replied.

*"Alright, sir. We have confirmed this. The officer is going to offer you an escort."*

"Thank you very much," he replied. The police car turned into the near lane and sped up. Both men shared a look to one another, then the police car got in front of him and they sped along. When they made it to the emergency room entrance, Ed jumped from the car and looked to the police officer with a nod. "Thank you."

"Any time, sir. I hope your wife is alright," the older, pale colored officer said.

*Must have been in this situation himself,* Ed thought to himself as he charged into the Emergency Room.

"Regina!" Ed shouted to the receptionist. The one positive thing about Livvy coming to her own hospital was that he wouldn't have to be saddled down with any foolish questions, having to prove his identity.

"Ed, right this way," the younger woman said quickly buzzing him through the door. "She's in room five. Ed, I..." she began.

"Stop it," Ed snapped as he rushed to where he knew Room five to be. When he got there, he saw Livvy laying on the bed, very pale with a gown on. She looked at Ed, her eyes red with tears.

"Ed" she began starting to cry.

"No," was all he could say as she held out her arms for him. He went to her side and hugged her gently as their sobs linked together in unison. He knew by her expression, by her tears that his worst fears were realized, despite his insistence that no one say it.

"I lost the baby," she cried. "I'm so sorry, baby. I—"

"You have nothing to be sorry for," Ed said looking her in the eyes and placing a gentle kiss on her lips. "This is not your fault. This... this was just... a horrible accident."

"I saw her, Ed," Livvy whimpered. "I saw her, and I got so mad. I was just screaming at her. It was like, like she was trying to push me. And I let her, and I got so mad. It's my fault, baby! I'm so sorry!" Livvy sobbed into Ed's chest as his arms held her close to him.

"Are you talking about...?"

"Yes," Livvy sobbed. Ed's eyes shut tight as he tried his best to soothe her, but unsure really what he could say or do for her, so he just held her and hummed to her while running his fingers through her hair.

"You know, we could always try again someday," he said after about twenty minutes of silence. "We give your body a chance to heal and everything, then we can always try again. We can make it work," he said.

182

Livvy said nothing. Her optimism all but completely crushed, and her spirit broken.

Three days later, Ed and Livvy sat in her OB-GYN's office. Livvy's eyes were bloodshot red, and Ed's face hard like stone as he looked at the doctor. Dr. Silver's hair was that of her namesake long, flowing, and completely silver with hard gray eyes. She and Livvy stood the same height, yet Dr. Silver was much more muscular and leaner compared the curvaceous Livvy. Despite her hard exterior, Dr. Silver had a warm way of speaking that endeared her to her patients. When she spoke, her tone was gentle and sad for the forlorn couple.

"Olivia," she began, "I am so sorry about this. I truly am. I do have some news for you. From what I can see of your physical, your miscarriage came from a combination of things. I can see from your blood pressure that you were under severe stress. Do you want to tell me what happened?"

"Yes," Livvy replied, squeezing Ed's hand tightly. "I... I ran into Ed's ex-wife. She was being so... and I just got..."

"Yes well, that was a contributing factor," Dr. Silver said sadly. "There was something else I saw though. In looking at your uterus, there is still some significant scarring. It looks like that is also another reason that you lost the pregnancy."

"So what do we do about it? How can we fix this?" Ed asked seriously.

"Ed..." Livvy began, and then stopped immediately before she could say anything else. "Can we, just talk about it when we get home... please?"

"That would probably be a good idea. We need to keep her stress at a low-level Ed. I know that you're upset, and you want to fix things, but it won't work that way. Olivia needs your gentle side right now." When Ed nodded calmly after taking a deep breath, she gave him a small smile. She then looked at Livvy and took her hand. "Olivia, again I am so very sorry," Dr. Silver offered her a sad smile.

"Could we..." Ed began to ask, "could we try again down the road?"

"Well, that's difficult to say," Dr. Silver sighed. "On one hand, Olivia, you are in great shape and I am very confident that you could carry a baby to term. However, that scarring is very tricky, and it is just impossible to be able to say yes or no for sure in even the best of circumstances."

Ed looked to the doctor and then put his arm around Livvy who stood up before he could settle in his embrace.

"Can we please go home now?" she said as she made her way to the door, not even bothering to wait for Ed to join her.

He walked with her down the hallway and then out into the parking lot. They did not speak a word to one another, not even when they got into the car. When he started the car, he sat there focusing on the steering wheel. Neither of them sure what to say to the other.

"Do you want to... do you want to end this now?" Livvy asked him.

"The fuck are you talking about?" Ed asked, shocked by the question.

"Ed, I can't carry your baby. I know you want another child, especially after everything with Eddie. If you want to—"

"Stop," Ed said abruptly.

He put the car into gear and drove them home without another word. When they got home, he parked the car, got out quickly, and then rushed around to her side, opened her door for her holding out his hand. She looked up curiously, but then took his hand and allowed him to lead her into the house. He led her up the stairs, still remaining silent as a sphinx.

"Would you like me to run you a bath?" he asked her quietly.

"Yes," Livvy said shortly. She wasn't sure what he was doing, or why he was doing it. Yet, she was ready for him to walk away. They had talked children so much, and he was so excited when she'd come up pregnant.

She began to get undressed when he went into the bathroom to draw her bath. He'd installed the large claw foot tub for her as a birthday present a week after he'd moved in. When she came into the bathroom wrapped in her bath towel, he was wrapped in a towel also indicating he would be joining her. He got in first and she followed, resting her back against his chest.

"I'm not going anywhere," Ed said after another moment of silence. "You're not getting rid of me that easily." His voice was firm, hard, and had a slightly dangerous edge to it. "Do I make myself clear?" he asked her sternly.

"Yes," she replied sheepishly. He reached out and grabbed a bar of soap and began to wash her back gently.

"Tell me what happened to you. For years now, there's been something you've been keeping from me. I want to know. Regardless of what it is or was, I'm not going to run away from you. I love you and that's all that matters. Do you understand?" he asked in the same stern voice.

"Yes," she replied, humming ever so slightly as he massaged her back while washing her. "I got hurt," she said simply

"How?"

"Martin," she said under her breath, just loud enough for him to hear.

"What about him?" he asked with an edge to his voice. "What did he fucking do to you?"

"In the last few years of our marriage, he'd begun drinking a lot. We were losing the ranch. I'd been begging him for years to give me a baby, but he always said it wasn't a good time. Well, finally, I got pregnant. When he was sober, he acted happy to almost indifferent about it but when he was drunk, he yelled at me all the time and became violent. He told me that I was trapping him by being pregnant and that it was my fault the ranch was failing because I was always pressuring him." She looked over her shoulder to meet his eyes. When he looked at her, he saw that she had no more tears in them, and neither did he.

"Usually, I just stayed quiet. He'd thrown things at me while he was drunk. Spit beer at me, threw an open bottle of beer at me once. Almost busted my head wide open. I just tried to stay out of his way when he was drunk most of the time. Well one night, I don't know what changed. Maybe I was just in a bad mood, or maybe he'd said something particularly mean. I really don't remember. All

I do know is that he started in on me and I started yelling back. The next thing I knew, he punched me in the stomach as hard as he could."

Ed growled a feral, angry growl as he gripped the bar of soap into a mound of mush. He shook angrily as he let her words wash over him.

"He punched me, and it hurt worse than anything I'd ever felt in my entire life," she said finally, looking to him for his reaction. He simply continued to clean her with the mush that used to be the soap.

"Why did you never tell me about this before?" he asked in a softer, gentler tone.

"I don't like to think about it," she replied. "I'd never felt so unsafe before and when I think about it, it reminds me of that time. Except for now," she said leaning against him. "You've always made me feel safe. I think... I think I feel even safer now that I've finally told you about it."

"You are and will always be safe with me," he said to her gently.

"I'm sick of this shit, Ed," she said finally. "I'm sick of the power they have over us, that they hold over our heads. That... that fucking beast killed our baby, Ed. And that, that drunken bastard killed my other one. I should have one beautiful child and another one on the way. They've both been murdered and for what? Because *those things* just felt like it." Before he could say anything, she sniffled trying to fight back the threatening tears. "And this, this bullshit system is set up to let people like her thrive! Do you know why Martin didn't go to prison?"

"Why?"

"Because his father is rich, and he claimed that he was so drunk he didn't remember what happened. But he remembers, Ed, I know he does. The last time I saw him at the mall, there was something in his eyes, in his smirk. Oh, he remembered! I just... I just want to see him suffer for that! Just like I want to see that goddamned monster of yours suffer!" she shouted angrily. "And why the fuck not? Why not that fucker who was supposed to be your lawyer, but gave into everything she wanted? And that fucking conquering hero free lawyer of hers! And can you answer this question for me why is her family, and that little fat demon spawn of hers allowed to get away with this? They tried to ruin us, Ed! They ruined our chance to have a happy life!" she cried out looking to him, continuing.

"They destroyed our chance at a happy life. They killed our babies she is going to be living happy and fat and comfortably off of your hard work for the next eleven years of our lives! And then, if she sends that monster to college, good luck if you ever have any money to retire on! They're trying to destroy us!" Livvy growled. "Why is that right? Why?" she yelled.

Gone was the warm, loving brown eyes that he'd gotten lost in. They looked twisted, with sadness and pain. He was unable to judge her, or even feel fear. He felt the exact same.

"It's not right," he said. His voice low and thick.

"Do you remember Craig Jackson?" she asked him.

"Of course, I do," he said. "Every single day."

"What happened to him when he tried to take from you? What did you do to him?" she asked seriously.

"I killed his black ass," he growled.

188

"That's right! That's my baby! You killed his black ass! He was going to take you from me before I could even have a chance to have you! Was that right?" she asked.

"No," he said, with more conviction in his voice this time.

"No, it wasn't!" She moved her hand over his thigh and between his legs taking him into her hand causing him to gasp. "They keep taking, and taking, and taking from us. I am tired of it, baby. Aren't you tired of it?" she asked sweetly.

"Yes..." he moaned as he grew more excited.

"So what are you going to do about it, baby?" she asked him as she began to stroke him faster the splashing of the water from her movements was the furthest thing from their minds. "What are you going to do? I have you so hard right now, Daddy and guess what? You can't do anything because I have to heal. That cunt, and that bastard and their little friends have done this to us. What are you going to do about it?" she asked, stroking him faster and harder now. He shuddered in her grasp biting his lip for a moment.

"I'm going to make them pay!" he cried out loudly as his climax hit him suddenly and without warning. She continued to stroke him harder than before causing a second wave of orgasm to hit him before he was even finished with the first. She gently rubbed him as his body went limp in the water.

"I hope so, baby. I am tired of this. I am tired of being used as their punching bags. Tired of us being hurt by their lies and their bullshit. It's enough," she said pulling her hand from under the water, his excitement still coating her hand. She licked the remnants from her fingers and kissed him gently.

"I'm ready for bed, honey," she said. "Let's go to bed. Alright?"

"Okay," he replied subordinately, following her to the bedroom after they dried off, he laid with her in still silence. For two hours he lay with her, his eyes wide open. Even after her breathing went soft, automatic with sleep, he was still wide awake. Her words replayed over and over in his mind.

*What are you going to do about it, baby? They keep taking, and taking, and taking from us.* Echoing over and over. He gently massaged her stomach, and he felt sadness cover him like a blanket. He held her close, placing a gentle kiss on her forehead.

"It's not right," he said to himself, continuing to massage her empty womb softly. "It's not right," he said again. "No more. I'll get them for you. I swear to God... I'll get them."

# CHAPTER 14
## *VENGEANCE*

Two months had gone by, and the agony that they both felt from the miscarriage had become another part of their daily lives. Livvy insisted Ed go back to work after a week, needing the time to herself to be able to heal. After a month, she went back to work as well. They didn't mention the incident again. When six weeks had gone by, neither felt interested in revisiting their sex life.

Ed felt terrified at the idea of causing her any harm. Livvy simply had no interest. When she noticed that he was aroused, she gladly satisfied his desires in ways that she knew wouldn't make him nervous for her health. She hated the routine, yet she loved him for being willing to go through with it. One night at dinner, while he cleared the dishes, she looked at him with a warm smile.

"I love you Ed. You know that right?"

"Of course baby. Why're you even asking me that?"

"Because," she said sadly, fresh tears falling down her cheek. "I'm turning into her. We aren't having sex anymore. You're afraid to touch me because I made our

baby die, and I'm afraid for you to touch me because..."
she began to sob.

He put the dishes down and went to where she sat
and got down on his knees, taking her hand, resting his
head against her chest so that she could hold him.

"You are nothing like her Livs. You hear me?
Nothing. Yeah, I'm afraid that you'll get hurt again, but this
wasn't your fault. It was her. It was all her. And you have
no reason to put that blame on you. That's on her, and that
piece of shit Martin. Do you hear me?" he asked her
fiercely.

"But Ed..."

"No 'buts' Liv. You're the perfect wife. You're
gorgeous. You're amazing. You're the best woman I've
ever known in my life. God... I wish we had met earlier.
Then I never would have had that demon in my life, and
you never would have met that punk ass baby killing piece-
of-shit."

"Oh Ed," she held him close, her tears pouring
from her cheeks onto his shaved head. He trembled with
fury at the pain and blame that she carried within herself.
He released a gentle breath, pulling away just to give her a
gentle kiss.

"Let me run you a hot bath. I'll make you some tea
and you get some sleep. Alright?" When she gave him a
tearful nod, he stood up and went up the stairs. As the
water ran into the tub, he felt a fresh wave of fury run
through him that he hadn't remembered experiencing
before. Normally, he would want to scream at the top of
his lungs, roaring like a tiger at any trespasser into his
domain. Now, it was different. The fury that was normally

white hot was cold, cruel, calculating. He knew what he had to do to make her feel better. He'd been thinking of it since the night after they'd found out their dreams of a baby was no more.

*What are you going to do about it, baby?"* she'd asked him that night. *"They keep taking, and taking, and taking from us.*

The words replayed over and over in his mind, the same as they'd done on that fateful night. "It's not right," he said to himself as he put his hand under the running faucet, ensuring that it was the very temperature that she preferred. "It's not right," he said again. "No more."

"What did you say baby?" Livvy asked, sniffling as she entered the bathroom wearing her bath robe. She took it off and hung it on the back of the door. She went into the nearby cabinet and pulled out a bath bomb and dropped it into the water.

"Huh? Oh, nothing," he replied kissing her softly on the lips. "Enjoy your bath. I'll have your tea ready in the bedroom when you're finished."

"Thank you Ed," she hugged him gently, placing another kiss on his lips before she slipped into the water.

He left the bathroom, pulling the door closed behind him and went to the kitchen, his mind running through a plan.

*It's fucking enough!* He roared to himself internally. *No, fucking more!*

Later that night, he laid beside her, her arm and leg wrapped around his body as she slept soundly. Ed lay on his back, staring at the ceiling, unable to get the plan out of his mind.

*It's enough.*

*You're goddamn right it's enough! But what're you going to do about it? What? Are you all talk? You just going to let your wife live in fear forever? Or are you going to be man enough to protect her? Fuck, she'd do it for you? Wouldn't she? She'll be happy you're willing to do this for her. Won't she?*

"Yes. She will," he replied aloud. He disentangled himself from her, careful not to wake her. He pulled on a pair of boots, black jeans, and a black sweatshirt and a spare set of clothes. He then grabbed his keys and wrote her a note and left it on the nightstand.

*No more.*

*-E*

He remembered the address to Martin's that he'd seen looking through her scrapbooks. A letter that came with her original nursing license had the old address on it. Ed put the address into his GPS and drove off, a single purpose in mind.

Martin still lived on the land where the ranch was, except now it wasn't a ranch it was a ranch style house with a lot of land and nothing more. Ed kept to the back roads, finally pulling onto the property after an hour of driving. The house was pitch black, but he saw the truck parked in front of the house.

"No more," Ed repeatedly said to himself like a mantra. He pulled up a few feet from the truck and killed the engine and lights. Then he opened the glove compartment and pulled out the handcuffs he'd walked out of his job with. He checked to make sure he had the cuff key, popped the trunk, then got out of the car and inhaled the humid late-night air. It was going to rain soon and a cold grin spread across his face.

He wore black leather gloves, and plastic bags with rubber bands over his boots and a dark folded bandana to cover his face. He went to the front door and found that it was unlocked. He slipped inside keeping his senses about him. He went to the master bedroom and saw Martin sleeping with beer cans sprawled all around him. Ed walked over to him and slapped his face.

"Martin? Martin, fucking wake up, you bastard!" When Martin didn't stir, Ed put the handcuffs on him, then went into Martin's drawer, rolled a sock into a wad, and shoved it in his mouth before wrapping a handkerchief around the gag. Ed picked him up from the bed and carried him out onto the lawn. Using his foot to open the trunk, he unceremoniously tossed Martin into the trunk and shut it. He knew that he was passed out drunk, he wouldn't wake up any time soon.

"Livvy, wake up."

Livvy groaned weakly when she felt a hand on her shoulder, shaking her gently.

"Come on, baby, wake up."

"Leave... me... alone," she groaned weakly.

"Livvy, baby, you need to wake up. Right now," Ed said again, a bit more forcefully.

Livvy groaned loudly, irritably opening her eyes to look to her husband. His eyes were dancing with excitement, but not joyful excitement.

"Ed, what are you doing?" she asked with a yawn.

"Get dressed and come with me," he said shortly. "Right now. I have something for you to see."

"Ed, will you please tell me what's going on?" she asked with a yawn.

"I'll tell you in a minute. Come on, get dressed. Let's go."

She let out another loud groan and rolled out of bed. "Edwin White, you'd better have a good fucking reason why you're waking me up for something other than sex! It's fucking..." she glanced at the alarm clock beside their bed, "two thirty in the morning!" she hissed.

"I know. Put on jeans and a sweatshirt," he commanded.

Livvy grumbled, pulling on the clothes he'd ordered her to and followed him downstairs.

"Ed, where the hell are we going?" she asked as irritation threatened to take control of her any second.

"To the basement," he said simply.

"Alright Ed, why in the hell are we going to the basement?"

"Baby, trust me. Just come on. 'No more'. Remember?" he replied in a mechanical voice.

She followed him unsure of what to think. He led her past the washer and dryer, the deep freezer toward the small room he used as his exercise area.

"Ed, what's this about, baby? You're scaring me," she said nervously.

"There's nothing to be afraid of, baby," he said in a cold voice, stopping in mid step, turning to face her. "I'm

196

going to make sure you're always safe. I promised you that before and I let you down."

"You didn't let me down, Ed," she said softly, massaging his cheek. His expression was hard, but his eyes still danced an evil, macabre silhouette.

"I did," he disagreed. "Well. Now. I'm going to make it right."

He opened the door to the basement to reveal Martin seated on Ed's bolted down weight bench in the inclined position, so he was sitting upward. His arms were individually handcuffed to his bench press bar with a total of five hundred pounds to weigh the bar down, and the safety clamps wrapped around the bar to ensure it did not move. His ankles were cuffed to the bolted down metal of the bench where his leg press was, completely naked, and unconscious.

"Ed, what is this?" Livvy asked him anxiously. "Why is he—?"

"No more, my love," he said methodically. "It's partially his fault that our baby is dead. He is going to pay for it. I thought you would want to watch."

Upon further inspection, she saw the propane torch, bolt cutters, a box cutter, and Ed's circular saw all laid down neat and tidy in the corner. Ed reached into his pocket and pulled out four tourniquets and made his way toward Martin's prone body and proceeded to tie the tourniquets at Martin's wrist and ankles, just above the handcuffs. Then he checked to make sure the gag was still firmly in Martin's mouth. When it was to his satisfaction he moved on.

"Ed, honey what are you going to do?" Livvy asked nervously. "You're—"

"Baby, it's going to be alright," Ed repeated. "I love you. He is going to pay for hurting you." Ed opened up the nearby first aid kit and pulled out the smelling salts, cracked it to release the pungent scent of ammonia, and placed the small container under Martin's nose. Martin turned his head from side to side before waking up with a snort. When he tried to speak, it was muffled by the makeshift sock and handkerchief gag. When he tried to pull against the cuffs only to cry out in pain as the unforgiving metal of the ratcheted handcuffs dug into his skin. He looked to his left and right, finally becoming aware of his predicament, then looked first at Ed and then at Livvy. She could just barely make out his words, even though the translation was almost completely lost thanks to the gag.

"What the fuck is going on?"

"Martin, I... Ed, what are you trying to prove?" Livvy asked nervously.

"We are no longer going to be victims to people like him," Ed said coldly. "He punched you in the stomach and killed your first baby. Remember? Well, he isn't going to get away with it. Not for a second longer. He killed your baby, now..." Ed walked over to the corner and picked up the Bernz-o-matic and lit the torch. "I'm going to make him suffer."

"Edwin, don't you do this!" Livvy hissed as Ed walked toward Martin.

"It's not going to be fast for you, Martin," he spoke coldly. "Oh no. It's going to be good and slow." Ed glared at him. "How could you? How could you punch your pregnant wife in the stomach? How?" Ed roared and punched Martin on the right side of his face with a vicious left hand. "You murdered your own child, and then have the nerve to walk up to my wife as though you have not a care in the world after all of these years?" Ed growled and turned the knob on the torch so that the flame was thin and blue and threatened to put the flame to Martin's crotch.

Martin screamed in terror in his gag, unable to move away from the heat. Ed moved the flame just close enough before he could burn him. The smell of burning hair in the air invaded Livvy's nostrils.

"You don't like being a victim, do you, Martin? No, no you don't. You don't like this at all. Too bad really. I'm sure Livvy didn't want to be your victim. Did you, baby?" he asked looking over his shoulder.

Livvy was frozen in a combination of terror and fascination as she watched her new husband bring the hot blue flame to Martin's trapped left hand burning the middle finger knuckle causing Martin to scream in agony through his gag. Tears started to stream down his face as his eyes went wide with fear.

"Did you want to be his victim, Livvy?" he asked again, looking back at Livvy again.

She brushed tears from her face. "No," she said simply.

"See that?" he yelled, running the blow torch over Martin's naked thigh, singing his hair. "She didn't like it. She never liked it. But that didn't matter to you? Did it?" he asked running the bright blue tip quickly over Martin's nipples causing him to scream even louder in anguish into the gag.

"I don't think he likes being a victim, honey. I wonder if he cares that you were a victim all of that time. What do you think?" He kept the flame on his nipple for a few seconds causing his cries to explode from him, only to be captured in the fabric as more tears poured from the captive Martin's eyes. The scent of burning flesh tingled her nose. "It's too bad," Ed sighed. "If he would have just considered your feelings, and how his actions affected you, he wouldn't be in this situation." Ed settled the torch on Martin's other nipple the stench of burning flesh growing thicker in the air as Martin appeared to be ready to pass out from the pain.

"Are you not enjoying yourself, my love?" Ed asked her as though they were at the opera and not torturing her ex-husband in her presence.

"Ed, I don't think this is a good idea," she began. The smell of burning flesh and hair was repugnant. However, she had to admit, seeing Martin in agony the way he was did make things better for her.

"Do you want me to stop, baby?" Ed asked in a disappointed tone. "I can't just let him go now you know."

It took her a moment to speak. In a flash she remembered their married years, the constant mixed signals, and alcoholic rages. The screaming, the lazy and uninterested sex life, his complete condescension for her feelings. The arrogant look of disregard as she lost their baby thanks to his actions. The look he'd given her outside of the courtroom, the same look he'd worn in the mall.

Her humanity was replaced with intense hatred as she stepped forward.

"No, Ed. Don't stop," she said in a casual tone. "After all, I did say it earlier, didn't I? The same as you did 'no more'. Continue, baby," she said coldly.

Martin's eyes bugged out of their sockets as Ed stepped forward with a cold, cruel glare.

Ed proceeded to burn Martin's finger tips and toes until all total twenty fingers and toes and thumbs were black, burned nubs.

"Why did you do that, baby?" she asked curious.

"For one, it would hurt," he said coldly. "For two, he will not be able to be identified. She gave a nod of understanding as Ed put the torch down and picked up the box cutter. "Let's get down to business shall we?"

"Do we still have a shot of adrenalin?" Ed asked Livvy fifteen minutes later. She shook her head no, and Ed grunted in disappointment. Martin was barely conscious Ed had cut his eye lids off so he could not close them after burning off the identifying features of his fingers and toes, and the tattoo on Martin's back which caused him to scream even louder. Despite the gag, his screams began to grow in intensity.

"We should soundproof this room," Livvy said shortly.

"Good idea, baby," Ed replied.

"I want to try," she said stepping forward, and holding her hand out. Ed smiled at her and handed her the box cutter. Livvy had to admit as she stepped forward and slapped Martin in the face harshly, that he looked very creepy with his eyes rolling into the back of his head with no eyelids to cover them. She slapped him again and he started to grunt and cry as agony and terror surged through him.

"Do you realize how long I have been afraid of you, Martin? Yes. You. Some drunken monster that murders his own child because he blamed me for every little thing wrong that ever happened in your adult life! But you wanted me to be afraid. Didn't you, Martin?" she asked in a soft, sing-songy voice.

Martin began to sob shaking his head 'no' frantically.

"Do not lie to me, Martin. You knew. And you loved it. You loved the power you had over me. You laughed at me when you punched me in the stomach. You remember that?" she shouted. When Martin shook his head again, Ed stepped forward and placed a masterful, and accurate punch to Martin's stomach causing him to grunt loudly in pain. Livvy smiled warmly.

"Thank you, Daddy. This is such a great present you've gotten me," she said looking to Ed affectionately. She stepped forward and claimed his lips with hers moaning softly into the kiss. When she broke the kiss, she looked at Martin angrily.

"It's partly because of you," she said with an acidic tone, "that I can't give my daddy what he deserves in full." She swiped the box cutter past his face with a malice that surprised and aroused her. Martin screamed loudly in agony as she saw the bloody mess that had once been his right eye pouring down his cheek like thick, viscous, crimson tears.

Livvy looked to the bloody box cutter in her hand as though transfixed.

"Is something wrong?" Ed asked calmly.

"It's the same color it was when I... when I lost the baby," she said flatly. After a few seconds she looked at Ed, his eyes hardening. "Daddy. Hurt worse. Please? For princess?" she looked to him with a sad face, combined with a pouting lip. The sadness in her eyes at the memory brought a fresh burning of fury through him as he looked to the scene.

Ed wasted no words. He took two gliding steps toward Martin and threw a monstrous punch just below his left ear at the jaw bone. The sickening crunch rang through the basement as Martin released the howl of a wounded animal. Livvy purred lightly when Ed repeated the process to the right side of Martin's mouth. Thunder rolled as rain pounded the house, as though tears for the innocent fell from Heaven. Livvy smiled an evil smile at the scene before her, licking her lips seductively when her lover looked back to her with his fists dripping blood from the captive man's face seeking her approval.

"Thank you, Daddy," she said in a husky tone, a familiar fire beginning to burn inside of her. The excitement of the situation, the look of dangerous fury toward a common enemy on her husband's face brought a damp feeling to her.

She reached out and gripped his crotch with a feral grunt, kissing him hard. His attempts at protest were stifled by her tongue as she kissed him deeply, manipulating his body outside of his clothes. She broke the kiss, keeping a grip on him.

"Let's finish him," she said, her lips inches from his. "We have a lot of time to make up for."

Two hours later, the two lovers lay curled up together in their bed, sweaty after a violent round of love making that had started in the shower. He had attempted to remain gentle, but she wouldn't allow it. She drove him on, goaded him to give her what she wanted. And he'd obliged her in every way she demanded. Below where they lay in the basement, rested the mutilated, dismembered husk that had once been Martin Rogers and tools that had been used to perform the ghastly task.

Bloody pliers lay among a pile of teeth, a chainsaw lay haphazardly along with Martin's appendages, and a grinder covered in the gore that had once been Martin's face.

Livvy curled up naked against Ed's nude body. She'd wanted him so badly. She massaged his sleeping face affectionately, happy that she had given him everything that he'd deserved.

"You did this all for me?" she asked in a soft, gentle tone. "You knew he hurt me, what he did to me and you did this all for me." She placed a gentle kiss on his lips. "I'll have to return the favor." She snuggled against his chest. "Soon."

"How are we going to get rid of his body... err... I mean what's left?" Livvy asked at breakfast the next morning. The initial exhilaration had worn off, and she looked at Ed curiously. For a brief moment, he looked different to her. He was like a glacier he didn't appear to be phased in the slightest by what happened.

"Part of the reason why I cooked his fingers and his toes was so there was no way to identify him," he replied as simply as though he were talking about hunting. "I pulled out his teeth so there would be no dental records, and I filed his face down to the bone so they wouldn't know what he would look like. Blood type can belong to anyone so that isn't unique or identifying. Was his DNA ever put in the system?"

"No," she said shaking her head, not trusting herself to speak. She could feel his eyes on her, and after a few seconds Livvy's eyes locked with his. He looked at her with such a gentle, loving gaze she began to feel shame. "Not unless it was after we were separated. I don't think he would have for any reason though."

"Ed, we... you... you killed him," she said finally.

"Yes. I did," he said simply, offering no other words.

"Do... do you even care?" Livvy asked him, her voice raising in octave. "Does it even bother you that in our basement you chopped up and tortured my ex-husband?"

"Did it bother him that he tortured you throughout the years of your marriage?" he retorted in a quiet voice, barely above a whisper. "Did it bother him that he killed your unborn child because he was a drunken asshole? It did not appear to. So no Livs, it does not bother me that I tortured him and mutilated him. Not in the slightest. I slept soundly."

"But Ed—"

"I did it for you, Livvy," he said in the same gentle tone. "The look on your face when you told me about the baby, the nightmares that you've had all these years because of him? I only did what the law wouldn't do," he said going back to eating his eggs.

"What do you mean, Ed? What are you talking about? Vigilante justice?" she asked, trying to calm herself as hysterics threatened to take the place of rational thinking.

"Martin Rogers ended a life. I've balanced the scale."

"Was it like this when, when you killed Craig Jackson?" she asked timidly.

Ed looked up at her with surprise for the question, then anger covered his face before he spoke. He took a deep breath to calm himself, and serenity washed over him again. "At first, I felt guilty," he admitted. "When I was wheeled into that operating room, I was hoping that I would die. I thought that was my punishment for taking a life. When I was under though, I had a vision."

"A vision of what?" Livvy asked curiously.

"I could see all of the things that Craig Jackson had ever done in his life. He murdered his own cousin for being in a rival gang, then he murdered a blind woman, her dog, and her caregiver all for a gang initiation. He'd raped the eleven-year-old sister of another rival gang member he was going to murder the wife and son of an investigating police officer before he was caught. What he was in prison for? The drive-by shooting gone wrong? That was barely the frosting on the cake of what an evil bastard that kid was, and all before he turned twenty-five. That, coupled with the fact that he was going to kill me? My feelings of guilt did not last long.

"Why would you ask me that?" he asked sadly. "Last night, before I went to get Martin…"

"Ed, I don't want you to feel guilty about killing Craig Jackson. I'm glad you did. I wouldn't have you here with me now. It's just—"

"Just what?" Ed interrupted. When she didn't respond right away, he cleared his throat. "I did it for you, Livvy. But I understand it's a lot to take in. If you're going to call the police, I ask that you allow me missing person's time of twenty-four hours before you call them."

"Ed, I'm not calling the police. I'm not some disloyal cunt like that pig ex-wife of yours!" she shot back, her blood beginning to boil. "I'm just trying to come to grips on this if that's not too much to ask? I mean Christ, I hated that bastard downstairs. He's a monster… was a monster. I just… I've never seen anything like that before that's all. Alright?"

"Okay," Ed replied simply.

They were silent for a few moments before she purred, "You did that just for me?"

"I did."

"What's next?" she asked with a smile.

Ed grinned at her finishing his food.

"We clean up. I say we take a trip up the coast today. Dump various bits and pieces here and there so that finding him is almost impossible. We'll stick to back roads in rural areas to make it that much harder. When I went into his place I had plastic bags on my feet so that avoids them finding trace evidence of our place there. I also had on gloves. He had his door open, so I didn't have to force my way in. I just lifted him up out of his bed and carried him on out."

"You mean he didn't try to fight at all?" Livvy asked and then shook her head in disappointment in herself that she didn't get it sooner. "He was passed out drunk wasn't he?" she asked.

"Yes," Ed replied. "He was starting to wake up when I got him in the house and still not fully woke up when I cut all of his clothes off.

"I was just thinking," she said, "do we still have those plastic contractor bags?"

"Yeah, a whole box full."

"This is what we should do then get a brand-new deep freezer. I do not want that bastard anywhere near my food, then freeze him. Then, get that woodchipper you've been eyeing all this time. Nobody will see anything since we have the tree line the whole way around and the house blocking anyone seeing into the back. Use the contractor bags to catch whatever flies through then we take the trip. We'll go up the coast and toss the teeth in the ocean." She smiled coldly. "We'll also get a new luggage set to keep the bags in. If we do get pulled over, they probably won't think to look in the luggage. And guess what? We can put some clothes over the plastic if they do."

"That's brilliant baby." He chuckled. "I think I've created a monster."

"I think we both had a hand in creating this," she said with an evil smile.

"You know they are going to come and talk to you about this right?" he said seriously.

"Yeah, I know. Martin had a lot of people that hated him," Livvy replied. "I'm just one of a few. What should I say?"

"Lie with the truth," he said calmly. "Law enforcement are trained to sniff out lies. They're like a man-pig-dog mix," he said with disdain. Since he'd left his corrections job, his hatred for law enforcement had increased dramatically. "So you tell them that you hated him, and that you've had a restraining order for years against him and that whenever you saw him at the mall it scared you because the restraining order had run out."

"But wouldn't that be me admitting—"

"No," he interrupted. "You're just stating how scared you are of him. Never mention him in the past tense that is a dead giveaway. When you go to show hatred though, that's when you bring up the baby. And then after that you should be good."

"That's smart," she said with a smile.

"Yeah well, I was a CO for a while. CO's are smarter than cops by a lot. We had to do the same things the cops do on the streets, but it's harder when you're still surrounded by the people involved. You get to know how they got caught, and why. So you learn ways to beat it if it were you."

"Careful," she chuckled teasingly, "you sound like you've got pride in that thin barb-wired line."

"Fuck that," he hissed in annoyance.

She threw back her head laughing loudly. "I love you, baby, but it's so easy to push your buttons. I think that's why I love you so much," she purred. "My sexy, impulsive tough guy."

Ed stood up and moved around the table with the grace of a cat and wrapped his arms around her from behind, massaging her breasts through her nightgown bringing a moan to her lips. She moved her hands over his and purred.

"Let's get to work. Fun later," she said firmly. "We need to at least get him frozen. I do not want my house to smell like Martin Rogers." She didn't let him remove his hands from her breasts, however. "We get that done, and we can have some fun before we get back to work. Make sure we get a lot of ice too. It takes a few hours for a new freezer to get cold," she said.

"So I suppose we're showering separately then too right?" he chuckled.

"Yes. You're going to leave now to get the freezer, the ice, and the woodchipper. Your truck should be big enough to carry all of them."

"What're you going to do?" he asked.

"I'm going to start cleaning up down there. It's a mess. I'll use the bags and everything too. When you get back and have everything all set up, if I'm not done, you're helping," she said placing a kiss on his lips.

"Alright, baby. I'll be back."

Later that day, Livvy moaned loudly in desire from the pain he inflicted as she pressed her hips into the air to receive him while she rested on elbows. She looked over her shoulder, past her own naked back to her lover, her protector as he grunted in pleasure. The sight of his hard, ebony upper body so firm and glistening with sweat from the effort of pleasing himself with her body, threatened to drive her mad. She adjusted her right arm between her body and the bed to massage her sodden ecstasy. The duality of his assault upon her while she massaged herself a few short inches away drove her over the edge and she felt her climax's intensity saturate everything in its path.

"Oh my God!" she screamed as her body, wracked with this new wave, caused her to go limp. She was barely aware of his continued thrusting and movement before she heard his bestial roar. The feeling of his explosion somewhere other than she was used to with him caused a second, intense climax to overwhelm her.

He slowly, gently, removed himself from her. The movement, while still so sensitive, caused him to cry out as their bodies collapsed onto the bed. He was barely aware of the sheets soaked with their combination of fluids as they lay upon one another.

It felt like an eternity before she could speak again. She was hardly aware of his arm over her. His breathing, finally more rhythmic than erratic, warmed her.

"God... that was... wow," she gasped lightly.

"Are you alright?" he asked her with concern.

"Better than alright. I swear it feels like every time gets better than the last." She chuckled. "How do you do that?"

"I just do," he replied massaging her stomach gently.

"She has to be longer than he was. You know that right?" her tone informing him of the change in subject.

"I do," he replied.

"Good. I want her to suffer. She deserves to. For everything that she has done to us," she said firmly. "I need to make her suffer, Ed. I need her to... hurt. And even that isn't good enough."

"I understand," he replied with a soft kiss to her neck. "And she will. I promise you."

"No. I promise you."

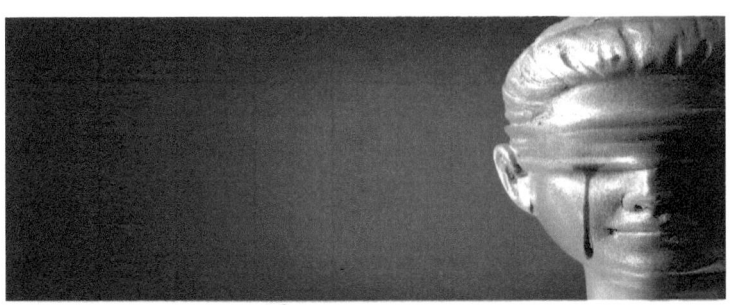

# CHAPTER 15
## *FOREVER AND FOR ALWAYS*

The following night, they were in her car driving toward the coast with their bags packed. It'd taken up until mid-afternoon that day to be satisfied with the freezing of Martin's body. They'd carefully placed the contractor bags so that when the frozen parts were placed in the woodchipper, more would go into the bag than would not. The combination of rain, wind, and scavengers would handle the rest.

She'd called a little inn she knew about on the boarder of Maine and made reservations for the following morning.

"Are you sure that it won't look funny? Us leaving like this?" she asked nervously from the passenger's seat.

"Of course not," he reassured her. "We're still allowed bereavement time, we need to get away from it for a few days, especially since we sort of just went back to life as normal. It will look completely normal to anyone, especially if they have been through it also." Their hands were interlocked as they drove, and he pulled her hand to his face and kissed her knuckles gently. "Don't worry. It's going to be fine."

Every fifty miles they drove along the coast, when it was clear, he would stop and remove a bag from the trunk, poke holes in it for decomposition reasons, and toss it into the water, then continue on their route. When they finally arrived in the state of Maine, all that remained was the bag of teeth that they had purposefully saved for last. She rolled down her window, and opened the baggy and let the teeth scatter out into the dawn-soaked roadside.

"That's that," he said after a few minutes. "He's gone."

"Putting the bags in the ocean was smart," she said calmly. "There won't be anything to find."

"And some sea creature doesn't have to work as hard for a meal." He snickered. "Now all we will have to deal with is when the police question you about his disappearance. That will be easy."

"And if something goes wrong?" she asked mesmerized by the dawn.

"It won't," he replied shortly.

"But if it does?" she said firmly.

"I'll take care of it."

"How?"

"I will take the blame. I threatened you to cover it up. Simple as that," he said emphatically.

"No." She looked at him. "That will not happen, do you hear me, Ed? It won't."

"Livvy—"

"No, Edwin!" she said, her voice raising. "I will not let them take you away from me. I would rather us both died first!" she growled. "Don't you ever say anything that stupid again, do you hear me? I'm not some disloyal whore like that first bitch you married do you understand me? I

214

married you and I'm your wife! That means, for better or for worse, which makes me a real wife! So, that's not going to happen! I may have times when I'm a complete bitch, but goddammit I'd never turn my back on you! So don't you dare think to turn your back on me! I had better not hear you say anything like that again!"

"So what do you want to do then? If something does go wrong?" he asked her seriously.

"We will cross that bridge when we get there. But I mean it as sure as I'm breathing don't you ever let that thought enter your head again, do you understand me?" When he didn't respond she pulled her hand from his and gripped his shoulder tightly, digging her nails into his shoulder.

He looked down to where his flesh was being pierced and did not flinch.

"Do you understand me, Edwin White?"

"Yes. I understand," he responded in the dull tone of a scolded child. "I'm sorry." A single tear slipped from his eye, yet he did not move.

"It's okay, baby," she replied lovingly, removing her nails from him. "I can't think about you being taken from me. I just can't. It drives me crazy, absolutely crazy. I've spent a year away from you, I will not have that happen again. Not for anything. We are together forever and for always. That's what you promised me."

"Yes, I did," he said.

"And you always keep your promises."

"Yes, I do."

"Good. Then never, ever, let me think that you are going to leave me again. If we have to," she cupped his cheek, kissing his lips, "we will go out in a blaze of glory. We will make Bonnie and Clyde look like a couple of Ed and Livvy wannabes." She giggled softly giving his cheek a gentle pat. "But before we can even think about that, we have a lot of work to do," she said, her tone turning serious again.

"The bitch?" he asked.

"No. Not yet. I have made a list. It must be followed exactly, baby. And when I say exactly, I mean exactly." Livvy looked at him seriously. "They want to fuck with us? We will make them suffer. All of them."

"Mrs. White, my name is Detective Glatt, and this is my partner Detective Wade. I wanted to say first off, we're very sorry to bother you during this difficult time." The older detective wore a well-pressed brown suit. He'd unbuttoned the suit coat exposing his slightly protruding belly, and his muscular chest. His slightly tanned skin indicated to Livvy that he'd either just returned from vacation, or he was just naturally dark. Detective Wade looked considerably younger and wore a much more casual khaki-colored pants, blue shoes, and a black turtle neck style sweater with his badge hanging from his neck by a military dog tag style chain.

They'd returned home after being gone for four days. Ed was right that the police would talk to her, and she was grateful for his council on the situation. She felt her heart pounding anxiously as the second detective hadn't taken his eyes off of her since she'd come into the office and taken a seat at Detective Glatt's desk. They'd called for her shortly after Ed had left that morning, asking her to come down to the station to answer a few questions about Martin since he'd gone missing.

"Yes, it is a difficult time. You mentioned on the phone this was about my ex-husband?" she asked casually.

"Yes ma'am," Detective Glatt agreed. "Mr. Rogers hasn't been seen in almost a week. He disappeared from his home without a trace, but his truck is still parked outside of his home. Now, when was the last time you'd seen your ex-husband?"

"I saw him about a year ago at the mall. He scared me to death," she said with a slight shudder. "Our marriage was quite abusive, and I had a restraining order against Martin that was allowed to expire by the court last summer."

"I bet that upset you didn't it? The restraining order being allowed to run out after two years was it?" Detective Wade asked, watching her with scrutiny.

"Yes, it did upset me, Detective," Livvy replied with a scathing tone. "I just told you that he was abusive in our marriage. How would you feel? Or is it considered policy by your department to treat a victim like a suspect?" she asked immediately causing Detective Glatt to shake his head vehemently.

"Absolutely not, Mrs. White. That is not the case at all."

"Can I please speak candidly, Detectives?" Livvy asked.

"Of course, Mrs. White. This isn't an official interrogation we're just asking some questions to rule things out, that's all," Detective Glatt replied.

"Martin was a sweet man when we first met. I suppose I stopped being what he wanted somehow along the way. He hurt me badly, and I left and that's it. I've made my peace with it, and I've moved on. I've just lost my baby with my new husband I don't make it a point to seek out my ex-husband for any reason. Alright?"

"I apologize, Mrs. White," Detective Wade replied. "I wasn't trying to—"

"I understand, Detective. It's your job to search every possible angle." Her eyes began to grow misty as she put a hand to her head. "I'm sorry, I'm just... I'm still very emotional right now and—"

"Mrs. White, we totally understand," Detective Glatt replied. "We have just a few more questions and you can leave, alright?" When Livvy nodded in response, Glatt cleared his throat. "Do you have any idea where Martin would go if he decided to just... leave?"

"Well, when he drinks he likes to wander," she replied. "One time he got drunk and then just walked through the woods. I found him passed out on one of the hiking trails. It was very scary. Other than that, I wouldn't know. It's been years since I've even seen our old home. Like I said, we haven't been married for quite some time and I didn't associate with him at all."

"Of course, Mrs. White, of course," Detective Glatt replied. "I am so sorry to have wasted your time and if we have any other questions we'll be in touch."

"I actually have one final question." Detective Wade said confidently. "Has Ed ever dealt with your ex-husband? I mean, at all, like at a store, or bar, or anything? We looked into you and Mr. Rogers, Mrs. White." He chuckled. "Yet another night of his binge drinking and—"

"Actually, no he hasn't. Ed has never dealt with him up close before, he doesn't even know what Martin looks like," Livvy replied reaching for a nearby tissue to dry her eyes.

"Oh come on!" Detective Wade exclaimed. "Do you seriously expect us to believe that?"

"It's the truth," Livvy replied, her voice turning cold as steel. "I barely even talk about Martin to Ed. Ed knows nothing about anything about my marriage to Martin other than we were married out of college and we got divorced when our business, I'm sorry *his business*, went under. That's all I ever told him and will ever tell him about my ex."

"And he has never thought to ask you about—" Detective Glatt began but was frozen to silence at the glare Livvy shot at him.

"What do you think, Detective?" She looked to his left hand, noticing his wedding band. "You're married. I am sure that you and your wife have argued countless times over things that she doesn't tell you. Why do you think we hide things from you?" Tears began to swell in her eyes and fall down her cheeks furiously. "Because we love you idiots. You get these mindsets, these ideas that you need to protect us with your big muscles and your loud mouths. Well Ed is exactly the same way from the same macho man mindset." She laughed softly as her tears flowed. "If I told him that Martin used to beat me, and made me lose my baby, Ed would go crazy." Tears started to free fall down her face as she glared at the detectives angrily.

"So I decided to protect him as best I could. I decided not to tell him anything more than he needed to know about my marriage to Martin. When I saw Martin, I never told Ed about it, not ever. Like I told you before, I saw him for the first time at the mall that day. He wasn't nice to me, but it wasn't anything I couldn't handle. I never reported it because I want Martin to move on with his life... just not with me, nor near me. If I were to come to you people about it, it could make things harder for Martin. I just want him to move on. Because if he moves on, than I can keep moving on! That's all I want don't you get that!"

She put her head in her hands, trying to hold back sobs. Her shoulders started raising and lowering to the rhythm of her agony. The two detectives looked at one another and then back to the now sobbing woman. Another man stepped forward wearing dark blue uniform pants and a white shirt with a badge and various other trinkets indicating his rank. His reddened skin, and his scarred, hardened face matched his muscular body: all commanded respect.

When he stepped forward, the two detectives went quiet. Livvy looked at him, tears still in her eyes with a defiant glare.

"Mrs. White, I am Captain Marvin Harris. I am very sorry for you having to go through this. Please accept my, and my department's apology for this," he said, sending a scathing look to the two detectives. "If you would like, we can have an officer drive you home and..."

"No. I'll be fine," she replied, composing herself as best she could. "My husband is nearby. He can be here within five minutes." She pulled out her phone and sent a quick text message then looked at the detectives, then back at the captain.

"I hope you are able to find Martin," she said brushing her tears away. "He isn't always a bad man, just when he drinks."

She stood up from the chair and gave the detectives another look of disgust before turning her back to leave, walking at a normal pace brushing tears from her face as she did. When she got outside, Ed was sitting in his car waiting for her patiently with a worried expression. She got into the car without a word and he drove off.

"Those fucking detectives," she grumbled angrily after they were a few miles away from the station.

"What happened?" He looked at her, noticing her tears. His hand rested on her thigh protectively.

"Well they tried to make it all about me, and then when they had nothing, they tried to make it about you," she replied simply.

"Did you make sure to mention him in the present tense and not the past tense?"

"Of course, don't worry. I was more worried about them trying to come after you," she snapped.

"So what did you say?"

Livvy recounted the discussion with Ed. His eyes narrowed hearing how the detective Wade tried to grill her. He was grateful that it wasn't an official interrogation because he knew things could only have been worse for her.

"I'm glad it was just an interview and not an interrogation. It could have been worse," he recalled his thoughts to her.

"I could handle it," she said simply.

"I know you could, baby," he said proudly. He knew she could do more than just handle it she would survive long after him if everything went south.

"Thank you for protecting me," he said with a gentle smile. "You're the only person that ever has."

"Because I'm the only one that's ever truly loved you, Ed," she replied staring out into the blue sky, almost as if she were in a trance. "People tell you that they love you, but they only want something from you, nothing more. They knew they could get you to do whatever they wanted if they promised you love. It's the only thing you've ever really wanted, and you've never been shy about expressing that." She chuckled lightly.

"Yeah, I guess," he replied flatly.

"You big grouch." She snickered lightly. "I wasn't accusing you I was just stating a fact. All your life you have just wanted to be loved. Your father, your mother, hell your sisters and your brother, all you've wanted is to be loved by someone. All your life, people have let you down when it comes to love and that's not right. And that's why I was brought into your life." She smiled warmly. "The same as with me. People have been letting me down all of my life and have never loved me the way I deserve to be. That is why you were brought into my life." When he turned off the road to take them home, she felt a slight swell of pity.

"All of these people, and none of them will ever really know what it's like to be loved." She reached a hand to his shoulder and massaged him gently. "But you and me? We now know what it's like. We're among the lucky ones. And now that we know, we will never, ever let it go."

"So what now?" he asked her softly. No matter what he tried to do, he couldn't disagree with what she was saying. "Everything you're saying makes sense. But what do we do now?"

"We stick with the plan," she replied simply. "We'll have to be a bit more cautious as they'll be watching us. But we're going to stick to the plan. That bitch is going to suffer for what she did to you, hell that little monster of hers should suffer to."

"Eddie?" he asked, confusion etched on his face.

"Why not?" she asked. "He's been just as disloyal as she ever was. Do you remember? All through your divorce all he did was lie about you. You only have supervised visitation because he told people that you abused him." When he didn't respond, she sighed softly.

"My poor dear heart. My poor, poor baby. You didn't know?" she asked.

"He wasn't allowed to be in the court," he said. "How could I have known?"

"Well that's what he did."

"How do you know? Why did you never tell me?" he asked her, his voice starting to rise ever so slightly.

"My sister Jeanie, remember? I told you that she was her therapist. She told my sister everything, through the entire time. I'm sorry, Ed."

"It's alright," he said. "She couldn't ever say anything, I totally get it."

When they pulled into the driveway, he shut the car down and let out a sigh.

"He stopped being my son a long time ago, didn't he?"

"Yes, he did," she said, giving his neck a gentle caress.

"Good. Makes me feel better."

"Better about what?" she asked curiously.

"About not being sad for what we're going to do." His face was impassive.

"Good," she said leaning forward to kiss him gently. "Once we finish this, we can leave this place behind, Where we never have to be reminded of all that they took from us, not ever again. Do you hear me?"

"I hear you, baby," he said with a warm smile. "When do we start?"

"Soon, baby. Very soon."

"I love you, Livvy."

"I love you too, Ed. Forever and for always."

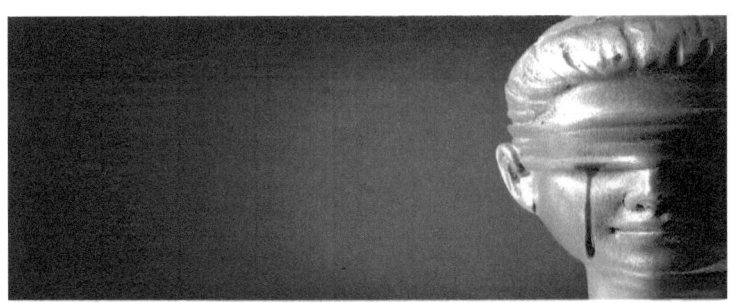

# CHAPTER 16
## *PLANNING AND EXECUTING*

Eddie sat playing his handheld game system, not even bothering to turn the volume on the game off or even down. He sat at the table with Ed doing all that he could to pretend that his father wasn't there and looking at him.

"So, how's school going?" Ed asked quietly.

"Fine," the boy replied shortly, not bothering to give up on his game at all.

"So..." Ed began.

"Don't call me 'son' okay? You're not my dad and you haven't been my dad in a very long time if you were ever my dad at all. I don't even want to see you," the boy huffed angrily, not turning his game off.

"Fair enough. So why did you come?" Ed asked calmly.

"Because Mom says that I have to... something about court or whatever. You're not my dad anymore, Edwin," Eddie said coldly.

"You know, for being nine you definitely act very grown up," Ed said with a smirk.

225

"Well, my dad teaches me a lot," he said with a grin when he saw the quick flash of pain in Ed's expression. "Travis has been more of a dad to me than you ever could." Eddie nodded. "He said he's going to adopt me one day so he can always be my real dad." Ed looked at him with a slight nod.

"Old Travis," Ed said with a slight nod. "Well I used to tell you that Travis couldn't ever be your real father. Just look in the mirror first and foremost. I told you that he couldn't ever teach you to play football, or baseball, or anything like that because the guy would probably be dead by now. I guess I was wrong."

"Mr. White!" the moderator, a young blonde-haired woman with too much make up and not enough shirt hissed.

"So you want Travis to be your father? Fine. Tell your mother to shoot me the paperwork from the court to sign. I'll sign over my rights and he can adopt you. I'm not going to keep trying to be your dad if you don't want me to be."

"Good," the boy replied. "Because I do not want you to be. You hit my mom and you were mean to me. I hate you," the boy said, a look of hatred in his eyes.

"Alright, I think we should..." the moderator began.

"I never struck your mother, son. Not ever. I probably could have been nicer, but I was trying my best to raise you properly and I wasn't all that nice about it. For that I am sorry, but I always tried my best to be a good father to you."

He grinned bitterly shaking his head.

"I stayed awake with your mother all while she was pregnant with you. When she slept, I was still awake because I just wanted to see you. You only really cried when you were taken out of my sight, and that made me smile. I fed you when she couldn't feed you, I bathed you when she couldn't bathe you, and I worked jobs that made me miserable to give you a good life." Ed nodded lightly. "I did all of that for you. You can hate me all you want, at this point, son, I can't change your mind. I can't fight for you if you don't want me," He shook his head, standing up slowly.

"Don't worry, Eddie, you'll never have to do this again," Ed said making his way to the door.

"Wait, Mr. White! You still have time on your visitation," the moderator protested.

"No offense, young lady, but I don't give a damn anymore. He doesn't want to do this, and why should I keep subjecting myself to this, or him?" He looked at Eddie who had started back playing his game and put his headphones in. "He doesn't care. He could get the news in an hour that I'm dead and it wouldn't even shake him."

"Mr. White, he is young and is on the cusp of puberty. Your divorce with your ex-wife was very hard on him. You just have to give him more time and I'm sure that everything is going to be alright."

"Lady, spare me alright? This kid has hated me since the divorce was going on, no matter what I have tried to do for him. His mother has been using him against me from the day he was born, and this is the final nail in the coffin," Ed growled angrily.

"Mr. White—"

"Spare me your psychobabble alright? You people did this," he said, his voice thick with contempt as he pointed at her. "You took her word against me, made me out to be the worse person alive, and took my son from me. You helped her do this. No more. No more. Get me the paperwork so that if her boyfriend wants to adopt him, he can. I'm not going to play this game anymore."

"If that is what you truly want, sir, then that's fine. I'll speak to the courts and find out exactly what needs to be done. How do you know that this man even wants to adopt Eddie?" the woman asked.

"I'm just going by what the kid says. Consider it the last thing I ever did just for him, and trust me lady... there is a very long list of things. A long list indeed." He grabbed his jacket off the coatrack and went to the door. He looked over his shoulder one last time to see the strange boy that had once been his son and made his way to his truck and started it up ready to head off when he looked into his rear-view window and saw Laura and Travis sitting in their car talking.

Unable to control himself, he got out of his truck and made his way toward their car, his eyes blazing.

"Hey!" he roared out to the car his eyes narrowed. Travis and Laura looked toward his booming voice and both exited the car. Ed glared at Travis, gripping his hands into tight balls of fury.

"You have something to say, Ed?" Travis questioned. The older man was easily three inches shorter than the massive man before him, wearing a black pin stripped suit with a blue shirt and red tie. His silver hair was complimented by a mullet style haircut with a long flowing rat tail in the back. The glasses he wore, and the way his lips curled around his teeth gave Ed the impression that he was a rodent walking upright wearing a suit.

"Fuck yeah, I have something to say! To both you and the walking trailer park over here!" he roared gestured toward Laura. "How fucking dare you trash bag pieces of shit turn my own kid against me!" he boomed. "You made up every single lie you could possibly conceive and then you convince Eddie that they're true too?"

"I don't know what you're talking about, Ed," Laura replied in a cool, coy voice. "I never once—"

"You lying fucking bitch! You know I never laid a hand on you!" Ed exploded. He took a step pointing at her when Travis stood in his path and put his hand up.

"Ed, I suggest you—"

Ed's eyes blazed with anger, but his tone became quiet, and subtle. "You even remotely make me think that you're about to make physical contact with me, Travis, and I swear to God—" Ed started.

"You swear to God what, Ed?" Travis asked, opening his suit jacket ever so slightly to expose an over the shoulder gun holster with an arrogant grin.

"Is that right, Travis?" Ed questioned as his heart beat feverishly, sending burning hot lava to ever part of his body as his muscles tightened, begging for him to allow them to react. "You really think you having a gun worries me?" His laugh sounded foreign to him. The smile that Travis had on his face when he showed Ed that he was armed seemed to fade ever so slightly. Laura watched nervously, seeming to think that Travis being armed would unnerve her ex-husband, not enrage him further.

"Do you really think that means a damn thing to me? If you were going to pull that burner, you would have done so already. Sorry 'Old Man River', but you cannot fucking intimidate me." Ed took another step toward him, causing him to take a step back. Ed chuckled coldly.

"You're a fucking pussy, Travis. Some white trash mother fucker that plasters NRA on everything he's got and carries guns thinking that it's going to scare people away from them." Ed shook his head. "I could fucking end you right here, right now with the slightest bit of movement before you could reach into that coat to pull that burner." He shook his head. "You're a pathetic piece of shit, the both of you." He looked toward Laura. "You turned my kid against me. There's a special place in hell for you, you evil fucking-" he took a deep breath, trying to control his anger. "You can go to hell Laura. You, and every single sack of shit that has worked with you to try and hurt me."

He looked over his shoulder seeing Eddie being led out of the building by the moderator. She stopped short looking to the scene that she'd interrupted.

"You want him to adopt my boy? Get me the fucking paperwork and I'll sign it," he growled. "I'm through playing this bullshit game with all of you. Every single last one of you mother fuckers." He spit a wad of phlegm between Laura and Travis and made his way back to his truck, revved his engine and drove off, spinning both rear tires with loud squeals.

"Did that fucker pull his gun on you?" Livvy asked as she removed her robe to get into the tub with Ed. He'd been home for about an hour when Livvy came in from work and saw that he was in the bathroom soaking in the tub and had decided to join him. While she was getting undressed and asking about his day, he informed her of the altercation.

"No, he didn't pull the gun. He just showed it to me, thinking that he was going to scare me. I think he shit his pants when I didn't even step back," he replied to her as she placed a kiss to his lips and laid her back against his chest.

"He's going to pay for that," she said simply. "Nobody threatens my man and thinks they're going to get away with it." Something in her tone told him that disagreeing with her wouldn't be the best of ideas, so he remained silent for a moment.

"Eddie told me how much he hated me, and how he wants Travis to adopt him. I told them that I would sign the papers. He's no longer my son," he said plainly.

"I'm so sorry Ed. I really am. I know this is a stupid question but, are you okay?" she asked him as she adjusted herself against him so that she was pressed up against his waist.

"Indifferent," he replied. "I don't really care."

"Good," she said. "Then, as we agreed, he is no better than the rest of them."

"Fine by me," he said. "The little bastard is dead to me," he said in a cold voice. "He really had the nerve to tell me that Travis was a better father than me."

"He hurt you. You're angry right now, but he hurt you. That makes me want to punish him all the more," she said, rubbing her hips against his, causing him to moan gently. "I'm going to make this all right for you, baby. I promise you."

"How much longer?" he asked.

"What do you mean?"

"How much longer until we can go after them?"

"Soon. Very, very soon. I just need to figure out exactly how we can do it without ruining us."

"Do you have a plan?" he inquired.

"I'm getting there. Nothing for you to worry about. As soon as I figure it out, I will let you know. But you are going to love this. I promise you."

"Alright," he purred as she continued to move her hips against him. He pressed his lips to her ear lobe and nibbled gently. "I want to finish them. Every single last one of them."

"I know, baby. I know," she said as she pressed against him again, then released a hiss of pleasure as she felt him enter her. "Don't you worry, we are going to end this soon." She rolled her hips against him, releasing another groan of pleasure. "And when we do, we are going to go somewhere that no one knows us, and we can start all over again." When she rolled her hips on him again, he released a louder moan as his hands began to caress her breasts feverishly.

"Now, you lay right there, and you let me take care of you, baby," she purred as she rolled her hips over him again. "You've had a hard day, let me make it better."

The next morning Ed stood in front of the mirror, not seeing Livvy in bed next to him, he assumed that she'd gone to work. After finishing his workout, he'd decided it was time to shower and shave. As he guided his razor over his face, he stared into his own eyes and then down the long trail of scratches on his chest. They'd gotten very passionate the night before, and rough.

His thoughts returned to the scenes from the night which he used to feed his workout. He could hear Eddie's dismissive, hateful words toward him, and the threat made on him. He wasn't worried about the police since there would be no way that Travis would risk telling the police that he had attempted to threaten Ed with a gun.

When he finished his shave, he got into the shower and let the hot water wash over him. As his body gave way to the sensation of heat, it washed all of his thoughts away. After getting out, he heard the front door open and close. He quickly dried off and wrapped the towel around his waist.

"Livs? Babe, is that you?" he called out curiously.

"Yeah, honey, it's me."

"Did you go to work today?" he called out walking down the stairs and stopped short at the sight of her.

Her face was dirty as was her disheveled, and colored hair. Her clothing was torn in random places and her lip was bleeding.

"What in the hell happened to you?" Ed asked her seriously inspecting her closely. She smiled to him and took his hand gently.

"I was taking care of a few things, the same as you did for me that's all." She smiled. "Is there anymore coffee or did you not make any?"

"Umm, there's coffee," he said curiously. "I'd like to know where you were and why you look like you got run over at club hell though."

"Let's just say Christmas is coming early for you this year, baby." She giggled warmly as she kissed the scratches on his chest and melted into his arms. He held her close to him and chuckled lightly.

"What do you mean?" he asked looking at her curiously. Seeing the look on her face, she could see realization connecting in his mind and she nodded to him in affirmation. "You went after that bitch last night? I can't wait to hear about that!" he said with a chuckle.

"I'll tell you. Later though because right now, you do realize the police are going to come after you and want to talk to you and that's my fault. So we're going to have to do this very, very quickly. We're going to have to push our timeline up very fast."

"So why are we doing it now?"

"Because I can't stand to see you hurting. I know what that little monster said to you hurt you, and she caused it. She's the whole reason why we aren't going to have a baby. I'm tired of waiting. I want to get this done and I want her to hurt. Do you understand me?"

"Yes, I do," he said with a warm smile. "So how will we get away?"

"Like I said," she smirked giving him a gentle kiss, "I'll take care of that."

"Alright, so where is she?"

"I found a place to take her. She can scream herself insane and it won't matter. No one is going to hear her. Don't you worry about that."

"How did you get her?" he asked her calmly.

"Oh my god, Livvy! Yes!" he roared loudly as he gripped her hips as he exploded inside of her. She fell on top of him, his muscular arms holding her close to him as their chests heaved against each other. She rolled off of him with her back to his chest and cuddled against him as his arm wrapped around her.

"How do you feel now, handsome?" she asked dreamily.

"I feel... fucking... amazing," he said with a loud yawn.

"Good, really good." She smiled. "That's the way I want you to feel for the rest of your life."

He mumbled something inaudible and Livvy just chuckled lightly as she felt his grip on her lighten indicating sleep.

"You're so cute."

She waited another hour. When she was sure that he was asleep, she slipped from his embrace. She went into the bathroom and pulled a bottle from the cabinet and smiled at the temporary hair color bottle. She grabbed her hair straightener and plugged it in. While it began to heat up, she began to rub her hands through her hair, then began straightening her curly hair to ensure that the length would partially cover her face if it weren't in a ponytail. She then entered the shower and began to wash her hair, then put in the temporary hair color, turning her hair jet black. When she was satisfied that the color was set, she turned off the water and began drying off.

After examining herself in the mirror, she smiled evilly, then pulled on a pair of tight jeans, a white t-shirt, and a pair of black boots that she knew, if Ed were awake, would get her clothes torn off of her in a round of love making that would get her pregnant again.

She made sure to move without making unnecessary noise, got to her car and drove off. Her eyes set on the road with intense purpose. The look in Ed's eyes when he came home made her so angry, she was almost unable to contain herself.

"You should never have to look like that," she said out loud, her voice resonating with a harsh pitch. She knew what she needed to do, she just needed to know where her target would be. When she stopped at the red light, she signed into her false Facebook page to look up Laura.

"Stupid cunt." She chuckled. "Can't do a damn thing without telling the whole world about it." When she found what she was looking for, she shook her head. "Getting drunk when you're supposed to be parenting, huh? Doesn't seem to me like anyone is going to miss you anyway."

The two-hour drive did nothing more but fuel her hatred as she had nothing but time to focus on everything that she experienced about Laura White from the first time she laid eyes on her her nasally voice, her sense of entitlement that allowed her to cruelly suggest that it was Ed's job to wait on her hand and foot, the lies that she told in her attempts to ruin Ed's life, and the look on her face as she caused the death of her baby.

"Fucking cunt," she growled as she said it again, pressing her foot harder on the accelerator. She pulled into the bar's parking lot and shut the car down. She began checking her hair in the mirror, ensuring that her hair hung over her face just enough to fully conceal her. Satisfied with her hair she reached into the console for a pill bottle and dropped it into her purse and made her way into the bar. She saw Laura sitting alone with a drink in front of her talking to the bartender, obviously completely drunk.

"And do you know what that asshole had the nerve to say to me, Ted?" she said to the female bartender.

"Laura, honey, my name is Sarah." The bartender snickered. "I think you may have had enough."

"No, I'm alright. I promise! Anyway Cindy, he said that I was a lying cunt that never parents! Can you believe that? That evil black bastard! How dare he!" She drank her drink down in one gulp and nodded and pointed to her glass. "Another rum and coke!" She chuckled.

"Alright, Laura honey, I'm going to have to cut you off," Sarah the bartender said. "You've had enough."

"I'll tell you when I've had enough, dammit! My money is great here!" She chuckled. "That bastard is paying me child support, you know? I was able to get his entire pension and still be able to get the kid and my disability money! Stupid fucker really thought he could fuck with me?" She hiccupped. "Come on, one more rum and coke. There's a damn good tip in it for you." She chuckled as she shook her glass lightly.

Sarah looked to her and then to the glass then took it and filled it. Laura laughed lightly going into her purse and pulled out her credit card.

"Thank you, honey. Now you listen to me when you swipe this you give yourself thirty dollars okay? I mean it!" Laura blurted out loudly. When her drink was put in front of her she sipped it and shuddered. "This is strong just the way I like it!" She laughed loudly. "So yeah, stupid bastard. All he had to do was just keep working and keep his mouth shut. Now look at him! He's with some stupid bitch that can't even give him a kid. You know she tried to get tough with me at the mall? I left that bitch bleeding!" She laughed loudly.

"Stupid bastard. I don't even know what I saw in him! Oh well, I got a kid out of it, and that boy hates him! I have to try and talk Travis out of wanting to adopt him though," she said quickly.

"Why would you do that, Laura?" Sarah asked.

"Because if Travis adopts him then I don't get any more child support! I was going to go to court in a month or so and see if they would amend the payment arrangement to get more! One of my friends found out that he got a few more contracts for his self-defense business or whatever he's doing. That could get me at least another six hundred a month." She grinned coldly.

Livvy gripped the table as tight as she could until her knuckles turned white hearing Laura run her mouth the way she did. Livvy, at least, was able to take solace in the fact that Sarah the bartender looked disgusted by Laura's display and told herself that it was because of her admission. Her thoughts were interrupted when Laura pulled herself up from her stool.

"Okay fine! I'll go home! Let me just get my keys and—"

"No, Laura," Sarah said sternly. "You are not driving home. Give me your keys, you can get them tomorrow."

"Well how the fuck am I going to get home?" Laura asked in a loud, confrontational tone.

"I can either call you a cab, ride share, or you can get a designated driver," Sarah said in a patient, calm tone.

"I can drive her," Livvy said walking toward the bar in a sweet tone. "I was coming in for a drink, but if she lives close by, I haven't had anything yet. I can give her a ride."

"That's sweet of you," Sarah said. "She lives a few blocks away so she's not far."

"No problem," Livvy purred lightly, putting an arm around Laura while she fiddled with her purse and keys, oblivious to the conversation going on involving her. "Come on, sweetie, let's get going so you can get some rest."

"Oh that's sweet of you," Laura said, barely able to notice who she was talking to. When they made their way to the entrance, Laura looked at Livvy curiously. "I've fucking seen you before haven't I?" she asked angrily.

"I don't know what you're talking about, dear," Livvy replied sweetly, moving her from out the door into the parking lot.

"I swear I've seen you before." Laura grunted as Livvy pushed her a little bit rougher toward the car. Livvy's demeanor, with every step, darkened.

"Laura, you are going to get in the car and you're going to shut your fucking mouth, or I swear to God I am going to make you fucking suffer more than I already intend to," Livvy snarled.

"Wait a minute!" Laura yelled as they got to the car. "You're—"

Livvy's eyes narrowed and took a fist full of Laura's hair and slammed her head first onto the roof of her car. Then she opened the passenger's side door. When Laura attempted to protest again, Livvy slammed her head into the roof of the car a second time and watched her collapse into the front seat.

"Good. Now shut the fuck up," She slammed the door and quickly moved around to the driver's side and drove off. "And fortunately for me, and unfortunately for you, this tiny ass hick town hasn't discovered parking lot, or traffic cams yet. And I know that dive bar doesn't have shit either. You've fucked up for the last time bitch!

"So when do we get to get started?" he asked her anxiously. The way Livvy told the story, he pictured Laura, now, sitting in some dank basement somewhere scared out of her mind. The thought brought a warm smile to his face.

"As soon as I get something to eat and cleaned up and you get dressed," she said placing a soft kiss on his lips. "I have all of your toys there for you that you will need. You won't have to worry about the police until tomorrow. Of course, you wouldn't have been seen anywhere near her, so you won't have to worry anyway."

Ed smiled at her. "Then you go ahead and get cleaned up. I'll make you something to eat. Did you start on her without me?" he asked.

"Now would I do that, baby?" Livvy asked innocently.

Ed looked to her with a sly smirk and Livvy smiled lightly.

"Well, I may have indulged myself just a little, but believe me, honey, I would never take that thrill away from you."

Ed kissed her softly on the lips, running her fingers through her hair.

"Babe, how did you get all roughed up like this if you were able to get her in the car like you did?" he asked calmly.

"Well, she woke up when I took her to the surprise, and she tried to fight me. I guess she thought that because she has more weight than me she could take me." Livvy giggled. "Stupid bitch didn't know what her ass was in store for. She wanted to talk about me getting *my* ass kicked?" Livvy snorted lightly, shaking her head. "I'm going to take a shower. Do you think you can make me some tea, eggs, and sausage please?"

"Of course, honey," Ed replied. "Thank you," he said quietly.

"For what, honey?"

"For always looking after me and..." He tried to find the words and then laughed lightly. "How do you say, 'Hey thanks for capturing that bitch of an ex-wife of mine so we can torture her!'?" He laughed. "Think Hallmark has a card for that?"

Livvy kissed his lips gently, massaging his cheek. "Listen to me," she said sternly. "You, for one, did the exact same thing for me. And, for two, I told you I'd always do what I could to take care of you and do what I thought was best for you. I meant that. You always keep your promises, and so do I. We're going to deal with these bastards who've hurt us, like I said, and we're going to finally be able to live like normal people."

Ed nuzzled his cheek into her hand and gave her a small nod. "I'll get some breakfast made."

"Thank you, honey," she purred lightly. "I love you, Ed, forever and for always."

"I love you too, Livs," he replied.

# CHAPTER 17
## VENGEANCE IN JUSTICE'S NAME

Downstairs, Livvy knew his heart was racing with anticipation while trying to wash the last few dishes sitting in the sink. She couldn't help but smile when she heard a second glass fall and shatter, then loud frustrated cursing followed. She laughed quietly as she walked back toward the doorway and took in a deep breath to hold back the snickering that would follow if she didn't.

"Alright!" she called out trying not to spit her tea through her nose. "Bring me the travel mug for my tea and I'll just eat on the go."

"Are you sure?" he called out from the kitchen doing, what she guessed, was sweeping up the shards of glass on the floor.

"Yes, Edwin, I'm sure." She chuckled. "If we don't, you're going to end up breaking every glass we own and I sure as hell can't have that. I like those glasses. Hurry up so we can go." She shook her head at him lovingly when he brought in the mug and placed a light kiss on the knuckles of his right hand. "Geez, you're like a damn kid at Christmas. Not like I can blame you, of course." She selected a comfortable, casual tie dye dress and tied her hair into a ponytail.

"Make a left coming up," Livvy instructed three hours later. By the time she'd gotten out of the shower, Ed had her tea, eggs, toast, and sausage waiting for her. He didn't bother to burden her with questions, allowing her to eat in silence.

He followed her instructions to the letter and realized she was taking him on another route into Maine.

"We're a few miles from the inn," she replied before he could ask the question. "I drove up there last night, found a place to stash her and then drove back to come and get you. I figured it would probably be better if we did this further away."

"Good idea. She never got to say your name to the bartender right?"

"Nope. I barely gave her a chance to even see me until we were out of the bar. Plus, it was dark, so I don't think she got that great of a view of me anyway. That's why my hair looks like this so that way they couldn't identify me. And even if they did, so what? We got outside, she realized who I was, and she stormed off simple as that. Of course, we are going to arouse some suspicion now," she said looking out the window.

"Maybe we shouldn't go back," he said. "Maybe we should stay up here?"

"I paid for the room in cash. But I ended up giving them my real name since it was the same guy behind the desk as before so I couldn't just lie. If we do stay up here, then we are going to have to find someplace else to stay."

"Clean out our bank accounts so we have money," he added. "Too bad we can't just open up new bank accounts, at least for a while, we could invest the money and live off the interest."

"I don't think it works that way in full, dear," she replied in a patronizing, teasing tone. "You're right though, we do need to have a bank account and still use the internet. But and it's a very large but... use it only when at the house till we pick up and move on. No sense giving them anything to worry about or figure out. Only look up normal married couple shit like home décor and recipes. Even porn if you like," she winked as she said. Using it on our phones, or in hotels or libraries, that's stuff we need to stay away from so they can't trace us. That'll mean likely losing the cell phones too," she replied.

"I already have mine turned off," he said.

"Good boy." She chuckled. "Paranoid much?"

"Absolutely. I worked in the system, remember? Luckily, they don't have enough suspicion for phone taps or anything like that, but it's a good start. We can get some burner phones that will do us better good if we need to keep touch with each other."

"Good, baby," she replied. "The only thing that sucks is, we need to get new identities," she replied. "We certainly can't go on as us once they start looking for us."

"What about the rest of them?" he asked her curiously. "The kid, the lawyers, and all of them. What are we going to do about them?"

"I suppose they will get a little bit of a reprieve," she said. "For now. But do you think that we're jumping the gun? All they'd have is suspicion, it's not like they'll ever find her body on either of us."

"Yeah, but you'll have her DNA in your car. We'll have to get it detailed to make sure that's taken care of. I would say that cameras in the area could fuck us over, but the only one that I know of is on the traffic light on the main street. Did you go through the light, or go away from the light when you came home?"

"I don't remember, Ed," she said, her voice taking a slight edge to it. "Through it probably."

"Ok, so if that camera were working it could have seen her in the car, but it's not definite. It's not like that hick town has the same quality cameras that the big cities have. They can barely afford to fix roads. Shit now that I think of it, I think it's just there for show." He smirked.

"I didn't even know there was a camera there," she offered. She looked to him after a few minutes, taking a superfluous sip of her empty travel mug. "Do you think we'll be able to come back home?" she asked.

"Well, they'll come after me to question me about her disappearance. They'll even start to ask questions about both of our exes going missing so close together. I say we have at the most, maybe a week before the questioning starts."

"Alright then," she said. "I don't want to finish her off too fast, though," she said. "I want her to really suffer," Livvy purred. "Do it for me, Daddy. Please?" she asked in a soft, sing-songy voice.

"Don't you worry, baby," he growled. "I have no intention of letting her off easy. We can maybe get back up

246

here when things start to get a little bit hairy and finish her off."

"I'd like that." She smiled evilly, massaging his thigh. "Tell me about how bad you're going to hurt her for us you, me, and the baby." The sudden change in her made him moan in delight. She'd switched the game almost mid-conversation and it made his anticipation for what he was about to do grow. He moved his hand to her thigh, pulled the fabric up the dress up ever so slightly for easy access to her bare thigh.

"First, I think I will do what she tried to accuse me of in the first place," Ed grumbled, giving her thigh a tight squeeze.

"And what is that, baby?" she asked in a soft tone, taking his hand, and moving it between her legs. She released a moan when he realized she wasn't wearing any panties, and the anticipation was driving her wild as well.

"I'm going to take this right hand of mine," he pushed his fingers inside of her with a quick, rough thrust, "and I'm going to punch her right in her fucking face," he growled coldly. "I'm going to make her bleed, just a little, of course."

"I like the sound of that," she cooed lightly. "What else?"

"I think, after I've knocked out a tooth or two, we should start pulling her fingernails out one at a time. Then, go to her toenails."

"We have that stuff," she said. "Like I said, I got most of your toys except the woodchipper and the freezer," she replied.

"Where did you get everything else?" he asked calmly.

"I stopped at Wal-Mart." She chuckled. "I even got your blowtorch and stuff. I paid cash and kept my head down from any prying cameras, that way there's no chance to trace the cards too and what was on the receipts." She smiled.

"Good girl. Anything else we need, I'm sure I can manage."

"You're an artist you know." She moaned softly when his fingers continued to work within her. "A true artist. I want you to make her sing for me, baby. Make her sing just for me."

"Don't worry about it, gorgeous. When I'm done, she will sing a song the likes of which has never been heard before. I promise you."

He turned onto the dirt road he was instructed to turn down and chuckled at all of the bumps that he had to navigate.

"You really found a nice, out of the way type of place, didn't you?"

"Of course. I know this area pretty well my family used to vacation out here when I was a kid. No one will be around here for a few more months. This cabin is always deserted, nothing we have to worry about."

"Good." He grinned as he continued driving. "This reminds me of the *Evil Dead*." He laughed lightly.

"You mean that stupid *'Join us'* movie that you're always trying to get me to watch?" she said with disgust.

"The very same."

She shook her head. "Ed, don't you dare ruin this for me," she said pushing his hand further between her legs. "You don't want me to dry up do you?"

He grinned lightly. "Sorry, baby."

He navigated the dirt road. When he saw the cabin in the distance, he couldn't help but tremble with delight.

"It does seem quite chilly this close to the ocean this time of year, doesn't it?" he asked.

"Very much so. Too bad for her she wasn't wearing very thick layers last night." Livvy chuckled.

"Tragic," he agreed.

They pulled up to the cabin. Ed killed the engine and stepped out of the car. He inhaled deeply and stretched before he let out a deep breath.

"I love the smell of the ocean," he said with a grin.

"Maybe when we leave we will live near the ocean so we can smell it all the time."

"On the west coast," he said. "Seattle, or northern California," he said with a nod as he locked eyes with her and sucked her juices off of his fingers.

"You dirty boy! If you want more, you're going to have to earn it," she purred lightly.

"Is that right?" he asked raising a brow.

"Yes it is. What're you going to do about it?"

"I could just take it," he said, mock seriousness in his voice.

"Yes, I'm sure you could. But if you earn it, I just may make it better." She winked moving onto the porch.

"Fair enough," he replied walking toward her as she opened the front door to the cabin.

"Yeah, this place looks exactly like the *Evil Dead* cabin," he said with a grin. The main room had an old bookcase along the wide wall with dusty old paperbacks neatly stacked on it, a dusty looking couch with a sheet that belonged on the couch, thrown eschew on the floor. A bear skin rug lay on the floor facing the door that had seen better days, a buck's head on the wall, some floor lamps, an old coffee table, and a few chairs scattered around. She closed the door behind him shaking her head.

"Enough about that stupid movie," she said. "I hate it when you have it on, it gives me the damn creeps."

"Well, it *is* a horror movie," he chided her taking off his coat. "Even the one they made a few years ago wasn't all that bad."

"If you want to get laid tonight, I think you should stop talking about that stupid movie," she said seriously.

"What movie?" He chuckled, moving to the fire place on the near side wall. He collected an arm full of wood that lay in a nearby box, tossed it into the fireplace and started to build a fire. "Is she asleep down there do you think?" he asked curiously.

"Possibly," she said. "I will go and check on her." Livvy went to the trap door in the far corner and lifted it open slowly with a grunt. "That fucking thing is heavy. Well the kerosene heater is still on," she replied making her way downstairs seeing the faint glow easily in the darkness.

As she walked down the old wooden stairs, the creaking protest and the darkness made her shudder memories of her older cousin Allan torturing her with ghost stories swam over her. She pulled the hanging chain and the tiny 60-watt light bulb illuminated the basement.

There sat Laura White, still tied to an old wooden chair with her head hanging low. Livvy walked forward and noticed the slight bruising on Laura's flesh from trying to pull free and was pleased to see the thick layers of duct tape on her wrists and ankles had held despite what Livvy knew to be extensive pulling for freedom. The duct tape also kept her mouth firmly covered as well, much to the captor's delight.

She looked to the back wall at the workbench that already had a multitude of old, rusty tools that would be Ed's instruments in the grizzly symphony he would soon conduct, as well as tools that she had purchased for him the night before. She turned and made her way back up the stairs glad to see that Ed had got the fire started.

"So she is still down there. Looks like the poor thing tuckered herself," Livvy reported. "Are you hungry?" she asked.

"Actually yes, I think so," he replied. "I could use some lunch."

"Alright, well I picked up a few things last night for us also. So we won't be starving."

"I love you, baby. You always think of everything." He kissed her gently.

"Well I have to take care of my man, now don't I?" she asked. "Do you think we can get started soon though? I am so excited!"

Ed grinned evilly. "I'd love that. My hands won't stop shaking. I hope I don't get performance anxiety."

"Oh I don't think you will, baby. I really don't." She leaned forward to kiss his lips, taking his hand into hers and sliding it up her skirt again. "Just think about what you're going to get after this first round."

Ed grinned, the lust in his eyes unmistakable. "Did you get me knives and stuff?" he asked curiously.

"Come downstairs and see. But not too loud. I want you to be surprised."

Ed nodded in compliance, walking with her to the basement, careful not to be too loud. He walked around Laura while she slept and checked out the workbench. He was happy to see the jars full of old rusty nails, old pruning shears, hunting knives, paint brushes, paint, and thinner, and various other tools. He nodded lightly in appreciation and then began to inspect what had been purchased for him.

Fishing knives, fish hooks, replacement reels, peroxide, rubbing alcohol, tweezers, pliers, a small propane torch, scissors, and rubber tubing. He looked to Livvy and smiled.

"You did perfect, baby."

"I did?" Livvy asked. "I didn't know what all you would want. I told the man in sporting goods that you were going on a fishing/hunting trip."

"You did great. Between what you bought and what's already here, this is going to be perfect." He looked to the corner seeing the fuel can. He claimed it and was instantly delighted to feel that there was still fuel in it. "Oh wait," he said to himself. "Kerosene space heater, of course there is fuel, Ed, you dumb ass," he said to himself with a soft smile.

"This is going to be fucking fun," he said, reaching for the scissors. He looked over his shoulder at Livvy and smiled. "So do you want to be my special helper for this?" he asked with a grin.

"You know I do," she said with a grin.

"Good. Grab me the tools I ask for and... hmmm first, take off your clothes," he said with a grin.

She didn't waste time asking questions. She could feel all reason and rationale leave her as he picked up the scissors and began to work them in his masterful hand to test them out. She pulled the straps to her dress down and exposed her breasts. When her arms were free, she pulled the dress all the way down, standing before him completely naked.

"Good girl," he said admiring her flawless physique with curves where they should be. "Now, let's get down to business."

He walked around so that he stood directly in front of Laura and without wasting a word, threw a short right hand to her jaw snapping her head back. Her eyes snapped open, whimpering loudly from the contact.

"Oh good," Ed smiled lightly to her. "You're awake. I was truly hoping you would be. I would assume that you must have a hell of a hangover I mean with all of the drinking you did last night. Am I right?"

Laura's response was muffled by the duct tape, a laugh rose within his chest shaking his head.

"I'll take that as a yes." He smiled and moved her hair from her face gently as he once did a long time ago, mockingly. He rose his baritone voice to a bellow full of booming bass as he continued. "So one would assume then that yelling like this would cause you a massive headache? Not to mention my 'wake-up' love tap?"

When Laura closed her eyes tight from the yelling, he laughed looking over his shoulder at Livvy who smiled back at him. She stayed behind him, allowing him to hide her. He could see by the look on her face that she was a completely submissive mood. He could feel the thumping in his groin as he looked over Livvy's gorgeously naked body.

Ed turned back to Laura and slapped her harshly across the face relishing the fact that she closed her eyes in a painful wince. Tears fell from the assault. Ed simply looked at his palm and dismissed her for the moment while she started to sob.

"Well, if you think that hurts you are in for a nice long lesson," he said with a grin. "Do you realize the pain you caused me all of these years? Do you? Saying I beat you. If I had, this is just a taste of what that would have felt like you sick bitch. You caused me far more pain that you can ever fucking imagine."

Her muffled replies were only given life by the look of anger in her eyes.

"'What type of pain have you caused?' you ask?" He chuckled lightly. "Where to begin, you fucking sow? Where the fuck do I begin?" He slapped her hard across the face again. "Before we get started though, I want you to see something."

He stepped aside so that Laura could see Livvy's naked body. Her ripe, full, forty-two D breasts were the perfect mix of perk and hang. Her stomach was the perfect mix of lean and curve. Her thighs thick and delicious. Ed smiled evilly.

"Do you see my Livvy right there? See, that is a perfect woman right there. Turn your back, Livvy, and don't move until I tell you to."

She complied, turning around revealing her rear.

Ed moved to her and began to massage her gently. "See this ass? This perfect, perfect ass?" he smiled. "Turn back around, Livvy."

She again complied.

"This is the body of a real woman, you see? Even her pussy is nice and tight, not hanging with excess fat from sitting on her ass all day with fake back issues. Let's do a quick comparison shall we?" He stepped forward, slapping Laura in the left side of her face then rebounded his hand into a fist connecting with the right side of her face, then methodically cut the neckline of her shirt all the way down to her waist to expose her hanging belly, and slapped the wobbly, hanging flesh. Afterward, he cut her sports bra at the cleavage and pulled the tattered clothing off of her.

"Now let's compare shall we?" he laughed coldly looking to her breasts.

Livvy could barely resist the urge to laugh at the whimper of humiliation that came from her. Ed slapped her breasts roughly, leaving a handprint.

"You're right to laugh, Livvy. Look at this circus freak!" he roared slapping her belly again. "I'm not a slim Jim, but damn, you have a gut that's bigger than mine! I can do fifty sit-ups and crunches, I bet you can't even do one, can you? Oh, wait you say you have a back problem. Yeah, I forgot that I already mentioned that fake bullshit, right? RIGHT?" he roared slapping her face roughly. "Bullshit! You're just a lazy sack of shit that's what you are!" He laughed coldly, slapping her belly again, leaving a massive handprint that would likely bruise on her flesh. "Woo! Look at that blubber go! I bet it would wobble all night if I let it, wouldn't it! Shit, Mama Weasley got nothing on you!" he grinned and moved over to Livvy and lightly massaged her stomach.

"See that, Laura?" he purred. "Your shit wobbles for seconds on end. Livvy? Barely a movement whatsoever. Just the way I fucking like it! Hell! Livvy isn't skinny. She's curvy, she takes care of herself. She at least puts forth the fucking effort! That's the most disgusting thing about you! You don't even want to try. If you had real injuries, or if you were sick, it could be understood. You though? You're a liar. A fake. You just do this just be-fucking-cause."

Laura glared at him scathingly, her speech muffled as she launched a tirade at him.

"See, I can only image what you're saying something pedestrian and without any sort of wit or knowledge behind it no doubt. You are about as good at verbal judo as you are fucking that's for damn sure."

Livvy couldn't help but release a loud yelp of laughter.

"She's right to laugh at you, Laura." He moved back to Livvy, running his fingers through her hair. "I want you to nod for yes, and shake your head for no, Laura. Do you understand me?"

She huffed angrily, and Ed merely smiled.

"You won't comply? Well, perhaps I can persuade you." He stepped forward and slapped her again in the face causing her to whimper again weakly.

"Nod for yes, shake your head for no. Understood?" When Laura glared at him defiantly, he smiled. "Oh, you're going to be difficult! I love that. You know this so-called hair that you seem to be so proud of?" he asked. He roughly grabbed a fistful and cut it roughly with the scissors. Laura's whimpering intensified as he sawed through her hair with some difficulty. When he finally got the massive tuft of hair separated from her head, he saw where he had caused her to bleed slightly.

"Now," he said holding the hair up for her to see. "Are you going to cooperate?" When she nodded, he smiled. "Excellent. Now, do you suck Travis' dick?" he asked.

Laura's eyes widened at the question and a quizzical mumble came from her.

"Why?" he asked. "Well, it's real simple. I'm proving a point. Now answer the question do you suck Travis' dick?"

Laura nodded slowly.

"Often?"

She shrugged her shoulders and gave a slight nod.

"Well," Ed snickered, "good for him. Well, was good for him. You know how you would hardly ever suck mine? Do you swallow for him too?"

Laura shook her head no and he grinned.

"Well, Livvy sucks my dick all the time. Don't you, Livvy?" he asked.

"Yes, Daddy," she said submissively.

"And you love it don't you, Livvy?"

"Oh yes I do, Daddy," she answered.

Ed gave her a scolding look and she cleared her throat.

"Yes, I love sucking your dick, Daddy."

"And you love swallowing me, don't you?" he asked.

"Yes, Daddy," she replied. "I love to swallow you."

Ed nodded lightly. "Why don't you ask Laura the same question that you ask me all the time?" Ed looked at Laura coldly when Livvy stepped forward and slapped Laura across the face, resonating a loud smack of flesh on flesh and duct tape.

"How could you have this—" Livvy reached out to massage Ed's throbbing member through his jeans. Ed pushed her hand away and unbuckled his jeans and pulled his hardness from their restraint. Livvy purred and wrapped her hand around his thickening shaft. "—and not appreciate it?" she asked angrily. "How could you not fuck him for months at a time? How could you not suck this dick, and do everything you could to please him? He worked for your fat ass, did everything for you! How could you not appreciate him?" Her timid tone with Ed turned into a voice of rage as she addressed Laura.

"Do you know how long I craved this cock?" Livvy purred, stroking him harder. "I would go home and dream about him fucking me! You had him and you made him feel like he was nothing! You bitch!" Livvy slapped Laura hard across the face again causing Laura to whimper.

"That's enough, Livvy," Ed replied patiently. "Show her what you mean," he ordered.

Livvy instantly went down on her knees, giving Laura an evil smile before taking him into her mouth. Ed's eyes closed lightly, yet he forced them open to glare at Laura who had closed hers. Ed shook his head and grabbed Livvy's hair and pulled her away from him. Livvy looked to him with a sad pout but complied with him. When she started to stand, he shook his head.

He pulled off his boots, shirt, pants, and boxers. He walked over to Laura and grabbed her roughly by the hair on the same side he'd cut her hair to maximize her pain. Her eyes shot open and tears streamed down her already mascara painted cheeks.

"I am trying to prove a point to you, Laura. Closing your eyes defeats the purpose. Now, if you want to see Eddie again, I suggest you pay close attention. Nod if you understand." When Laura didn't nod, Ed grabbed the bottle of rubbing alcohol and opened it. He poured some of the liquid into the cap and poured it into the wound on her head causing her to open her eyes and scream. "Do. You. Under. Stand?" he asked empathically.

She nodded vigorously and he smiled.

"Good." He moved back to where Livvy remained on her knees. "Continue."

He kept his eyes on Laura as Livvy pleasured him. As she continued on, he couldn't help but close his eyes, moaning loudly.

"When I come," he moaned, "do not swallow."

Livvy moaned, continuing on as she was expected to. When his moans grew louder, Livvy knew her treat was coming. When he exploded into her mouth, she kept latching on him so not to lose a drop. She looked up to him and slowly pulled herself away.

"Now, show her your present," Ed said. Livvy stood up and squatted down to open her mouth to show Laura the fruit of her labor.

"This is, of course, intensified for the situation. I would have been satisfied with this you know? You didn't have to swallow, but you could have at least let me finish. Hell, how many times did I let you come in my mouth? In my face? All the time. You couldn't even let me enjoy it. As soon as you knew I was into it, you pulled away and expected me to finish you off like you're Queen fucking Sheba," he bellowed. "Do what you want with it, Livvy."

Livvy closed her mouth and looked at Ed, and then back to Laura. She looked back at Ed, and then at Laura with her eyes narrowed and spit Ed's leavings into her face with a look of disdain.

"You disgust me you fucking bitch. I fucking hate you!" Livvy growled. "How dare you take him for granted? But I should thank you. If you hadn't, I wouldn't have him to let him know what a real man is supposed to feel like."

Ed couldn't contain himself he laughed loudly looking at Laura's face as the mixture of saliva and semen dripped down her face.

"You know, Livvy doesn't really like you, Laura. I can think of a number of reasons why." Ed shrugged lightly. "So, did you like the show, Laura?" he asked politely. When she shook her head no, Ed chuckled. "Well that's no surprise. I mean, you saw how to really suck dick and you know with having half a brain, to please a man with that much skill will elude you for the rest of your days. Oh well, blame your mother." He walked over to his pile of clothing and pulled his boxers back on. "By the way, I expect a thank you card for my genetics. If it weren't for me, Eddie would probably be an idiot freak just like you." He looked at Livvy curiously.

"Are you cold or are you alright to stay this way for a little while?" he asked.

"I'm fine, Daddy. Are you going to hurt her more?" Livvy asked.

"Oh, absolutely. I was just checking on my baby that's all." He kissed her deeply with a moan. "I want you to be nice and comfortable. Daddy takes care of his baby girl." He smiled lightly.

"Now we have a few more things to discuss, Laura," Ed said calmly, and then stopped and looked at her stomach. "Laura, are you knocked up?" he asked with a smirk. Laura looked to him, tears in her eyes and nodded lightly.

When Ed looked back at Livvy, she looked back to him. He then turned back to Laura curiously.

"Let me get this straight. You're pregnant, yet you went out drinking. Is that what I can assume?"

She nodded slowly, tears in her eyes.

"Well it's obvious to us that, despite whatever mutant you could be carrying, that you don't deserve that mutant. Is that right, Livvy?"

"That's right, Daddy," Livvy replied in a dangerous tone.

"Didn't she kill our baby?" he asked calmly.

"Yes she did, Daddy." Livvy shuddered as her heart began to pound. "She came up to me in the mall with her monster child and she knew she was upsetting me. She didn't stop. She kept messing with me, making me mad.

Then I lost the baby right there. I looked up when she was walking away and she laughed. She was even laughing about it last night at the bar!" she said, tears falling from her eyes. "But I bet she isn't even pregnant!"

"Well, let's find out shall we?" Ed growled coldly. Laura began to protest angrily, unable to get the words out. Ed walked forward without another word and brought down his powerful right fist into her stomach once, twice, three, four, five times. Each punch was angrier than the last. Laura began to cry loudly, even with her gag her moans of pain rang loudly.

"I hope you're bleeding now, bitch," he growled. Looking at her jeans, he reached a hand out to lift her stomach so that he could see her waist line and cut her belt and then the button of her pants. He then unzipped her pants and laughed.

"Those are the same pink, holy panties you had from when I first moved here! And you pissed yourself? God you're disgusting!" He punched her stomach again harshly, then took a step away from her and placed a kick to her stomach with enough force to knock her back in her chair. Her cries of agony were loud as momentum sent her onto her side. Ed shook with fury as he watched her lay in a heap.

"You fucking monster!" he roared angrily. "You pull me away from my friends and my family, alienate me, make me have to work shit jobs just because you don't want to work at all? Turn my son against me? Murder my unborn child and laugh about it. Fuck, and for what? Because you want to be a spiteful cunt? Well guess what, you fucking beast? Tonight is the night for retribution! You are going to answer for every single, solitary thing you have done against us! You're going to fucking pay! You'll never see Eddie again do you understand me? Never! Count down the minutes, bitch, because they're you're last!" he laughed manically. "They are going to be the most painful you have ever had. When I'm done, you're going to beg me to kill you." He looked over to Livvy, her eyes were narrowed to slits.

"Right now though, I'm hungry. So you will get a nice little reprieve," he said, walking over to the fuel can, then got an idea. He picked up the discarded scissors and began to roughly cut Laura's hair, her muffled protests only fueling his rage. After a few moments, there were tufts of hair all around her, her head in some places balder than others. He then grabbed the nearby paint brush and poured a little of the contents on the paint brush and made two small strokes on her shoulder where he noticed for the first time a tattoo.

"'When you settle, you accept what you don't deserve,'" he read out loud. "Interesting. You know I saw that somewhere online. You must have seen it too and figured you would take it as a mantra. Is that right? Well, no matter. See, you don't deserve to have that put on your body. You weren't the one that settled, bitch, I was. How you can think you were ever on my level is beyond me. Just because I allowed it, doesn't mean that you ever were." He grabbed the torch off of the workbench and ignited it.

"You don't deserve that tattoo. So let's see what we can do about that shall we?" Laura began to scream against her gag as Ed touched the flame to the tattoo. The fuel that coated the tiny section of her skin instantly reacted to the heat and accepted its nourishment.

Ed held out his hand, and he felt Livvy take it almost instantly watching the burning flesh with a sickening fascination.

"Fire. It cooks our food, heats our homes, and negates bullshit." He chuckled. "Isn't it lovely?" he asked.

Livvy purred. "The only thing about her body that could ever be lovely." She chuckled.

"I agree. And look, using the paint brush keeps it nice and controlled," he said with a smile. "She'll probably pass out from the pain soon, which will be pretty fine by me." He looked to Livvy and kissed her softly. He reached his hand down between her legs and grinned broadly. "So you approve?"

"Yes, I do." Livvy walked around to Laura's front and saw a dark stain forming on the crotch of her pants.

"You avenged our little one," Livvy said looking to him in love struck awe. "Thank you, Daddy."

Hours later, Ed and Livvy made their way back down to the basement. They'd made love when they went upstairs more passionately than ever. Afterward they slept peacefully in each other's arms, not wanting to be apart. Livvy woke first and began to cook, knowing that he would be hungry again. When she woke him, they enjoyed their steak dinner in silence. Both of them were able to ignore the muffled whimpers coming from the basement.

"Are you alright?" he asked, breaking the prolonged silence.

"I'm fine," she said quietly.

He looked to her curiously shaking his head. "You're not acting fine. Are you sure you're alright? Did I go too far down there?" he asked calmly.

She looked at him incredulously shaking her head. "Don't you ever think that again, hear me?" she said angrily. "There isn't enough in the world you can do to her! I'm just, I miss the baby. We would be about ready to welcome her to the world by now, you know?"

"I know," he said.

"Now she knows how I felt when Martin did what he did to me if she was even pregnant at all. And that is something that I will never forget. Thank you, Ed." She smiled at him through a wave of tears.

"You're welcome, baby," he said, making his way to her to hold her close. "I'm ready to continue, when you are?"

"Can I do some things to her too?" she asked.

"Of course, honey, you owe her just as much as I do. If not more." He kissed her gently and led her back to the basement, softly by the hand.

Laura still lay on her side, shuddering. Ed could smell the blood mixed with urine coming from her and a cold smile spread across his lips. He walked over to where Laura lay, bent at his knees, and lifted the chair up.

"Sorry to have left you laying in your own mess, but, well I needed to take care of a few things. How are you feeling, Laura?"

Laura looked at him with absolute disgust and hatred but did not respond. Ed nodded with a grin.

"Good. And how is your shoulder?" he asked, pouring rubbing alcohol into his hand, and cupping it into her burn causing her to scream. "Excellent." He smiled, looking toward Livvy. "Are you ready, honey?"

"No, not yet. Do a few more things first, please?" she asked. "I love to watch." She smiled.

"If that is your wish," he replied reaching for his trusty paint brush and poured more fuel on it then began to run the paint brush over her left arm from wrist to shoulder. She tried in vain to pull away from him. "Oh, that won't be necessary now will it?" he asked with a grin while picking up the propane torch. He ignited it and teasingly let the blue flame brush over her knuckles. The hairs were singed off instantly from the kiss of the fire.

When Laura whimpered and tried to pull away again, the fuel on her wrist caught the slightest bit of flame causing it to leap from the torch and follow the trail up to her neck/shoulder area where Ed had stopped the line. She howled in pain as Ed and Livvy looked on. She tried as hard as she could to wiggle free but was too tightly bound by the tape. The two lovers watched with evil fascination as the flames ate away at her skin.

"I want her to hurt more, Daddy. Please?" Livvy asked in her soft, girlish tone.

"Of course, honey." Ed looked to Laura and grinned coldly. "Let's see if we can fix one of nature's worst mistakes, shall we? Ed asked.

"Her face. Destroy it," Livvy replied.

Ed nodded and grabbed one of the knives on the work bench and glared at Laura.

"Listen up I'm going to cut that tape off of your mouth. Don't bother screaming because, well to be frank, no one is going to hear your ass. Not like anyone would bother with you anyway. You're a waste of life, a waste of air. I'm doing society a favor." He grinned and threw another short punch to her jaw before roughly cutting the tape from around her mouth. Livvy snickered seeing that he'd cut her skin.

"Fuck you, Edwin!" Laura roared. "Fuck you! You sick fucking bastard! You're going to go to prison forever! I hope you like getting ass fucked, you—"

Livvy drew her fist back and connected with the bridge of Laura's nose causing blood to squirt as the cartilage collapsed. Livvy shook her hand limply as though to shake the pain from the punch from her hand.

"You okay, love?" he asked her, checking her hand.

"I'm fine," Livvy replied.

"Is it broken?" Ed asked cautiously.

"I don't think so," Livvy replied flexing her fingers gingerly, inspecting her hand.

"That was a damn good punch though, really. I think you just caught the sweet spot better than a lot of people can!." He smiled at her with pride. "When this is over, I'll show you how to throw a proper punch so you don't have to worry about a break."

"You sick bastards," Laura whimpered, the blood making her voice sound thick and nasally. "You're going to—"

"We're going to hurt you some more, and have fun with you before we kill you," Ed replied. "Now, honey, what would you like me to do to her?" he asked.

Livvy went to the workbench and opened up the package that contained the fishing knife. She then slapped

Laura harshly, then grabbed her top lip. Laura began to hiss and fight, screaming.

"No! No! Stop it!" Livvy kept a tight grip on the tender flesh. She brought the knife up and Laura began to fight harder. Livvy simply pulled her lip further out from her body and made quick slices, causing her to scream loudly as more blood flowed. Ed smiled at Livvy, then looked at Laura.

"She's such a quick study. Don't you agree?"

"Ffffuck you, Ethhhwin!" Laura screamed, her speech distorted from the blood and injuries. Ed looked at her with a mock look of pain.

"Laura, I'm hurt. Really. But, think of it this way, you're paying a debt."

"Wha ffffucking debt you psycho?" she roared as blood flowed heavily from her mouth onto her bare chest. "Wha haff I done to you?"

"Do we need to go over this again? Wow, you must be quite delusional if you think that everything you've done since the day we met is actually even remotely acceptable."

"I luft you, Ethwin!" Laura screamed. "Why can't you understan ththat?"

"Oh, you loved me?" Ed asked, his tone turning icy.

"Yesth! I did efferything I could to make you happy!"

"Oh, you did? So guilt tripping me into staying here when I was miserable was love? Or, what about you stealing Eddie from me all because I disagreed with you taking him to your father? Or what about lying about being abused? Do you realize how many fucking women die because they report abuse, and no one believes them? Yet you, for a free meal, and a free roof over your head, made

268

up lies about me to destroy my name. You turned everyone in my fucking life against me because of your petty fucking lies! You destroyed my life! But you were trying to make me happy? You're a piece of fucking shit Laura," Ed growled, and drilled Laura in the face with a hard right hook to the chin, knocking her and the chair over.

"I hope you enjoy your handy work bitch," Livvy growled. "Because of the shit you did to him, you made him like this." Livvy stomped on her stomach with all of the power that she could muster before stomping on her again.

Ed put a hand on her shoulder. "Baby, I thought you said you wanted her to suffer more?" he asked.

"Oh, I do," Livvy replied. "I want her to hurt bad."

"Ffffuck you!" Laura roared spitting blood on the floor as she did. "Fffuck both of you! I hate you, you Black son-of-a-bitch!"

"I may be," Ed chuckled, "but I'm not the one that's going to be dead within the next two days now am I?" He picked up a jar of rusty nails and the drain cleaner smiling at Laura. He unscrewed the cap to the drain cleaner, put a hand on her wrist and inserted the nail under her finger nail causing her to scream loudly.

"Smarts does it? Hurt just a little?"

Her screams echoed off of the stone walls of the abandoned cabin as he inserted nails under all of her fingers and toe nails. Then Ed put some kerosene on the paint brush and began to brush over her nipples.

"No! Ed! Ed, please don't do this! You've done enough! I forgive you, Ed!" Laura cried.

"You... forgive... me?" Ed asked her incredulously. "You forgive me?"

"It's the first—" she began.

"Shut the fuck up!" he roared, pouring more kerosene on the paint brush and began to brush over her entire chest and stomach. "I've got your forgiveness right here! Let's see if we can cook some of that fat off of your belly!"

"Ed! Please!" Laura cried.

Ed activated his torch again and tapped it onto her stomach. Laura screamed loudly in anguish as the flames consumed her flesh. Ed watched with horrific admiration as she lashed about, unable to put the flames out.

"Honey, are you going to let her burn up?" Livvy asked curiously.

"Not my intention. However, I may have used too much fuel."

Laura screamed in savage woe as the flames continued to eat at her flesh.

"I do not want her dead just yet," Livvy said to him simply.

Ed looked around and quickly grabbed a nearby blanket to smother the flame. The flames had been allowed to burn for twenty seconds, and he nodded lightly. Livvy bent down to inspect Laura as she whimpered in agony.

"It's not good at all, but not life threatening for what I can see. I will say that she is probably going to have a horrid infection," she said. "If she lives through the night."

"But, she isn't going to live that long," Livvy growled, noticing Laura going into shock. "Wrap her up with the blanket. Keep her warm. I want her to hurt more. There's no way in Hell she gets to die before we're done," she said, looking at the scalded flesh of Laura's body.

"That burn is going to hurt like hell," he said with a nod. "Although, there is one way she could die that will be most horrible. Disgusting, but horrible."

"And how is that?" she asked him curiously.

He washed his hands, finally feeling his stomach starting to lurch in revulsion. He'd allowed Livvy some privacy as she was unable to handle it. The disgust on her face was almost too much for him to deal with. He could hear her in the shower, he wanted to say something, anything, but wasn't sure how she would receive him.

"Livs..." he said finally, unable to keep the silent treatment going for so long.

"Yes?" she asked curtly.

"Say something. Please?" he asked.

"What goes on in your mind?" she asked suddenly. "What goes through your mind to think to do something like that?"

"Babe, you told me that you wanted to make her suffer. What is worse than that?"

"It's not that it happened to her," she said fiercely. "I'm glad that it happened to her. I loved watching her choke to death! But, what seriously makes you think of something like that?" When he didn't reply, she pulled the shower curtain back so she could look at him. "Who thinks to do something like that with a nail and kerosene?" When Ed stayed quiet, she shook her head. "Fucking insane."

"You have to admit, it was inventive," Ed replied. "Duct taping her mouth shut and..."

"Okay! Okay!" she shouted. "That's just wow!" she shook her head. "I'm not mad at you, I promise. Hell, I think it was a great idea. It's just fucking disgusting, absolutely disgusting. I actually think it's kind of funny," she replied shaking her head as Ed sighed.

"Believe me, I was grossed out by it too. But what matters is that she finally got what she had coming to her," Ed replied.

"Yes, that's absolutely right," she said with a nod. "Thank you, baby. You did amazing, absolutely amazing. Baby, would it make you feel bad if I told you that you scared me just a little?"

Ed couldn't help but chuckle. "What do you mean?" he asked intently.

"How do I know you won't get mad at me and... and hurt me?" she asked.

"I would never do anything like this to you, not ever," he said looking toward her. "This is just for us to get back at those that wronged us and that's all. Besides, I am scared of you also," he said.

"How do you mean?" she asked curiously.

"For one, I'm the one that's done all of the killing. You could easily tell the police, or anyone else, that I forced you or something along those lines. They're dead so they can't testify against you, and look at where we live nobody down there is going to give me a fair shake. It would be your word against mine and your word will probably mean a whole lot more than mine."

"I suppose you're right," she said after a few minutes of silence. "But I married you because I'm in love with you. I would *never* betray you like that. Not ever."

"And I wouldn't betray you either," he said slipping into the shower with her. "Livvy, you are my soul mate, the one person that I was made for. Remember? There is no way I would ever turn on you."

"I know, Ed, I'm sorry," she said, placing a kiss on his lips and wrapped her arms around him. "It scares me how, how turned on it makes me. You turn so forceful so... it's just something... I never expected. I knew you would always protect me and be here for me, but..."

"I know," Ed said massaging her cheek. "I think we shouldn't waste any time. I think we should get rid of her body and start making our way out of here."

"I agree," she said kissing his neck gently. "It's sad though," she sighed lightly, "I really liked that house." She chuckled lightly.

"Yeah, me too." He smiled. "Do you think we can get through to Canada on our passports?" he asked curiously.

"Yes, we could. No one would know at first, of course when word got out they would be none too happy." She chuckled.

"This is going to be the real rip isn't it? Getting out of this in one piece without going to prison."

"We shouldn't have to worry about that anyway. Martin and Laura were the worst excuses for human beings to ever exist," she said heatedly. "We did the world a favor taking them out of it!"

"I agree. Unfortunately, all this world seems to do is allow people to get away with murder. Why didn't the

273

police ever go after that bitch for making you lose the baby? And why did they let that bastard Martin get away with killing your first baby? It's fucking bullshit enablement!" he growled.

"Well baby, no more from them," she said triumphantly. "No more."

"That's right. No more." He kissed her lips gently. "I did it all for you, baby."

"I know. Thank you, Daddy."

# CHAPTER 18
## *ESCAPE*

"I've been thinking more about it," Ed said a few hours later.

"About what?" Livvy asked curiously.

"About how we're going to get the hell out of this," he said calmly. "We're going to have to be very smart about it. We can't just instantly pull our accounts that will arouse more suspicion and bring them down on us."

"I was thinking the same thing," she said with a nod. "My expertise is medicine; law enforcement is your thing. So what should we do?" she asked.

"We're going to have to slowly and surely pull our money, we are also going to have to make sure we can get rid of her body quick." He thought for a moment.

"That's a good plan. Do we buy another woodchipper?" she asked curiously.

"No," he said shaking his head. "That will arouse suspicion like a sore thumb." He rubbed his eyes lightly. "I will have to find somewhere to dump her off," he said, his face contorted with deep thought.

"Ed, what are we going to do?" she asked him again, her voice starting to sound anxious.

"Don't worry," he said with a grin as she could see the figurative light bulb go off in his eyes. "I have a great idea."

"Care to clue me in?" she asked curiously as he began reaching for his clothes quickly, throwing them on while laughing.

"You say you grew up around here right? You know the area?" he asked.

"Yes," she said looking to him as though he were insane. "My brothers used to play in the woods all the time. Why?"

"Because I am going to go on a little hike. Livs, are there any caves in the woods?" he asked.

"Well..." she thought for a moment, "yes, these woods are full of them, but..." Her eyes lit up wide and she smiled warmly. "You are a genius, baby."

"Thank you," he said with a grin. "How far in the woods are the caves?" he asked calmly.

"That's the problem," she said sadly. "They're at least a few miles in."

"A few miles? Hmmm... No problem. We still have a few hours of night left I can rig up a little sack and drag her through the woods. I will take more of the kerosene and take her into the cave. First thing though." He began to pull his clothes off again. "Need to get rid of a few things first."

"The teeth?" she asked with a purr.

"The teeth," he replied.

"With hindsight being twenty-twenty, you should have done it while she was alive. Would have hurt more."

"True. Oh well, live and learn."

"I'm coming with you," she said sternly.

"No. You're not," he said simply.

"Why the hell not?" she asked angrily.

"You're going to walk a total of God-knows-how-many-miles at night in the woods in a sundress and light shoes?" he asked her seriously. When she got quiet, he nodded at her lightly. "Trust me, you're safer here. I'll take care of this, no problem. I will be back in a few hours and then we'll make our way back. If you can, why don't you straighten up a little bit downstairs, okay? Just in case."

"Fine," she said resentfully.

"Baby," he said sadly kissing her gently. "I'm not trying to say that I don't want you to come. Believe me, I really want you to come with me. But you aren't dressed for this part and we still need to straighten up downstairs. If you don't want to, that's fine. We'll still have to make sure our presence here is minimal at best though either way."

"You're right, baby," she replied. "I'm sorry I just... I don't want you to have to do this alone that's all."

"I know, honey, believe me I know. But we also need to work this out as best we can." He kissed her softly again. "I love you."

"I love you too, Ed."

It was after one in the afternoon, and Livvy paced nervously through the cabin. She'd attempted to call his cellphone, but he didn't answer. She remembered him saying he'd turned it off and telling her that it would be a while before he got back. He'd also said not to worry. Her mind began to run miles and miles of scenarios that frightened her.

"What if he fell and hurt himself?" she whimpered to herself. "What if someone caught him? What if there was a bear? What if..." She ran through a mile of 'what ifs' in her mind, shaking in terror. She almost leapt out of her skin when her phone rang with a number she didn't recognize.

"Hello?" she asked in a shaking voice.

"Mrs. White?" questioned the unfamiliar voice.

"Yes. Who is this?"

"Mrs. White, this is Detective Wade of Manchester PD. Is now a bad time?" he asked.

"Actually, Detective, it really is," she said.

"Well, I do apologize. However I was trying to get in touch with your husband and no one has seen him, and I cannot reach him on his cell phone. Do you know where he is?" he asked.

"Yes, we needed to get away for a few days. Losing the baby still is... is still a very painful subject. So, we needed to get away."

"I see. Well, Mrs. White, it is very important that we speak with your husband much sooner than later." His voice had a small hint of warning to it.

"What is this about, Detective?" she asked.

"Laura White, his ex-wife, has gone missing and I wanted to discuss this with him."

"Laura? Okay. Well we've been here for a few days now so, I'll let him know you called and need to speak with him," she said.

"That's it?" he asked sounding somewhat surprised. "You're not going to tell me how he wasn't there, question me on when she disappeared, or anything in that regard?"

"No, Detective," she said coldly. "It isn't *our* business when it happened. Besides, I'm sure you'll tell him when he comes in to see you. We should be coming home tonight."

"Where did you say you were, Mrs. White?"

"Goodbye, Detective," Livvy replied coldly and clicked the end button. She looked at Ed's number on her recent calls again, three hours since the first call. "Goddammit, Ed, where the hell are you?" she asked.

He arrived an hour later breathing heavily. When he walked into the cabin, she rushed to him and promptly slapped him in the face, tears spewing down her face.

"Where in the hell were you? You have been gone for so long!" she yelled. "I thought something bad happened to you! And that detective called and was trying to find you and... dammit, Ed, why did you make me worry like this?" she asked hysterically.

"Baby, I'm sorry. The caves were a bit further away than I imagined over pretty rough terrain carrying her fat ass, and then I had to build a pyre and make sure the wood was hot enough to burn her until there was nothing left. Plus, I had to go deep enough into the cave that when someone did see the smoke she would be burned up enough that it wouldn't matter. Believe me, it wasn't easy," he said patiently.

"Did it work?" she asked.

"I think so."

"I hope so," she said. "The police called and what if they trace the call and they know that we're in Maine and..."

"Shhh." He hushed her gently. "She burned just fine and dandy. I am sure of it. I partially waited until she burned out to check on her and then burned her again. There's no flesh on the bones hardly at all. Nobody came looking, thankfully. After I was sure that she burned enough, I smashed the shit out of the bones until they were next to nothing, then I put what was left in a lake. Don't worry, they aren't going to find anything. And even when they do, it's going to be so far gone it'll be just another cold case. Now, I suppose the detective wants to talk to me about her being missing?"

"Yes," she said, steadying her voice. "I told them we would be coming home tonight and that you would be in tomorrow sometime."

"Good. We want them to think we are cooperating in full." He nodded. "Anything else?"

"He seemed a bit surprised that I wasn't questioning him," she said.

"It's fine, I can deal with that. He's just fishing for clues. How long did you two talk?"

"Not even a minute or so?" she said.

"Alright good. Next time, make it a little less. Don't give him anything to go on. I'll go in and talk to him tomorrow and get this situated straight away," he said with a nod. "We'd better start making our way back now. While I'm doing that, I want you to start getting some money out of the bank slowly. Start spreading the rumor around work that we're thinking of moving for work. Apply for a job in any other state just to get a good paper trail going," he said.

"That way instead of just disappearing..." she began

"We do it good and smart," he finished for her, as they got on the same page. "That is why you are taking out the money. We're going to start shredding the credit cards slowly. Cell phones will be among the last things we get rid of. Also, start to slowly stop talking to people online. We need to *disappear*," Ed made air quotes when he said this, "but to do it right we are going to have to do it methodically."

"How do you know all of this, Ed?" she asked, moving to start packing their things.

"Because up until us, I was going to disappear for good. I was getting prepared. And, in prison, cons talk. Some are far smarter than most so they know how they fucked up and how to get away with it if they ever get out again. Being one of the only Black officers, many of the 'brothers' trusted me enough to just talk without worry I would go rat them out. I never did. Trust is hard to find inside, especially from a CO."

"You never told me that," she said to him surprised.

"It never came up," he replied. "I have some money in a safety deposit box that I'll pull out after I meet with the detectives. It isn't very much, but it will be enough to get us started. Do it that way open up a safety deposit box and put both of our names in it. Start to liquidate money and any assets we can live without into the box. They won't think twice about it at the bank, rich people do it all the time," he said with a nod. "Then, when we are ready, we will go in and close out the box."

"Alright. What if something goes wrong and they try to lock you up?" she asked.

"They have nothing but suspicion right now, and it is reasonable, but it isn't anywhere near enough to arrest me. They may be able to use the confrontation the other day, but any reasonable man would have had the same type of confrontation. No one can place me at the scene of her disappearance, and you won't necessarily stand out, plus the woman didn't ever hear your name, and you were in disguise. They'll be chasing their tails, especially with no body. Don't worry."

"How sure are you that everything is going to be alright?" She massaged his cheek.

"I'm completely confident that within the next thirty days we will be out of here. We will probably have to backpack like college students in Europe or take a train to get wherever we want to go. Nothing plastic can have our names on it. No driver's license, no credit cards, no nothing. We're going to have to go completely off the grid because leaving could definitely make them want to come after us."

"If you are sure we're going to be alright, then we're going to be alright. Let's go home."

He sat in the passenger's seat while she drove. He yawned loudly looking over to her affectionately.

"What? Why do you keep looking at me?"

"I don't know. I just can't take my eyes off of you," he said. "I'm sorry I got us into this," he said suddenly. "I'm not sorry for what I did to those people, not even a little bit. I just, I'm sorry that we have to uproot."

"Ed, enough of this talk. I could have had you take Martin back and found a way to explain this away. I got off on you hurting him for me. Hell, I got off on watching you hurt that ex-bitch of yours too. I'm not sorry about this either. The only thing I'm worried about is them separating us, that's all. I don't give a fuck about anything else."

"Alright, babe. You know what's funny? When we start talking all serious, you always tell me you don't want to hear that kind of talk." He chuckled.

"I know." She slapped his arm shaking her head. "I swear if you would just listen to me there would be no issue. Just keep your mouth shut and let us be us."

He let out a loud yawn as he curled up lightly in the front seat.

"You look so tired," she said. "Why don't you just go to sleep?"

"I can sleep when we get home, honey," he said.

"Babe, you are going to have a very busy day tomorrow. You are going to need to get all of the sleep that you can and dragging a buffalo through the woods to burn it up has to have taken its toll, even on you."

He released a loud yawn. "Yeah well, I did twinge my shoulder a little bit. She's gotten a lot fatter than I remember." He closed his eyes.

"Well I could have told you that," she said.

They fell into silence and he slept. She looked over to him after a short time and couldn't help but smile at how peaceful he looked despite what he'd done. She shrugged the thought off as quickly as it had arrived, giving his leg a gentle rub as she drove.

When she pulled up to the house hours later, she nudged him gently.

"Wake up, handsome," she purred lightly.

He slowly opened his eyes looking at her and smiled. "I love waking up to you."

"I do too," she replied. "Forever right?"

"Not long enough. I'd say forever with a side of eternity with a bit of ever after."

"God, you are so fucking cheesy." She laughed, shaking her head.

"Yeah, I can work with that." He opened the passenger side door and got out, stretching. He stopped for a moment, his face turning to stone.

"What is it?" Livvy asked when she saw his body go rigid, and his face harden.

"Someone's here," Ed said simply staring straight ahead.

Ed's blood ran cold when he heard the click of what he knew to be the hammer of a gun. He looked toward the shadows near Livvy's Garden and saw the silhouette of a figure with their arm held out aiming what he knew to be a gun at them.

As the figure stepped out of the shadows, Ed's eyes narrowed as he saw the Glock .40 pointed at them with Travis attached to the grip panel.

"Alright, Ed, where the fuck is Laura?" he asked, his voice shaking with anger.

Ed locked eyes with Travis and sized him up with his peripheral vision as he'd been trained to do. He'd never appreciated Travis' size until now while he was shorter than

Ed, Travis had dimensions that Ed had never noticed. Even for an older man, he had a muscular menace to him.

"I'm not going to ask you again," Travis growled, breaking through Ed's thoughts. "You can tell me now, or with a fucking hole in your leg. Your choice."

"Is that right?" Ed smirked. "You pull that trigger, you better put it in my head because I will fuck you up in ways that can only be described as biblical."

"You think you're so fucking tough, don't you, White?" Travis sneered, taking another step forward. "You run your mouth like you're so fucking tough, what about now, huh? I'm not a woman! I'll fuck you up!"

"Not a woman?" Ed roared with laughter slapping his knee. "You're right, you're not but you are the dumbest son-of-a-bitch this side of creation, aren't you? I never put my hands on her ever!"

"You lying sack of shit!" Travis roared thrusting the gun toward Ed, causing Livvy to flinch out of fear that it would go off. "I know what you did to her! You hit her, you fucked up her back, and you raped her!"

"What the fuck are you babbling about, you simple dumb fuck?" Ed asked taking a step forward, keeping Livvy away from the barrel of the gun. "She says it so it must be true? I suppose I'm a drug dealer too, right? I suppose I touched Eddie in weird places too, right? Use your fucking head, Travis! She has been playing your stupid ass all these years! I told you that the first time you started showing up to the exchanges! I never did any of that!" Ed took another step toward Travis, and quickly stepped back as Travis fired at his feet.

"You're so full of shit!" Travis shouted, firing at Ed's feet again. "You're going to tell me where she's at or I'm going to fill the both of you full of holes!"

"Tough guy, aren't you? You figure you're going to pull a gun on me, and I'm supposed to be scared? Fuck you!" Ed snarled taking another step forward much to Travis' shock. Ed's eyes and body shook to the same rhythm of adrenaline mixed with pure fury. "Come on, mother fucker! Pull the goddamn trigger! I double dog fucking dare you!" Ed snarled putting his chest up against the barrel.

"Ed! What are you doing?" Livvy screamed from behind him. "Stop it! He's going to shoot you!" Livvy sobbed loudly. "Don't you dare leave me, Ed! You promised!"

Hearing her sobs, Ed glared at Travis and took a step back and put his hands up passively.

"Listen to your wife, Ed. I'll put enough lead in your body to make you into a pencil," he said. "Now I know that you know where she is! There's no way she'd go missing and you not know a damn thing about it! If you don't start talking right now!" he shouted back smashing Ed viciously on the right side of his face with the gun, sending the larger man sprawling to the ground.

"Come on! Get up, tough guy! You ran your mouth for so long! Now you've got your chance right now! Come on and hit me!" Travis slammed his foot onto Ed's stomach causing him instinctively to pull his body into a fetal position. He rolled onto his knees, trying to pull himself up only to get kicked in the ribs roughly, dropping him back into the fetal position.

"Come on, Ed! You're supposed to be so tough, aren't you? You don't look tough from where I'm standing!"

"Stop it! Leave him alone!" Livvy screamed rushing to get between the two men. When Travis pointed the gun at her, she stood in front of him to protect Ed. "Get away from him!" she said with a scowl.

"Shut up, you little bitch," he replied, gripping her shoulder roughly and shoved her to the ground. "How does it feel? I had to hear all about how this piece of shit call Laura a worthless bitch all the time! How do you like it, White?" he shouted kicking at Livvy's retreating form, catching her on her buttocks. "You like seeing your bitch get kicked like the dog she is?"

Ed wasted no more time with words. He exploded up, throwing a hard right hand to Travis' jaw, sending him slumping to the ground. When Ed advanced on him, he pointed the gun at him only to have it kicked out of his hand, sending it soaring in front of the White's truck.

After the gun went flying, Travis charged his shoulder into Ed's already ailing midsection, then exploded upward with an uppercut sending the larger man reeling back, clutching himself. Travis exploded back up and brought his fist down to Ed's face, dropping him to the ground then looked frantically for his fallen weapon.

Ed groaned looking up, seeing Travis searching. He forced himself to his feet and charged into Travis sending them both down to the ground, throwing punches at each other relentlessly, neither noticing Livvy yelling frantically into her cell phone.

"Police? Help! This... this man is here, and he attacked my husband and me with a gun and they're fighting now! Please, send someone right now!" she bawled into the receiver.

As they rolled around on the ground, Travis' hand wrapped around something hard. Ed barely had time to register the rock in his opponent's hand connecting with the side of his head. He fell to the ground like a sack of bricks as the eruption of stars clouded his vision allowing Travis to mount his upper body.

"How do you like that, tough guy? Huh? How do you like it?" Travis raised his left hand and dropped it ruthlessly to Ed's face repeatedly sending his head rebounding off the unforgiving dirt surface. Ed's eyes threatened to close when he saw Travis' rock laden right hand aiming for his face. At the last possible second, Ed moved his head to the side and roared as white-hot agony shot through his body.

"Oh look at that, big guy!" Travis held up the rock and Ed could just barely see blood dripping from its surface. Travis brought the rock down a second time and Ed moved his head again, wrapping his right arm around Travis' wrist trapping his hand against his body. He then wrapped his right leg around Travis' right leg and brought his bent left leg to his midsection and used his body to reverse their positions allowing Ed to mount Travis.

Keeping Travis' rock hand pinned, Ed brought his left hand down repeatedly to Travis' face. Still securing the rock hand, Ed shifted his position to put the smaller man into an arm bar causing him to scream loudly as Ed threatened to shatter his arm at the elbow.

"Yeah mother fucker!" Ed roared as he gasped for breath. "Didn't know it would be like this, did you?" Ed ignored Travis' attempts to break the hold by pounding on Ed's legs. "That won't help you, muthafucker!" Ed laughed bitterly.

Before Ed could gloat any further, his eyes widened as Travis reached out and grabbed a second nearby rock and slammed it onto his shin causing him to scream loudly in agony releasing the smaller man's arm.

The instant he was free, Travis scrambled frantically for the gun where it lay. Ed pulled himself to his feet trying to run after Travis but was too late as the man grabbed the pistol and picked it up, turning it toward Ed and firing an off-target shot sending the advancing man to the ground causing him to grunt in agony feeling the burning metal open his flesh.

"Oh stop your whining." Travis laughed maniacally. "I only grazed you, you fuck! Now get up!" Travis yelled. "Come on! Get up!" Ed slowly stood up, raising his hands submissively.

"Yeah, that's right, boy," Travis said, breathing heavily. "This is the way you belong quiet for once. I should just put a bullet in you right now, but I want to know where the fuck Laura is, and you'd better tell me right now!"

"Oh my God!" Livvy screamed into the phone. "He's got his gun on my husband! Please get someone here quickly! Please? He's going to kill him!" she bawled into the phone.

"Bitch, are you talking to the fucking cops?" Travis roared pointing the gun at Livvy.

Rage flooded Ed's mind when the gun was pointed at his Livvy, with Travis' finger on the trigger while holding his hands up, his left hand shot out hitting Travis' wrist in

an upward motion to send the bullet harmlessly flying in
the air. Ed closed his hand over Travis' wrist and stepped
into his body putting his back between them. In one fluid
motion, Ed's right hand joined his left hand and brought
Travis' already injured elbow down onto his shoulder.
Travis howled in agony as the sound of his elbow
dislocating and his humorous bone exploding out of his
flesh. The gun fell harmlessly to the ground as Ed kept
hold of Travis' arm and, with all of his strength sent his
body into the front of the car causing him to rebound off of
it and to the ground in a heap.

Ed glared down at Travis' prone body and began to
kick at him repeatedly, roaring inaudibly hardly able to
hear Livvy's frantic voice.

"Ed! Ed! Baby stop! The police are coming!" she
shrieked at the top of her lungs. The tone of her voice
snapped him back to reality and he turned to look to her,
terror in her eyes holding her cell phone to her ear.
"Please, tell them to hurry!" she shouted furiously. "He...
he shot my husband and he fell, but he, he got the gun
away from him! Please, just get someone here, please!" she
bawled into the cellphone.

Ed turned from Livvy and looked down at Travis. He
had just enough rational thinking to know that his enemy
had passed out from the pain of having his arm shattered
and being stomped within an inch of his life. His upper
body rose and fell heavily as he caught his breath. He
turned from Travis' fallen body, picking up the gun and
ejected the magazine then pulled the slide back to eject the
chambered round and walked toward Livvy, dropping the

gun to the ground. When he was within arm's length of her, she dropped her cell phone and sobbed against him.

"Did he hurt you?" she whimpered.

"I was just grazed, I'm fine," he said kissing the top of her head.

"You're bleeding," she said looking to him. "Let me look at you."

"Baby, I'm..."

"Edwin White, I said let me look at you. I'm a nurse, remember?" she said in a forceful tone, her fear retreating. He opened the passenger side door and sat down allowing Livvy to inspect him.

The flashing lights and sirens appeared a few moments later, and the responding officers came from their cars with guns drawn.

"He's over there!" Livvy yelled immediately, moving from the car, pointing to Travis' motionless body.

"Are you hurt, ma'am?" the officers asked, not holstering their weapons yet, but lowering them to a ready position slowly.

"I'm alright. My husband is bleeding, but I think he's alright," she said.

When the officers saw Ed sitting in the front seat, they were slow to holster their guns, watching him carefully. Seeing them still holding their guns in Ed's direction, her eyes narrowed to slits. She was prepared to scream at them until she saw the ambulance pulling in behind the police cars. She gestured again to Travis' body.

"My name is Olivia White I'm the head nurse at Man Gen. My husband here, Edwin White, is the victim of this man on the ground's assault! Now put your goddamn guns away and get them away from my fucking husband and stop treating him as though he's the suspect! This one on the ground attacked us!" When the officers holstered their guns, she shot them another venomous look and turned her attention to the paramedics.

"It looks like he has a compound fracture to his right humorous," she stated. "My husband has injuries to the side of his head, and his left shoulder and leg. He has a projectile wound but it was just a graze so some stitches maybe but gauze and packing for sure. Otherwise, he's fine," she reported.

The EMTs went to tend to Travis while the responding officers questioned Livvy as to what happened. Ed saw another car pull up and saw two plain clothes detectives exit the car.

"Hello, Mr. White," the younger detective greeted. "My name is Detective Wade this is my partner Detective Glatt."

"Yeah, my wife told me about you two," Ed said gesturing to Livvy a few feet away speaking to the responding officers.

"You want to tell us what happened?" Detective Wade asked.

"We came home from Maine and he came out from my wife's garden holding a gun on me demanding to know where my ex-wife is," he replied flatly.

"And?" Detective Wade asked writing in his notebook.

"And what?" Ed asked in an irritated tone.

"And what did you say to him?" Detective Glatt asked.

"What do you think I said?" Ed replied, his irritation building. "I told him I had no clue what he was talking about. He attacked me, I defended myself, he grazed me with a shot, I broke his arm in self-defense."

"Looks like you did more than defend yourself," Detective Wade suggested, watching the EMTs put Travis onto a gurney.

"I did what I had to do," Ed replied, being careful not to become defensive. "He had a gun he'd fired on me. I didn't know if he had another gun on him or what. He could have killed my wife and me, he was convinced that I knew something about Laura's whereabouts."

"And do you?" Detective Glatt asked.

"I didn't even know she was missing until Livvy told me that you'd called earlier. We were coming home anyway, I was prepared to come in and talk to you tomorrow," he replied.

"Well, I suppose this was a blessing in disguise then," Detective Wade replied. "We are here, why don't we talk about it now?"

"I suppose if I say that it's a bad time because I'd been assaulted wouldn't swing well with you gentlemen, now would it?" Ed asked looking up to them.

"Well... we'd like to get it out of the way, sir," Detective Wade responded. Ed could hear the dripping sarcasm at the last word.

"I see. Well then, I suppose we could do this. However, I'm sure your superiors won't be happy that you interrogated, I'm sorry... questioned, me without me having any medical attention. After all, this man came onto my property with a dangerous weapon intent on causing myself and my wife physical harm." Ed kept his face impassive and steadied his tone.

"If that was what we were planning on doing, I'm sure he wouldn't," Detective Glatt replied. "However, we are perfectly happy doing this at Man Gen. We could speak to you while you get fixed up."

"If that is what you gentlemen would prefer. I'm willing to cooperate one hundred percent," he said, standing up from the seated position. "My wife will, of course, be driving me to the hospital."

"And we will be along," the younger detective replied.

"Excellent," Ed said. "One question, detectives... if Laura's missing, where's my son?" he asked.

"You do not have to concern yourself with that, sir. As the court order specifies that you have supervised visitation, your ex-wife's family is looking after him."

"Good," Ed replied. "So long as he's being taken care of, that's all that matters."

An hour later, he lay in the hospital bed alone. Livvy, being the Head Nurse of the facility, ordered the detectives to stay out of the room while Ed received medical care. However, to not arouse any further suspicion, she stayed out of the room while he received treatment as well.

"Well Mr. White, it looks like you got very lucky," the ER doctor replied. "If that bullet would have gone in at the angle it looks like, you would be in some deep trouble."

"Story of my life." Ed chuckled.

"Well you're going to need a few staples for the graze and especially for that gash on the side of your head since its pretty deep and still slightly bleeding," he said removing the gauze from his head. "Looks like your shin is going to be fine, bruised nicely but just fine. Nothing broken or fractured."

"Great," Ed replied sarcastically. "Oh well, it could have been worse," he said with a grin.

"Well we have your head wound cleaned out nice and good so I will get started on that," he replied. "I'm going to give you a local and get started."

Ed nodded wordlessly. He remained motionless when he felt the slight prick of the needle followed by the immediate burn of lidocaine then nothing as the doctor went about his work. He closed his eyes, ignoring the four clicks of the staples going into his head, then four more going into his shoulder.

"Your wife will most likely gauge when those can come out and do it herself?" the doctor asked.

"Yup," Ed replied. "She'll probably enjoy that." He chuckled.

"Interesting how wives can be like that, right Mr. White? Alright, you're all set. The detectives seem to be anxious to get in here," the doctor said darkly.

"Well let's not keep them waiting any longer," he replied. "Best to get this over with. Thanks, doc."

When the doctor left, the detectives entered. Ed sat up reaching for his blood-stained shirt and pulled it on gingerly as his shoulder instantly protested the motion he'd begun.

"Mr. White, you know that you have the right to have an attorney present, correct?" Detective Wade asked him.

"Yes. I know my rights," Ed stated. "I have nothing... really..." he looked at both men squarely, "to hide and being that this is just an interview I am free to end it anytime I want to unless you have probable cause to detain me."

"I almost forgot," Detective Wade said with a sneer, "you were a CO."

"I have a bachelor's in criminal justice as well," Ed replied. "Graduated number one in my class before I moved up here." He smiled.

"Good for you," Detective Glatt replied almost impressed.

"Thanks. Most frustrating two and a half years of my life," he replied giving the officers a venom fueled smile.

"Alright well, why don't we just get down to the nit and grit shall we?" Detective Wade asked. "Where were you the third of March at around eleven p.m.?"

"I was at home. I went to bed at about nine," he replied.

"Why so early?" Detective Wade asked.

"Well my wife and I had spent time together and I was tired. Plus, I'd had my visitation with my son. It was an emotionally draining visit, so I decided to go to bed early."

"I see," Detective Wade replied. "You and your ex-wife had some words at the end of that visit, from what we were told by the court ad litem."

"Yes we did. I'm sure that the moderator told you that my visit with Eddie wasn't the best. He said some hurtful things and I confronted his mother about it because I know that a lot of his anger toward me is centered on her influence."

"Why do you say that, Mr. White? Why can't it be that your son just doesn't like you?" Detective Wade asked.

Ed gave him a slight smile, hidden behind it a look of absolute contempt. "Because my ex-wife has made it her life's mission to slander my name and ruin my life with unsubstantiated claims of spousal abuse, child abuse, and sexual abuse," he replied. "Neither she, nor my son, have ever been discovered having injuries upon their bodies by my hand, yet she holds onto the story anyway. And with the help of her lawyer, and mine not doing his job, was able to convince the court of these claims. Hence, why I only have supervised visitation of my son and have no parental rights."

"If you are supposed to be such a monster, why weren't you incarcerated?" Detective Glatt asked curiously.

"No police reports to back her claims, and no physical evidence to back her claims," Ed replied. "However, she had Martin Lincoln as her attorney, and he was able to spin it nicely in her favor. She walked away with my pension, an astronomical amount of child support, and would have all but crippled me financially if it weren't for my wife."

"I bet that pissed you right off," Detective Wade stated.

"Wouldn't you be?" Ed asked him shortly. He cleared his throat. "My apologies. I do not mean to come off as hostile or disrespectful. I have had a very difficult night, and I am still rather upset by the judge's ruling."

"Understandable," Detective Glatt replied. "I'm divorced myself."

"So you know that the system has the cards stacked against the man no matter what," Ed replied. "Listen gentlemen, I'm going to be straight with you."

"Please do, Mr. White," Detective Wade replied.

"I still hold a massive grudge against my ex-wife. I moved away from my family and my friends to live with a woman who told me that she would work with me to build a good life. Instead, I got a woman who faked a back injury and did all that she could to get out of working. Then, she looked at me with a completely unreasonable opinion of what a man is supposed to do. Yes, I did tell her that I wanted a traditional marriage where I was the bread winner. But when the market went to shit, not to mention the highest inflation in decades, she knew I needed financial help and she wouldn't do anything to be my partner. So yes, I am still hurt and angry about this." He cleared his throat.

"When I decided to end the marriage she kept my son from me for almost two months and the courts did nothing because she decided to make up stories of spousal abuse and said she was afraid of me. She even used my previous trial against me and said that I had turned into a monster after the Craig Jackson incident."

"Did you?" Detective Glatt asked.

"I was a bit more nervous. Craig Jackson had gang ties and I was nervous about retaliation. I also had nightmares. That was part of the reason why I had to complete a number of therapy sessions. I did not turn violent or abusive," he said calmly.

"Sadly, the system decided that I was a monster. So I lost my son, and everything I ever had to her. So now she sits pretty on disability and my child support. Never has to work again a day for the rest of her life, and she throws it in my face. I'm not nice to her because I have no respect for her. She has hurt me more than anyone in my life ever has. Any reasonable person would feel the same way about her that I do."

"The question here, Mr. White, is simple do you know of your ex-wife's whereabouts?" Detective Wade asked in a slow, near insulting tone.

"No, I don't, Detective," Ed replied looking him in the eye without glaring or staring. "Like I said, I was asleep in my home at the time you gave me."

"Did you have anything to do with your ex-wife's disappearance?" Detective Wade asked him.

"No, Detective, I did not," Ed replied calmly. "I would, however, like to know where she is myself," he added.

"Oh? And why is that?" Detective Glatt asked.

"She's the mother of my son, sir," Ed replied. "Despite whatever feelings I have toward her are, my son deserves his mother. Is... is he alright?" Ed asked.

"He's fine, Mr. White," Detective Wade replied. "He's worried about his mother, but he is doing alright."

"Good," Ed replied, adding nothing further for a moment. "If you have no other questions, I would like to go home. I have some bruised ribs that need a hot bath to soak in and I am quite hungry."

"Of course, Mr. White," Detective Glatt replied. "One final question though," he added as Ed stood to his feet slowly.

"And that would be?" Ed asked.

"Doesn't it strike you odd that your ex-wife and your current wife's ex-husband go missing in such proximity of each other?" Ed looked to them and nodded.

"Yes, sir, it does strike me as odd," he replied.

"Well, being that you have a BA in Criminal Justice, tops of your class, what do you think about that?" Detective Wade asked.

"To be quite honest, I gave up on law enforcement the day I turned in my badge," he replied. "I'll say this though, I hope that you find them. They have families that love them and care for them." He nodded firmly. Ed made his way to the door turning his back on the detectives.

"Do you honestly expect us to believe that assessment?" Detective Wade asked angrily.

"Expect you to believe it?" Ed asked with his back still turned. "Does it matter?" he looked over his shoulder. "You'll believe what you want to believe, sir. It really makes no difference to me. The burden isn't on me to change your mind, it's on you to prove what you think." With that, Ed exited the room.

"I want to nail that smug son-of-a-bitch," Wade said to Glatt angrily. "He knows the law in and out, he knows how to evade our techniques."

"I know," Glatt replied. "He's smart, but he is also right we need something we don't have proof."

"There is no way it is just coincidence that both of their exes have come up missing!" he said in a raised whisper.

"But we can't prove it," Glatt replied.

"I'm not going to let this go. I'm going to catch them, they will slip up," Wade grumbled.

"The captain said that if we don't get anything substantial, we are to treat this like missing persons and that's what we are going to do," Glatt said patiently. "Now let's go. I want to talk to Travis Day. We also have to read him his rights." He caught the younger detective's incredulous look and shook his head.

"I don't want to hear it, Carl. Despite what your suspicions are, he went to those peoples' house and waited for them with a loaded gun, shot a man, and assaulted him. Now let's go," Glatt replied. When they went to exit the room, Detective Wade almost walked into Ed.

"Can I help you, Mr. White?" Detective Wade asked.

"Yes, actually," Ed replied. "Can I have one of your cards please? Just in case I need to contact you? You know... in case I hear from Laura or Livvy sees Martin," Ed asked politely.

Detective Wade looked at Detective Glatt incredulously and then looked back to Ed with a small smile, handing him a card.

"Thank you, sir," Ed said calmly. When the two men left, he smiled coldly and then walked to Livvy and gave her a slight nod.

"Ready to go?" he asked.

"I've been ready to go," she said hastily. She inspected the staples on the side of his head and sighed. "Jesus, that looks horrible. It's probably going to scar too," she said placing a light kiss on his cheek.

"It's no big deal. I'm alright." He put his arm around her and leaned over to kiss her cheek, then whispered, "I have a way for us to get out of this." He smiled. "Let's go home," he said speaking in a normal tone. "I'm starving and I want to get some sleep."

"Alright, baby," she replied watching him curiously, the sideways smile brought a curious look to her face.

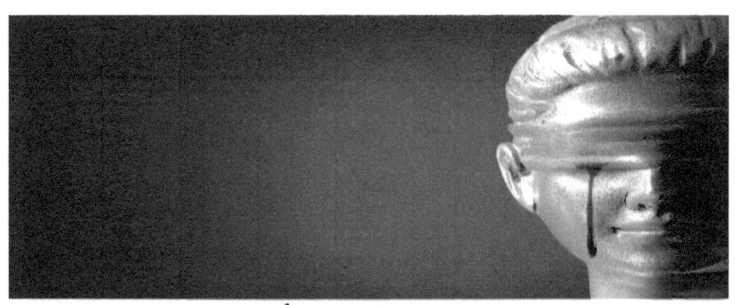

# CHAPTER 19
## *STRATEGY*

"That is fucking brilliant, baby," Livvy whispered, excitedly leaning forward to speak to him. He'd insisted on stopping to get something to eat. When they pulled up outside the out-of-the-way diner and saw there were hardly any cars in the parking lot, he knew it was perfect to discuss the plan.

"I hoped you would think so," he replied sipping his tea.

"So how do we do that? We got rid of everything," she said. "Plus, he may have an alibi for that night."

"Yeah, he probably does. And yes, we did a great job at getting rid of everything. Did you clean everything out of the cabin? And I mean like, everything?"

"I'm pretty sure I did. Why?" she asked.

"Let's just say that there's always some trace evidence. Even when it is cleaned up, there is still something left behind. They don't have enough to get a search warrant so that is on our side. What we need to do is push the suspicion off of us and put it onto Travis," he said.

"How do we do that?" she asked.

"Well, we get some luminol it's a chemical they use at crime scenes. We can use that and a black florescent light to make sure that we have nothing in the house, and the cabin. When we have that, we can clean up better. We will do the same thing for the wood chipper. Now, in theory, I think we can get the trace evidence on something... like gloves or something. Then, again theoretically, put it in his house or something. Hell, maybe even his car. If that doesn't work, we can always just make sure that we scrub everything down."

"Jesus, baby, you're like a mastermind." She laughed.

"Hell, you couldn't have thought you would have to do all of the thinking." He chuckled.

"I actually thought I would," she said with a teasing grin. "Strike one, you're sexy as hell. Strike two, you've got tons of brawn. Strike three you're sexy and brawny."

"You know flattery gets you everywhere." He said with a slight snicker. "Now listen, we have to be very careful with how we order this stuff. However, you work in the hospital and some of it you can get from labs if you just ask. But don't use anyone local. Do you have any friends out of state you may be able to call in favors with?"

"Yes, I think so," she replied.

"But will they be discreet?" he asked seriously.

"Absolutely," she replied. "I can call in some favors with some of my sorority sisters. They will keep their mouths shut." She looked at him curiously. "Honey, do you really think that we can do this without having to become fugitives?"

"Absolutely," he said ensuring that no one was listening in on their conversation. When he saw that they

304

were still alone except for the waitress who was talking on her cell phone, he whispered, "We just have to keep playing it smooth. We have to get that luminol quickly. We will go to the cabin first, although there is no official record that we were there so that will help. I just want to cover our tracks completely. House, including the freezer and the woodchipper, then the cabin and the trunk of the car just to be safe."

"Everything else, we will handle." When more people started coming in, they ended the conversation and ate in silence.

"Get your interior completely detailed tomorrow after work. Wash, wax, the whole nine yards. Take it to that old man's shop with all the college guys by the hospital. Tell him it's overdue," he said quickly. "I'll do the same. That'll take care of anything. But especially if they decide that they are going to check the traffic cameras near the bar if the fucking things work anyway. But, like I said, that is easy enough for you to get out of. You just happened to be in the same area, that's all. If they want to look further into it, we'll have the car detailed so it won't matter anyway. Plus no one in that bar is going to recognize you that well. Bartenders have so many goddamn people they have to serve they can't recognize someone that looks drastically different. If that bartender can, well we will figure it out."

"Jesus." She said with a short laugh.

"What?" he asked reaching gingerly for his wallet to pay the waitress and put her tip on the table.

"Why didn't you ever become a cop?" she asked. "I mean with the way your mind works you would have made a great detective."

"I hate cops. I only did the jail job because I was married to a lazy bitch."

"Well, why did you get your degree in criminal justice if you hate cops so much?" she asked curiously.

"I don't know. I thought I could make a difference in the system," he said. "Problem is, the system only works for people that have the money, aren't black, or in some cases have a vagina," he said seriously. "Look at the way the divorce system works a woman can essentially demand anything she wants from her husband in a divorce no matter how unreasonable. And nine times out of ten, she will get whatever she wants. Throw in a domestic violence charge, that the domestic violence advocates encourage the women to do, mind you, and bam a man's reputation and life are destroyed all because he didn't want to be married anymore.

"The real bullshit is that women like Laura? Like you said, they fuck it up for women that are abused. It's fucking evil horseshit." Livvy said, nodding in agreement. "It's bullshit. Martin actually abused me, and I didn't try to destroy him in court. I just wanted my share of what he sold the equipment and the back acreage for and that was it. I didn't want anything else from him."

"Exactly. The point is the system enables the weak, greedy, and corrupt. Meanwhile, the hardworking everyday Joe will have to bend over for a stiff dick up the ass, and like it. Not to mention that our liberties are being raped from us every day. I don't want to serve a system like that, not at all." Ed took a final sip of his glass of water and set the tip under the beverage.

"Well I'm glad you feel that way. If I had decided to do this with you as a detective on the case I would be finished." They shared a laugh as the waitress brought them the receipt back.

When they got to the car, Ed gingerly got into the front seat, his ribs and shoulder still bothering him tremendously. When they got home, Livvy helped him into the house and while he got undressed, she began to run a bath for them.

He slipped into the water first, as was the custom, and she got in after laying her back against his chest. She looked at the staples on his shoulder and kissed the closed wound gently.

"I was so scared when he shot you," she finally admitted, tears falling. "I was so afraid that was going to be it that I would lose you. If you were dead, I was hoping he would shoot me next." She turned to face him and hugged him closely. He put his good arm around her and kissed her forehead gently.

"All I could think about was if something happened to me, I wouldn't be able to help you. I was ready to kill him to keep him from coming anywhere near you."

"Look at us." She chuckled, brushing her tears aside.

"I know." He smiled. "Just goes to show, we are perfect for each other."

She rested her head against his chest as they lay in the water neither wanting to ruin the moment. After almost twenty minutes, she stood up and grabbed their towels. They laid in bed the same as they had in the tub and slept in each other's arms. There was nothing to say as they each slipped into the comfortable oblivion of sleep.

When they woke the next morning, they went about their normal husband and wife daily routines, with their own plans. When he returned home that evening, he could smell the delicious aromas of a steak and potato dinner and he felt his mouth instantly water.

"I'm home, baby," he called out, hanging his keys next to the door, and gingerly pulling off his jacket.

"Hi, honey," she called from the kitchen. "How was your day?"

"Wasn't bad. Yours?" he asked, making his way into the kitchen, and placing a kiss on her cheek.

"It was good. Long, but good. Were you able to get everything done?" she asked.

"Yes I did. Did you?" he asked.

"Yes. I put in a call to my friend Janet in Texas. We should have what we need in a few days," she replied.

"Good. I called a friend of mine today too," he said with a grin. "A friend that has a relative in Manchester PD."

"Oh?" she asked curiously.

"Yes. Let's just say we will be able to snoop onto them as they snoop onto us."

"What does that even mean, Ed?" she asked her irritability raising.

"It means that if those detectives do try and get anything on us, taps or anything, we'll know about it. They got turned down hard in court today trying to get warrants," he replied.

"That's good right?" she asked.

"Very good, kind of. They've already searched Martin and the bitch's houses. They found absolutely nothing, so that helps us. However, what keeps us from being in the clear is the fact that I know their tactics. So the judge, on one hand, says that they don't have enough to implicate us other than they are our exes and that they came up missing so close to one another."

"But?" Livvy asked when Ed was silent for longer than she would have liked.

"But... they are considering that I am former law enforcement and I know the rules. They are kind of in a quagmire about it. They don't want to look like they are going to try and target me because of my previous case, especially since it was a clear-cut case of self-defense. So the judge is kind of at odds. So the faster we get that stuff here the better. Since we have no paper trail for the cabin we are fine on that count. We just need to make sure that everything is okay in the basement and in the freezer."

"Well, Janet said that it could take about three or four days for it to get here," she offered.

"That should be plenty of time. We'll do some more cleaning in the basement between now and then." He massaged his shoulder gently.

"Are you alright?" she asked worriedly, already starting to unbutton his shirt to check his wound.

"Just a little bit sore that's all. I think it's just healing," he said as she kept her eyes on his shoulder.

"Edwin, were you trying to work out today?" she asked impatiently.

"Maybe?" he replied with a slight grin.

"Dammit, Ed!" she grumbled, resisting the urge to slap his staples. "You can't do anything for at least ten days until the staples come out!"

"How the hell did you know anyway?" he asked in a frustrated tone.

"Because you almost threw a staple, you jackass." She shook her head. "Thankfully, it's still in place so you don't have to worry about it. But if you pop it, I don't want to hear you whining."

"Fair enough," he answered, placing a kiss on her lips.

"How confident are you that you can trust this friend of yours?" she asked.

"Very. I got him through school, and I introduced him to his wife. The guy he has in the department here is his brother-in-law. They're a very tight knit family, we have nothing to worry about."

"What did you tell him?" she inquired.

"I told him that my ex had gone missing," he replied. "After Larry, my buddy, cussed her out for about five minutes, I told him that the detectives here were hounding us because your ex had gone on a drunken binge. He thinks it's bullshit, so he called his brother-in-law and he said he would keep an eye out. Apparently, this Wade guy has been reprimanded and even fired from some PDs because he couldn't just let things go even when there was nothing. So again, that's going to help us out. He's also had a litany of complaints on him for how he treats minorities, so that's another positive in our favor."

"Well, that's good. I want to leave here, but I want to do it on our terms. Not because we have to run."

"Same here," he said, rubbing the stubble on his jaw. "Well now we have to wait for the luminol. We have blacklights leftover from Halloween decorations last year, so that is no problem there. How much will she be sending?"

"She said that she would send a bit, she never really gave me an exact number. I told her I just needed some so she said she would take care of me. Apparently, people ask for that stuff more often than not, but it can be very expensive."

"Alright that is good then." He sat down in the nearby chair rolling his injured shoulder delicately.

"We're really going to get away with this, Ed?"

"I think so. But we need to think ahead also. Since Wade is trying to push, we are going to have to make him look bad." He thought for a moment and started to laugh.

"What's so funny?" she asked.

"Let's get a lawyer. Guys like Wade are going to watch who they're after, they turn stalker-like. We hire a lawyer so that we can make it look like Wade is up to his old tricks. That'll piss him off, but it will discredit him too. That way, they'll end up having to put the investigation to bed."

"Who should we get?" she asked.

"Your brother? I'm sure he could handle it." Ed chuckled.

"No. We aren't talking to him, he's a fucking asshole," she said stalwartly.

"Alright, well there's a guy that I know about named Boscoe Brown."

"You mean the guy that you couldn't afford when you were divorcing that cunt?" she asked.

"Yeah. I figure that I could do that, and he'll do a great job at tearing Manchester PD in half." He sneered.

"We can't do it right away though. We have to wait until he starts becoming to be a problem." She opened the oven and the smell of steak whiffed through the air.

"Absolutely. Damn that smells good."

"It had better." She winked. "I picked them up at the butcher specifically for you. Inch thick Porterhouse." She proceeded to waft the oven air toward him.

Three days later, when Ed came home from work, he saw a large, brown box sitting on the counter.

"Honey, I'm home."

Livvy came from upstairs hurriedly. "He's started following me," she said to him hastily.

"Wade?" he asked seriously to which she nodded. "Good. That means he's getting nowhere and is being stalled out, so now he is watching our patterns. I assume that the brown box is what we've been waiting for?"

"Yes, I just sprayed the basement before you got home. Well, I should say that I was about to when you pulled up."

"Good. Did you get the lights?"

"Not yet."

Ed went downstairs taking the big brown box with him, and went into the backroom then began to spray around, remembering where Martin's body had been and began spraying. He turned off the overhead light and flicked on the switch for the blacklight inserted just temporarily just for this. He saw the splatters mixed with what looked like streaks from previous cleaning with bleach where Martin Rogers lay.

"Well, it's not what I didn't expect," he stated looking on. "But not as bad as I had feared either." He went to the freezer, picked up the lid and looked in chuckling. "Well that's good."

"What is?" she asked curiously.

"Nothing in the freezer. Now we know the chipper will probably be about as bad, but that's something we can handle. I already put it up for sale online and have a buyer, I'm taking it there tomorrow."

"Well that's good I guess," she said calmly. "What do you know about the buyer?"

"An older lady, wants it for after the winter is up so that she can deal with fallen trees and debris."

"Alright, that's..." she stopped hearing the knocking coming from upstairs. "Are you expecting anyone, honey?" she asked cautiously.

"No." He walked to the door and looked through the peep hole and grinned. "Speak of the devil." He opened the door, part way and blocked the opening with his body locking eyes with Detective Wade. "Detective," he greeted.

"Mr. White. Glad to see that you're home." The detective nodded.

"You knew I was since you've been following my wife," he said dryly. "What do you want?"

"I'd like to speak with you. Can I come in?" Wade took a step toward the crack, but Ed did not move.

"No, I don't think so," Ed replied flatly.

"And why is that, Mr. White?" Wade asked with mock disappointment.

"Because I do not want to let you in, that's why," Ed replied with ice in his tone. "So why don't you get off of my property?"

"Mr. White," the detective replied, his tone take a slow, hostile turn. "You're going to let me into your home so we can have this discussion, or I will make life extremely difficult for you and your wife."

"Hmm, that sounds rather like a threat, Detective. I am morbidly curious though. Please do tell. How so? Oh and just so you know, my wife is about to call your captain right now and file a complaint against you."

"Oh she doesn't want to do that, Mr. White."

"Is that right, Detective? And why is that?" Ed asked with a smirk.

"Because I know that you killed your ex-wife, Mr. White."

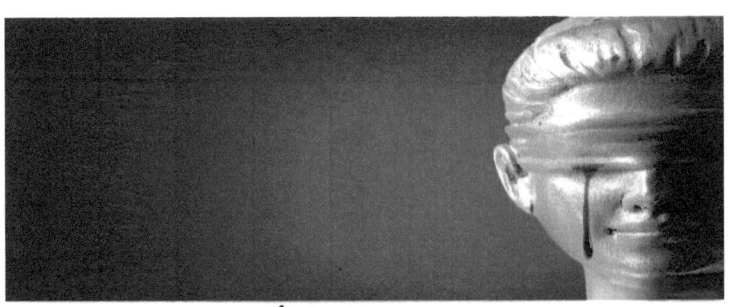

# CHAPTER 20

## *SWAN SONG*

"What did you say?" Ed said, looking at the detective as though he were insane.

"You heard me, Mr. White. I believe you murdered your ex-wife and your wife had something to do with it. I also believe that you did something with your wife's ex-husband and, again, she had something to do with it. Now, are you going to open the door or am I going to have to get unpleasant?" Wade said through clenched teeth.

Ed could see a wild look in the man's eyes. He looked over his shoulder at Livvy, then stepped back.

Wade walked in and closed the door behind him, looking at Ed and Livvy and gestured to the sofa in the living room.

"Go ahead, have a seat. We are going to have a chat, and I would like for the two of you to be nice and comfortable."

Ed gave Wade a look of pure hatred before leading Livvy to the couch and sat down. Wade looked at the leather easy chair and couldn't help himself he allowed a wide smile on his face and sat down with a loud sigh.

"This chair yours, Ed? Oh, I can call you Ed, right?" When Ed didn't respond, Wade chuckled. "Very, very comfortable chair. Thanks for the offer." He reached into his jacket and pulled out a pack of cigarettes and a lighter. "Do you mind if I smoke?"

"Do we have a choice?" Ed asked coldly.

"Good point." Wade lit his cigarette, took a deep breath, and blew his smoke into the air. "I did some checking on you, Ed. Seems you just bought that woodchipper you've got outside. Why would you be selling it?"

"Who says I'm selling it?" he asked calmly.

"Oh Mrs. Irene Robinson of South Highland Avenue. Very nice of you to take so much off such a practically new piece of equipment." He chuckled snidely again. "Yeah. Me." He shook his head lightly. "See, I knew there was something going on, but I wasn't sure what. So, I took the liberty of stopping by one day while you were gone and took a look around. Now, I don't want to hear anything about 'improper use of power' or anything about procedure. Nope, not interested in that discussion. Needless to say, nice blood splatter you have in your basement, luminol is amazing. I checked out the box before Olivia here came home and saw you had some shipped to you. Seems to me like you wanted to make sure the splatter had been taken care of.

"In any event, I took a quick squirt on the inside of your woodchipper and found some nice splatters in there too. So let me tell you how I think it worked either Martin Rogers, Laura White, or both, came here one night. You killed them in your basement, then you threw them into the woodchipper and somehow disposed of the body."

"You are insane!" Livvy shouted. "Get the hell out of my house, you bastard! Just because you have that badge—"

"Mrs. White, shut the fuck up." He glared.

"Get the fuck out!" Ed roared standing up hastily. "Or I will fucking throw you out!"

"Oh, you will?" Wade asked calmly. "You forget I'm a cop."

"And you have been told to get the hell out! I will sue the damn PD and you will be out of a job! You have no search warrant, no substantial evidence—" Ed exploded, taking a step toward Wade.

The detective reached into his jacket and pulled his department issue Glock .40. "Ed, I suggest you sit down and calm that temper of yours. I'm not some punk from the ghetto that you can take out with no issue, or some old man with delusions of grandeur. Now sit your five-dollar ass down before I make change!" Wade snarled gesturing to the couch with the gun.

Ed stood his ground glaring at him, his foot making a slight movement toward the detective. Wade looked at Ed with a surprised grin and pointed the barrel toward Livvy causing Ed to freeze in his tracks.

"Now, let me say this again sit your ass down or I *will* put a bullet between those perfect tits of hers. Next step and I put a bullet in her and then a bullet in your fucking knee cap. No one will believe a fucking word you say, and you'll be a gimp in prison for life."

Ed growled, but sat down slowly. His body rattling with fury, he ignored the pain in his shoulder and put his right arm around Livvy, holding her protectively.

"That's better. Now this is how it's going to happen I'll bring you in. You *are* going to admit everything and that will be that. But to let you know that I am not a bad guy I'll tell them that you turned yourselves in that way you won't have to worry too much about the death penalty. Juries love that whole 'seeking redemption' angle bullshit, believe you me. Now, do we have a deal?"

"You're insane!" Livvy cried out. "We haven't done anything!"

"Oh really? And how did those blood splatters end up in your basement? Huh? Why did you have a box of luminol shipped to your home? What about the blood splatters in your wood chipper? How did your exes disappear so close to one another? And why, Mrs. White, was a woman fitting your description the last one that the first Mrs. White was seen alive with?" He laughed loudly. "Sure, Eddie boy, you're smart. But you're no genius, that's for damn sure. So are you going to accept my generous deal? Or am I going to force option B?"

"You're wrong, Wade," Ed said, trying to speak reasonably. "We haven't done—"

"Enough!" Wade exploded as he shot to his feet, firing a single shot past Ed's head. "No more lying! You may have convinced yourself somehow, some way, that you've done nothing wrong! Maybe killing that kid gave you a taste for blood? Who knows, and who the fuck cares? You can lie to me, but I know the truth!"

"Ed..." Livvy whispered softly. He took his arm from around her with a slight grunt.

"Yeah, go ahead and discuss it amongst yourselves," Wade replied. "I have two sets of cuffs at the ready for you." Wade took a few backward steps away from the couple yet kept his eyes on them sternly.

"Ed," she whispered again, "what are we going to do?"

"I don't know," Ed admitted. "He doesn't have anything on us, and I'm not admitting to shit."

"What about the evidence he says he has?" Livvy asked.

Ed began to snicker, looking at Wade and then fell into full blown laughter.

"Ed? What are you doing?" Livvy shouted.

"What's so funny, Ed?" Wade asked with a laugh of his own.

"Are you off your meds today, Wade? Is that what your problem is?" Ed shook his head composing himself of his laughing fit, standing up to keep his body shielding Livvy. "You really think we're going to admit to anything? You executed illegal searches, including the federal offense of tampering with the mail! All for something you cannot prove! Blood splatters? Idiot, I work out and train in that basement! I do sparring down there, and it gets bloody! Not to mention that last year I went hunting and—"

"Do you think I'm an idiot, White?" Wade roared holding his gun on Ed again. "I know you did it!"

"That's twice now you've pointed that gun at me, Detective Wade. It didn't work out good for the last fucker that did that. You may want to—"

"Want to what, Ed?" Wade asked angrily. "Huh? You going to try and be a tough guy with me? With me?" he laughed coldly. "Illegal searches? It doesn't matter. I have you caught lock, stock, and barrel."

"Your evidence—" Ed began.

"It all comes together!" Detective Wade roared maniacally. "You know it! I know it! Anyone with half a brain knows it!" A loud thud coming from the doorway caught Wade's attention. He turned to his left and fired his gun toward the sound.

Ed took his chance ignoring the promise of agony, reached for the lamp on the nearby end table with his left hand and hurled it at Detective Wade. The detective took a quick step to his right to avoid the projectile and suddenly had Ed White's lowered shoulder drilling into his abdomen. The loud exhalation of air exploded from his mouth as his gun fell harmlessly to the ground. Ed then threw a hard right hand to the detective's jaw, then a left fist into his enemy's ribs.

Wade faltered weakly against the wall, dropping to one knee before exploding upward and punching Ed's injured shoulder causing him to roar loudly in agony and stagger backward. Wade threw another punch to Ed's shoulder, then finished his attack with an overhand left as soon as his defenses were dropped sending him to the ground.

"The hard way then." Wade smirked as he bent down to pick up his gun only to have Ed kick the gun away toward the front door. The detective glared angrily and kicked him in the face ferociously, then dropped on top of him throwing repeatedly blows to his face. As he reared his fist back for another blow, a bullet zinged past his head freezing him in place.

"Get the fuck off of my husband, you crazy bastard!" Livvy snarled.

"Crazy?" Wade laughed maniacally. "Crazy am I? We'll see whether I'm crazy or not! You're fucking killers!"

"Why the fuck are you so nuts over us?" Ed groaned weakly, turning his head to spit his blood to the ground. "We haven't done—"

"Liar!" bellowed Wade angrily. "You have the same look, he had! That same arrogant fucking look! Thinking you know everything there is to know about the law? Fuck you, White! You were never good enough to make it as a cop!" Wade went to reach for his ankle for his spare gun.

Ed threw his right fist as hard as he could, feeling the crunch of flesh on flesh as he knocked Wade to the ground in a motionless heap. Ed cried out loudly in pain, clutching at his shoulder as it seeped blood.

"Ed!" Livvy screamed, rushing to his side. "Are you alright?"

"Staples," he grumbled weakly.

Livvy rushed to his side Ed noticed her cellphone was on an active call. Before he could ask any questions, there was a pounding at the front door.

"Here! We're in here!" Livvy called out. "The door is open!"

The door opened and four uniformed officers made their way in. Livvy held up the phone for them to see. One of the officers picked up the discarded handgun and holstered it. Livvy pointed at the prone body of Detective

Wade as Detective Glatt entered the home looking at his partner's prone body in shock.

"That's the man that invaded our home! That's Detective Wade, your partner!" she said acidly to Detective Glatt. "He hurt my husband and shot at us!" she bawled.

"Goddammit, Ronnie," Glatt said under his breath in irritation.

"I want him arrested!" Livvy shouted. "He's been following me around and now this? He came in here ranting and raving like a fucking lunatic! I'm calling our lawyer!" she roared toward Detective Glatt who had barely taken his eyes off of his fallen partner. He shook his head in disbelief and looked toward one of the uniforms.

"Place Detective Wade under arrest," he said simply. He then looked at Livvy. "I'm... very sorry about this. I'd like you to come down to the station and give a sworn statement... if you don't mind?"

"After my husband gets medical attention. That bastard popped his staples," she hissed angrily, looking down at Ed who had his hand over his wound to stop the bleeding.

"EMTs are coming in right behind me," Glatt replied as the uniformed officers put the handcuffs on Detective Wade.

"Glatt!" Wade roared as he began to come to. "Glatt, it was them! It was them! Why... why the fuck are cuffs on me? It's them! They killed Rogers! They killed Laura White! They're murderers! Why are you arresting me!"

"Get him out of here." Glatt glared in disgust. Two uniformed officers forced Detective Wade out of the living room as he ranted and raved in rage.

As the EMTs came into the house and began to tend to Ed's wounds, Mr. and Mrs. White shared a look, and a small smile as he was helped up and walked to the ambulance.

"So let me get this straight," Detective Glatt asked the couple as they sat at his desk at the police department. "You say that you'd seen him following you, he admitted to you that he'd gone through your mail?"

"That's what my clients said Detective," Boscoe Brown said looking to Detective Glatt with hard eyes.

"Not to mention he was ranting like a lunatic saying that we were 'just like him' whatever that means," Ed said incredulously. "I kept telling him to leave if he didn't have a warrant and he wouldn't. He was pointing his gun at me, and at my wife. He was even posing as a woman on the internet acting like he wanted to buy my wood chipper!"

"Well, I'm not at liberty to discuss—" Glatt began.

"It doesn't matter," Livvy cut him off angrily. "We're going to sue this department! This is ridiculous!"

"Mrs. White—"

"Detective, I sincerely suggest you not address my clients any further..." Boscoe began to say.

"No, Detective!" Livvy roared. Boscoe looked down at her as she erupted, a look of sympathy for her pain on his face. "We have been cooperative in your investigation and what do we get out of it! Our home invaded, we were shot at, and my husband injured by one of the lead investigators! This is, this is disgusting! This is completely unreal!"

"You're right, Mrs. White," Detective Glatt replied. "And I am truly sorry," he replied looking to the Whites and then to their lawyer.

"I'm sure you are." Livvy glared at him and stood up. "I'm ready to leave," she said sharply, heading to the exit. Ed looked at the Detective and shrugged with a wince as he stood.

"You should see her when she's really pissed off." Ed laughed quietly making his way out after her.

"I will be filing paperwork first thing in the morning Detective. I am sure your Captain will not be happy," Boscoe said as he turned to follow the Whites out of the station.

"You know, this town is getting way too violent for me." Ed chuckled under his breath while Boscoe walked to catch up.

"Me too," she said as they exited the building.

"Okay you two," Boscoe said calmly. "You two go home. Like I said, I will file paperwork tomorrow. I'll call you when that's done and we'll go from there. Sound good?" he asked.

"Sounds great. Thank you Boscoe," Livvy replied reaching out to shake his hand.

"No problem," he reached out to shake Ed's left hand and gave them a smile. "When this is over and done, you'll be in a much better position than you are now that's for sure. Go and live wherever you want," he gave them a wink and began to walk off.

"You know he's right," Ed said with a grin. "Where should we go?"

"Out west," she replied simply. "Away from here. Maybe Washington state, we could get the ferry into Vancouver whenever we want to." She leaned over and whispered into her ear, giving it a slight nip. "Or need to."

"I like that idea," Ed purred lightly, kissing her lips softly.

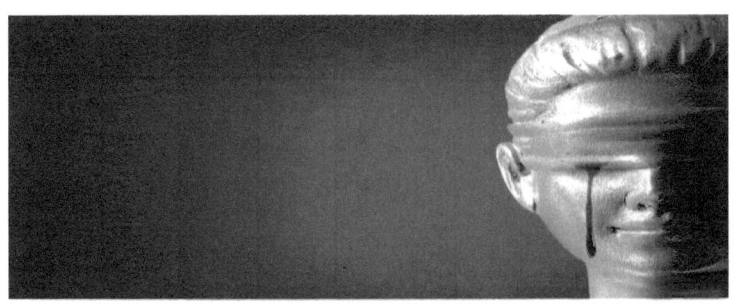

# EPILOGUE
## ONE YEAR LATER

Livvy sat in the parking lot with the driver's side door wide open as she'd put her shopping bags on the passenger seat of the car.

She rubbed the swelling baby bump and smiled warmly. Each and every time she looked at her belly, tears welled in her eyes from the children lost and the children she hoped would soon be. She couldn't help but smile at the events that had led to the comfortable point in their lives.

After leaving the police station, information leaked in the morning news about a rogue police detective unlawfully attacking, and detaining, individuals who had been all but officially ruled out as people of interest in a missing person's investigation. After a short trial and deliberation, the city negotiated a substantial cash settlement to avoid being held liable for the actions of a rogue officer.

The vision of former detective Donald "Ronnie" Wade being led in and out of court on television in handcuffs brought a wide smile to her face. When he was found guilty and sentenced to five to fifteen years in a psychiatric hospital for his crimes, she couldn't help but feel relief.

"Fuck the nuthouse!" Ed roared angrily. "He should be in fucking prison!" The scar on his right shoulder was a constant reminder of the detective, and of Travis who was given the maximum penalty of twenty years.

Ed, however, was still unable to gain custody of Eddie. Only the two of them knew he hadn't pushed as hard as he could have. Eddie hated him, and Ed resented him for it. Neither wanted anything to do with the other and she knew not to push.

After they'd made the cross country move, she'd discovered they were pregnant again. This time, with twins. Ed opened a martial arts school of his own while she'd settled into being a homebody, and even made the decision to get her teaching certification so instead of making rounds on the floor, she could train the next generation of nurses to follow behind in her footsteps.

She smiled warmly, as life was finally what she'd hoped that it would always be the moment she knew that she loved Ed White more than any other person she'd ever known. She ran her hand over her stomach again when suddenly a large SUV backed into her open door.

She screamed loudly in shock and terror, moving her body closer to the passenger's side seat, her arm cradling her womb protectively. When the SUV finally came to a stop, it lurched forward, and the driver stepped out.

The woman looked to be in her early fifties. Her dark black hair hung long in two pigtails, and her wrinkled faced heavily made up. When Livvy got out of the car nervously, she saw that she was easily ten inches taller than the short, thin woman. She wore knee high black boots with purple and black stripped leggings, and a matching-colored Catholic School girl style skirt, a white button up shirt that was unbuttoned around the navel with a silver-colored belly button ring with a purple jewel.

"You stupid bitch!" the woman shrieked. "Why don't you watch what you're doing!"

"What I'm doing?" Livvy replied in a confused tone. "My door was—"

"She opened the door while you were backing up, Anna!" an older woman yelled from the passenger's side seat.

"Yeah you did! You crazy fat bitch! What is the matter with you!" the small woman boomed. Livvy looked around, noticing a crowd was starting to form around them. She could feel hot tears of hormones, confusion, and frustration running down her cheeks.

"I don't have fucking time for this! You fucking cunt!" Anna cried jumping back into her car and speeding off.

"Hey! You can't leave the scene from an accident!" a young man called out.

"Someone get her plate number! Call the cops!" a young woman bellowed.

Livvy brushed her tears from her cheeks and pulled out her cell phone.

"Honey, are you alright?" a kindly looking older woman asked, noticing Livvy's pregnant belly.

"I'm... I'm fine," she said shakily. "Just a little rattled."

"Okay well, why don't you just have a seat, alright? My granddaughter is calling the police. Is there anyone I can call for you?" she asked.

"No," Livvy replied finding the number she wanted. "I'll call my husband."

"Alright, dear. Just wait here," the lady replied walking off.

Livvy pressed the send button. She listened to the ringing tone as her heart pounded within her chest. She knew he was in the middle of a workout, and he would answer her call. If she called when she knew he was busy, it had to be an emergency. Her left hand caressing her womb, and she could feel the babies kicking at her rapidly. They were worked up into a frenzy from the adrenaline burst. So was their mother, and so would be their father.

"*Baby? Are you alright?*" came Ed's deep, winded voice.

Her reply came in a soft, gentle, almost child-like tone. "DADDY? KILL?"

# BRYAN TANN

BRYAN TANN is the author of the *Dark Lands* Universe, *The John Baker Chronicles*, and many other works.

When he's not living in the rascally place he calls his mind writing books, he's studying martial arts, and being a loving husband, father, and grandfather.

To stalk Bryan find him on Instagram, Twitter, Facebook, Amazon, and many more social media outlets

Facebook:

https://www.facebook.com/AuthorBryanTann/

Twitter: @BryanTannAuthor

Instagram: author_bryan_tann

Amazon: https://www.amazon.com/author/bryanatann

## OTHER WORKS BY BRYAN TANN
*Invincible Heart: The John Baker Chronicles (a Permutation archives story)*
*Unbreakable Mind: The John Baker Chronicles II (a Permutation Archives story)*
*Bryce Kreed: The Enforcer (The Dark Lands book I)*
*Bryce Kreed: The Hunted (The Dark Lands book II)*
*Internal Anarchy: Poetry of an Existence Malcontent*

**Anthology Works Including Bryan Tann:**
*Crossroads in the Dark V: Beyond the Borders*
(contributed the Foreword) -Currently out of print.
*Santa's Naughty Elves*
*Painted Mayhem*

**Coming Soon:**

*A currently untitled John Baker Book 3*

*A currently untitled Bryce Kreed Book 3*

*The Concussion*

*Nerves of Steel: A Dark Lands Tale*

*An Everyday House Husband Saves His Bad Ass Super Spy Wife: No Really, That's What It's Called!*

If you or someone you know is being abused, there are people and facilities that will help you. The author and those who were involved in creating this story want you to know that you can reach out to the following for help.

The National Domestic Violence Hotline:

800-799-7233 or text START to 88788

Dial 911, and ask for help, or contact your local county sheriff's office and simply ask for help.

You can even contact your local county hospital. Any reports of domestic violence are investigated by local law enforcement. Do not allow yourself to be abused, nor your loved ones. If you cannot stand up for yourself, there are others who will help you get to your feet.